He moved cl
Camden bent   **d.**

What the hell was he doing?

It didn't matter that he was drawn to Grace Colton. Standing tall, he smothered a curse behind his hand.

She hitched her chin to the side. "Looks like the rain stopped."

It was a small torture to look at anything other than Grace. Puddles dotted the sidewalk and street. Sodden tablecloths hung limp. Awnings dripped. The downpour was over as soon as it had begun.

She stepped away, and his chest ached.

Sure, he'd stopped himself from kissing Grace this time. The question was: What would he do if he got another chance?

* * *

The Coltons of Grave Gulch: Falling in love is the most dangerous thing of all...

* * *

If you're on Twitter, tell us what you think of Harlequin Romantic Suspense! #harlequinromsuspense

Dear Reader,

I often get asked, "Why write romance novels?"

My answer is very simple. I believe that love is the greatest power on earth. I believe that good always triumphs over evil. I believe that there is strength in kindness. Despite the fact that some days it seems that my beliefs are wrong, I continue to write.

In *A Colton Internal Affair*, you will find a fabulous love story between an unlikely hero and heroine. Yet as I wrote this book and got to know both Grace Colton and Camden Kingsley, I realized that they are perfectly matched. They both have integrity and are driven to do the right thing—even if it means trying to deny their feelings for one another. As a writer, this has been one of the most satisfying romances I have written to date. I hope you love them as much as I do!

All of this is set in Grave Gulch, a town that's on the edge. With a serial killer on the lam and the knowledge that a forensic scientist falsified evidence, the last thing anyone needs is another scandal. But that's exactly what happens!

Whether you've read all the books in the Coltons of Grave Gulch series or this is the first title you've picked up, you'll meet a family that has its fair share of excitement and intrigue. At the same time, they're fiercely devoted to one another.

So, dear reader, sit back, relax and enjoy the time you've given to yourself to read this book. Because as a reader of romance novels, you and I know the truth. Everyone deserves their very own happily-ever-after.

Regards,

Jennifer D. Bokal

A COLTON INTERNAL AFFAIR

Jennifer D. Bokal

HARLEQUIN
ROMANTIC
SUSPENSE

Special thanks and acknowledgment are given to
Jennifer D. Bokal for her contribution to
The Coltons of Grave Gulch miniseries.

HARLEQUIN®
ROMANTIC SUSPENSE™

Recycling programs
for this product may
not exist in your area.

ISBN-13: 978-1-335-75942-9

A Colton Internal Affair

Copyright © 2021 by Harlequin Books S.A.

This edition published by arrangement with Harlequin Books S.A.

For questions and comments about the quality of this book,
please contact us at CustomerService@Harlequin.com.

Harlequin Enterprises ULC
22 Adelaide St. West, 40th Floor
Toronto, Ontario M5H 4E3, Canada
www.Harlequin.com

Printed in U.S.A.

Jennifer D. Bokal penned her first book at age eight. An early lover of the written word, she decided to follow her passion and become a full-time writer. From then on, she didn't look back. She earned a master of arts in creative writing from Wilkes University and became a member of Romance Writers of America and International Thriller Writers.

She has authored several short stories, novellas and poems. Winner of the Sexy Scribbler in 2015, Jennifer is also the author of the ancient-world historical series the Champions of Rome and the Harlequin Romantic Suspense series Rocky Mountain Justice.

Happily married to her own alpha male for more than twenty years, she enjoys writing stories that explore the wonders of love. Jen and her manly husband live in upstate New York with their three beautiful daughters, two very spoiled dogs and a kitten that aspires to one day become a Chihuahua.

Books by Jennifer D. Bokal

Harlequin Romantic Suspense

The Coltons of Grave Gulch

A Colton Internal Affair

Wyoming Nights

Under the Agent's Protection
Agent's Mountain Rescue
Agent's Wyoming Mission

Rocky Mountain Justice

Her Rocky Mountain Hero
Her Rocky Mountain Defender
Rocky Mountain Valor

Visit the Author Profile page at
Harlequin.com for more titles.

To everyone who serves their community with fidelity, bravery and integrity—this book is for you.

To John, always, for being one of those people.

Chapter 1

Grace Colton sat in the passenger seat of the patrol SUV. Sweat snaked down her back, and the straps of her Kevlar vest were heavy on her shoulders. Beside her, Brett Shea drove. His black Lab, Ember, was secured at the rear. The dog snuffled at the grate between kennel and seat, before letting out a soft whine.

She knew exactly how the dog felt.

Despite the fact that it was mid-September, summer still had Grave Gulch in its clutches. The dashboard glowed green in the darkened auto. Although it was 9:37 p.m., it was still seventy-eight degrees outside.

The air conditioning blew a weak stream of cooled air into the cabin, and Grace leaned into the vent. Tendrils of blond hair, which had hung limp around her face, fluttered. Sitting back, she shifted her rig. Grace knew every piece of equipment she wore and had taken the time to check each item before her shift began. Body camera on her chest. Mic head on the shoulder. She also wore extra ammo, a sidearm, a Taser, a collapsible baton, and a radio attached to her utility belt.

Brett took a left at an intersection. At the end of the block was Grave Gulch Park. A crowd of people—approximately fifty by her estimation—stood at the property's edge. Their chanting was unmistakable.

"Hey-hey! Ho-ho! Chief Colton has got to go!"

Grace winced.

"It's a hell of a thing," said Brett, turning left at another intersection. "Our job is to keep people safe, despite the fact that they hate us right now."

"I always thought that cops were the good guys," she said, her mouth dry. "It's why I joined the force—to do good and protect my community. But what do you do when the department is doing bad?" The conversation ebbed, and Grace glanced out the window. It had been revealed that Randall Bowe, a former GGPD and CSI analyst, had doctored evidence for years. His false findings had put innocent people in jail and let guilty ones go free—namely, a serial killer, Len Davison. The community was rightfully outraged, but that also meant the many Coltons in the department were also under fire.

She began, "It's just..." With a shake of her head, Grace said, "Never mind."

"We've got to know each other pretty well, working to catch that catfish last month. It's not like you to be speechless." He gave a quick chuckle to show that he was teasing, at least a little.

He was right. Usually, Grace was overflowing with words. "It makes me." She paused. "Well, upset." She glanced out the window again, seeing only her reflection in the glass. Like she had said, she'd become a cop to be on the side of right. Right now, everything in law enforcement seemed to be wrong. "I get that things happen, and the cops aren't always right. We're just as much Bowe's victims as the whole city."

"Hey, don't let these protesters get you down. It's this damned heat that's got everyone on edge. Isn't that right, girl?" Brett asked, addressing the dog.

Ember gave a happy bark.

"See, even she thinks it's the heat."

Grace gave an exaggerated eye roll, then glanced at Brett. He wore the same uniform as Grace. He had reddish hair, blue eyes and a way about him that made her feel totally secure. It was no wonder that her big sister, Annalise, was head over heels in love with the guy.

Grace had been so focused on her new job with the force for the past year that she hadn't gone on a decent date in months. Yet, she couldn't help but wonder if there was a guy for her.

"It just sucks that everyone's so hard on Melissa. I know she's doing her best, despite everything that's happened." Melissa Colton was the chief of police and Grace's favorite cousin. Honestly, that was saying something. Grace had a lot of cousins.

As an awkward kid in middle school, Melissa had stopped by to take Grace out for ice cream. Grace still remembered sitting in the passenger seat of Melissa's car, for the first time in her life feeling cool. From that day to this, Grace had been totally devoted to her older cousin.

Melissa was smart, dedicated to the GGPD and willing to work long hours to see that justice was served. In short, she was everything that Grace wanted to become.

Melissa had even found her own true love—Antonio Ruiz. Had most members of the Colton clan found their happily-ever-after? Except for Grace, that is.

"You and Melissa are pretty tight," said Brett, his words breaking through her reverie.

"She's my role model, that's for sure."

"She's a good lady."

The chanting protesters could still be heard. Sadly, Grace knew that they had a right to be upset. Still, the fact that much of the anger was directed at Melissa sat like a rock in her gut.

Glancing down an alley, she saw it, and her heart froze midbeat.

"Stop the car." A person, clad in a dark hoodie and jeans, had his hands on a window. He wore a backpack. From his build, she could guess the person was male.

"What is it?" Brett asked, his foot dropping onto the brake.

"I hope it's not trouble," Grace replied, her door already open. She pointed toward the figure, who stood near the window. Sure, it could be the homeowner, locked out of his house. Still, she was more than a little suspicious. "Sir," she said, directing her words to the man in the alley. "Do you need assistance?"

Even from where she stood, Grace could see his shoulders go rigid. He froze, his hands on the window. For a moment, she thought he was going to address her.

Without a word, he sprinted down the narrow alley.

Grace cursed. "I'll go after him on foot," she yelled over her shoulder to Brett. "You come around the block."

If Brett answered, Grace didn't hear what he'd said. She sprinted toward the figure, doing her best to ensure her footfalls remained loud on the quiet street.

The person glanced at Grace. She glimpsed the face: it was a male. Caucasian. Dark mustache. Then, he pivoted and sprinted to the far end of the alley.

Heart racing, legs pumping, Grace ran after the suspect. "Stop," she called out. "Grave Gulch Police." Sure, she was a rookie cop not even on the force for a year. Still, her training was fresh, so she knew what to do.

The first rule of policing: be clear as to what she wanted and to whom she was speaking. She tried again. "You, sir, in the black hoodie and backpack. Stop!" she called again. "Police."

The man never broke his stride.

Grace activated the mic on her shoulder. "This is Officer Colton. I'm in pursuit of a suspect in a possible breaking and entering." She gave her location.

Her radio chirped. The voice of the dispatch officer broke through the static. "Ten-four, Officer Colton. Do you have a description of the suspect?"

She recalled that single second when the man had looked her way. "Caucasian male," she gasped. "Black or navy-blue hoodie. Dark mustache. Height approximately five feet ten inches. One hundred and sixty to one hundred and seventy pounds."

Rule two: always get film of any interaction with the public—especially if the incident could end up in court. Slapping the control on her chest, Grace turned on her body camera.

Adrenaline raced through her veins. It gave her a surge of power, and she closed in on the suspect. Yet, the end of the alleyway loomed large.

Was Brett waiting with the SUV and Ember?

God, she hoped so.

Turning as he ran, the suspect glanced over his shoulder. His eyes were wide, and his nostrils flared.

How was she supposed to read his expression?

Was he afraid?

Angry?

Slipping the pack from his back, he whirled it around. The bag sailed through the air, coming right at Grace's chest. On instinct alone, she shifted her body and lifted her arm to block the blow. The bag connected. For a moment there was a flash of pain as the bag hit her, then an explosion of white filled her vision and agony rocketed through her wrist, her hand.

The bag hit the pavement with a metallic clatter. Grace stumbled, slowed and sidestepped the backpack.

Pushing the discomfort from her mind, she sprinted the last few yards. Bursting onto the sidewalk, she stopped short. There was no Brett, no Ember, no police SUV.

What made matters worse, the suspect was gone.

Camden Kingsley sat at his desk, located in the back corner of the Grave Gulch DA's office. As an investigator with Internal Affairs, he'd been relegated to no-man's-land between a supply closet and a conference room that nobody ever used. Honestly, he didn't mind the solitude. Being set apart allowed him to remain neutral—investigating the investigators.

Despite the large window that overlooked the street, the room was dark, illuminated only by the computer screen. A file filled the monitor, complete with a photo of a dark-haired man. A list of identifying information—name, date of birth, sibling, spouse—accompanied th picture. Camden didn't need to read anything: long ago he'd memorized every word.

Staring at the man's dark eyes Camden asked, "Randall Bowe, where in the hell are you?" For years, Bowe had worked as a forensic scientist for the Grave Gulch PD. During a murder trial several months prior, it was discovered that Randall had tampered with the evidence that implicated the accused, one Everleigh Emerson, when she was actually innocent.

After that trial, there'd been a review of all of Bowe's cases. And that's when the crap really hit the fan. When his crimes came to light, Bowe went on the run.

Aside from finding the forensic scientist who was on the lam, Camden's job was to discover what really had happened with Bowe. Sure, Bowe was trying to punish his wife for having an affair. He planted evidence in cases where he thought suspects had cheated on their romantic partners or rewarded faithful spouses.

It was a twisted retribution yet, there was one question that had plagued him from the beginning. What did the rest of the GGPD know about Bowe's misdeeds? It was the same question he'd asked himself every day for months now. So far, he didn't have an answer.

"Knock, knock," came a voice at his doorway.

Camden looked up. District Attorney Arielle Parks stood on the threshold. The DA was in her midfifties and kept her blond hair short. She wore a dark green blouse and an ivory skirt; both were creased from a long day at the office.

"What's up?" he asked, his eyes burning with exhaustion. "You're here late."

"I was just about to say the same thing to you. What are you working on?"

"Randall Bowe," he said with a sigh. As part of IA, Camden operated independently of all other city agencies. Since many of his cases ended up in court, he worked closely with Arielle.

The public was outraged about the whole Bowe debacle—and Arielle was a favorite target of the protesters. "Have you found anything?" she asked, her voice hopeful.

Camden shook his head. "Nada."

"Listen, it's almost ten o'clock. You should go home. Even people who work for Internal Affairs need to sleep sometime."

"I'm almost done," said Camden. He was the only Korean American man on the force. Sure, he sometimes felt that he had to prove himself. Yet, his long hours had more to do with his need to uncover the facts—any personal sacrifices be damned. "I'll be out of here in ten minutes, half an hour tops."

The light from his monitor reflected off the lenses of Arielle's signature tortoise-rimmed glasses. The older woman could have been looking at nothing or anything. The effect was slightly disconcerting. "What're you hoping to find?"

Camden paused and looked back at his computer. "The truth," he said.

"Are you any closer?" Arielle asked. She stepped into his office. The motion sensor turned on the overhead light.

Camden squinted at the glare.

"I keep wondering…" he began.

"What about?" Arielle asked, taking a seat on the opposite side of the desk.

That was one of the things he admired about the d'

trict attorney. She was as hungry for the truth as Camden. Did he really want to share his suspicions with the DA yet?

All the same, he was the one who'd alluded to his concerns. If he didn't want Arielle involved, he should've just kept his big mouth shut.

"We all agree that Bowe changed a lot of evidence on a lot of crimes," said Camden. He shifted his monitor so Arielle could see the screen. He pulled up an electronic copy of the initial arrest report of Everleigh Emerson. She'd been charged with murdering her estranged husband. Bowe's findings—fibers and hair on the murder weapon—were the cornerstone of the indictment.

The case went to trial. It seemed like an easy conviction for Arielle's team at the DA's office. Then, it came to light that Randall had fabricated the evidence linking Everleigh to the crime.

In the end, all charges were dropped.

Justice had been served.

The truth had won out.

It's just that the Emerson case—along with dozens more—left the Grave Gulch DA's office looking bad. The police department looked worse.

"What am I supposed to see now that I haven't before?"

"I keep asking myself *what if*," said Camden.

"Okay. What if?"

"Bowe's wife cheated on him. That's a fact."

"True."

"He forgives her to a point. But decides to punish those he sees as unfaithful spouses by falsifying evidence. Or to vindicate himself by altering reports to exonerate criminals who were faithful."

Arielle nodded. "Also true."

"He contacted Melissa Colton."

"True again."

"I just keep thinking." He paused. "What if Bowe wasn't working alone?"

Arielle's head snapped back, as if she'd been slapped. "What are you implying?"

He'd bet money that the district attorney knew. Still, Camden said, "What if Bowe had help from someone in the GGPD? What if it was Chief Colton?"

Arielle gave a short laugh. "You're kidding, right?"

Camden leveled his gaze at the district attorney. His stomach was tight, a rope tied into a knot. "I wish I was," he said, "but he hasn't been in contact with anyone else."

"Have you found any evidence to connect the chief to the investigations?"

"That's just it," said Camden. "Her name is all over the Emerson arrest warrant." He clicked open another file and one after that. "Her name is on all of these arrest warrants. And before you say it, I'll point out the obvious. She is the chief of police and involved in most every arrest."

"We know what motivated Bowe—his hatred of those who cheated on their spouses. What would Chief Colton get out of sending innocent people to jail?"

"I guess that's the biggest puzzle piece that's missing," said Camden. "A motive. I might be wrong. Still, I wouldn't be doing my job if I didn't ask the questions."

Arielle rubbed the middle of her forehead. "Keep digging, and keep me personally informed of anything you find. Don't talk to anyone else. The last thing we need is for your theory to get leaked to the press." She stood.

Of course the DA would be worried about the media,

the public image, the voters. Only a few months prior, ADA Evangeline Whittaker had faced serious public outcry. She'd been the prosecutor on one of the cases where Bowe had provided evidence. Despite the fact that Evangeline wasn't part of the DA's team anymore, the episode was still a stain on the office. More than that, Evangeline was gaslit and made to believe that she'd witnessed a crime on the streets. To him, it seemed like the whole town was on edge, albeit for good reasons. Yet one more incident could be too much. Camden said, "Discretion is my middle name. Anything else?"

Arielle began to shake her head. She stopped. "Actually, there is. Go home. Get some rest."

Camden laughed. "I can do that, too. Is there anything else you need that's work-related?"

"Sure, we all just need to hope that the GGPD isn't involved. This town's a tinderbox. One more scandal with the police and Grave Gulch is going to go up in flames."

Pulse pounding, breath ragged and short, Grace stood at the end of the alley. She scanned the street. Cars, parked at the curb, lined both sides of the road. A single streetlight, at the end of the block, threw a puddle of light on the sidewalk. The street was filled with businesses— a laundromat, a hairdresser, a barbershop—all of them closed for the night.

Yet the truth was undeniable. Aside from Grace, the street was empty.

The suspect had inexplicably escaped.

The block ran perpendicular to Grave Gulch Boulevard. Across the street was Grave Gulch Park. The wide lawn was surrounded by a wrought iron fence and protesters.

With a shake of her head, Grace turned her attention back to the matter at hand and the suspect who seemed to have vanished. Too bad she didn't believe in magic, which meant one thing: the guy must still be nearby.

She moved along the sidewalk, her steps slow and light. Grace paused at the fender of a car. Peering into the space between the bumper of one auto and the next, she saw nothing but pavement.

Slowly, she moved to the next car and the one after that.

There was a rustling noise, like leaves in the wind. She stopped. A shadow moved. It was her man.

Having hidden in the doorway of a business, the suspect darted onto the sidewalk.

"Stop." Still following protocol, she pursued and called out, "Grave Gulch Police."

The suspect didn't even slow, not that she'd expected any different.

She hit the mic on her shoulder. "In pursuit of suspect," she said, sprinting after the man and passing two people loitering at the entrance. "He's headed for the park's western entrance. Advise Detective Shea."

Dispatch responded, though their unintelligible words were nothing but noise.

At that same moment, the suspect turned. There was something in his hand. A flash of silver that caught the light. Grace could see a barrel. A trigger. He held a firearm, trying to aim at her as he ran.

"Gun!" she shouted, alerting anyone who might be nearby. "Take cover."

For Grace, time didn't slow as much as it shattered into a million pieces. She held her own sidearm, yet she didn't recall taking it from the holster. The suspect's weapon came up inch by inch. She understood that it was a small handgun.

Before the suspect had the chance to fire, Grace stopped, aimed and pulled the trigger.

There was the report of the gun. The flash of a flame was followed by the scent of a match-strike.

The suspect spun in a drunken circle. He staggered backward two steps, before falling face-first onto the concrete.

Bile rose in the back of Grace's throat. A couple—a man and woman she had barely noticed before—stood at the end of the block.

"Grave Gulch Police," she said to the couple. Her hands trembled, and her throat closed on the last word. "Stay where you are."

The woman began to wail. "Omigod, omigod, omigod!"

"Dude, you shot him," said the man. "You shot him!"

The young man approached the suspect, who lay on the ground, moaning. Grace exhaled. Thank goodness the shot wasn't fatal.

"That man's armed and dangerous," Grace said. Following all the safety procedures she'd been taught, Grace kept her own firearm pointed at the ground. She approached at a run. "Stay away from him."

The man knelt next to the suspect.

"For your own safety," said Grace, "you need to step away."

"Or what?" the young man sneered, while getting to his feet. "You'll shoot me, too?" He grabbed his girl-friend, still wailing, by the elbow. "Let's get out of here."

The couple ran.

Lying on the ground, the suspect held his shoulder.

Blood from the bullet wound leaked through his fingers. "I've been shot. I've been shot. Why'd you shoot me?"

"Where's your firearm?" Grace asked.

He continued to cry out. "I've been shot. I've been shot."

"Your gun." That was another rule. Make sure any suspect has been disarmed. "Where's your gun?"

"I've been shot." He gritted his teeth and spoke through the pain. "My shoulder. You shot me in the shoulder!"

Grace had paid attention to every word said at the police academy. She listened to every piece of advice given by senior officers. But nothing had prepared her for this moment. The sour taste of panic rose in the back of her throat. As if chaos was an animal, she could feel its eyes watching her in the dark—ready to pounce.

She scanned the sidewalk. A pool of blood surrounded the man. Yet, there was no firearm lying on the ground. Did the suspect have it still? What was she supposed to do next?

Grace knew. She had to get the suspect into custody.

"Put your hands where I can see them." She looked down the barrel of her gun, placing the suspect's chest in the middle of her sight.

"Put my hands where? How? I can't even move my damn arm." The suspect looked at Grace for the first time. "Aw, damn, I got shot by a little girl."

"Put your hands where I can see them." Her jaw was tight, and her words like flint.

The suspect lifted his palms. They were both covered in blood. She removed a set of flex-cuffs from her utility belt. One-handed, she slipped it around the suspect's wrists, before pulling the ends tight.

"Where's the gun?" she asked again. She slipped h

own handgun back into the holster. Until the firearm was secured, not much else mattered.

"I don't have a gun." The man's face was greasy with sweat. The front of his hoodie was wet. The coppery stench of blood hung in the air.

"Do you have any other weapons?" she asked, slipping on a pair of sterile gloves. Starting at his shoulders, she patted the suspect down. The man didn't have anything with him—not a wallet, and most definitely not a gun.

Standing, she actuated the mic on her shoulder. "There's been an officer-involved shooting," Grace said, before giving Dispatch the address. She ended with "Send an ambulance."

"An ambulance is on the way," the operator replied.

From her training and limited time in the field, she knew what needed to be done next. From her utility belt, Grace removed a wad of gauze.

"I'm going to apply pressure to your wound now," she said. "It'll help stop the bleeding until EMTs can treat you properly." A ragged rip in his hoodie made the bullet hole easy to find. She pressed the gauze onto the wound. Sure, she'd shot the guy. Still, he was part of the community she'd sworn to protect and serve. It was an oath that Grace took to heart. "What's your name?"

"Robert," said the man, his teeth gritted. "Robert Grimaldi."

"Mr. Grimaldi, can you tell me what you did with your firearm?"

"What firearm?"

"The one you pointed at me," said Grace.

"I never pointed no gun at you. Never."

Her patience was thin, yet she refused to be drawn o an argument with Grimaldi. Drawing in a deep breath, she counted to three and exhaled. "We both know that's a lie. Where's the gun?"

"How old are you?" asked Robert. It was then that Grace noticed the absolute silence. The protesters, little more than a block away, had stopped chanting.

Before Grace could wonder what that meant, there was a single *whoop* of a siren and the flash of blue and red lights. Brett stopped his SUV next to where she knelt on the sidewalk.

"What happened?" he asked, jumping from the driver's seat.

"Mr. Grimaldi drew a weapon, and I fired before he had the chance to shoot. He doesn't have the firearm on him now," said Grace.

"Anything else?" Brett asked.

Grace pointed her chin toward the alleyway. "He also threw his backpack at me."

Grimaldi said, "The little-girl cop is lying about the gun. I don't have a gun. I didn't have a gun. And you won't find a gun because it don't exist."

"We'll see about that," said Brett. Then to Grace he said, "I'll take Ember and do a search. If he threw the gun away or dropped it, Ember will find it."

Three more police cruisers approached, their sirens wailing and lights flashing. An ambulance followed. Police cars parked at the end of both streets, creating a barricade.

But it was too late.

She now understood what had happened with the protesters. Her pulse slowed, turning sluggish in her veins. They'd heard the gunshot and come—en masse—to investigate. More than four dozen people now stood just beyond the patrol cars. They no longer held prote signs. Now, they all had cell phones. What was worse, they were recording the incident. Dread pooled in her stomach.

A duo of EMTs approached. One carried a stretcher, and the other had a medical kit. "We can take over from here, Officer," a tech said.

Grace stepped to the side. Her head swam, and her legs were weak.

"What's going on?" one of the protesters yelled. "What happened? Did you shoot that guy? Hey, lady, I'm talking to you."

"Just ignore them." Brett grabbed Grace by the elbow and led her to the side. As they walked, he spoke. "It was a legitimate shoot. He drew a weapon. You had no choice but to fire. Let's go and find that backpack and then the gun."

It seemed that Robert Grimaldi had noticed the protesters, too. It didn't matter that he still lay on the ground, or that he was being treated by the EMTs. He yelled to the crowd, "The girl cop shot me. And for no reason."

The mob began to boo.

It was then that Grace knew an undeniable truth. Sure, things had been bad for the Grave Gulch Police Department before tonight. Yet, because of her, it was about to get a whole lot worse.

Chapter 2

Police dogs on leashes sniffed the ground. Blue and red lights atop cruisers strobed. Grace knew that most of the force had been called to look for Grimaldi's missing gun.

So far, nothing had been found.

Sitting on the rear bumper of an ambulance, Grace's heart thumped with each flash of the lights.

An EMT stood at her side and examined her injured arm. "Can you open and close your hand?" he asked. His echoing voice sounded like it came from the opposite side of a canyon. Moreover, she felt as if she were watching the events unfold and not actually a part of the action. From somewhere in the back of her mind came a single word. *Shock.*

She'd seen it before in victims of car crashes and crimes alike. It was a detached disbelief that something awful had occurred. Just putting a word to the sensation thrust Grace back into her own body.

The EMT watched her. She knew he'd spoken yet couldn't recall what he'd said. "I'm sorry. Can you say that again?"

"Can you move your hand?"

Grace spread her fingers and then closed them to a fist.

"Can you roll your wrist?" the EMT asked, rolling his own.

She imitated the motion.

"Any pain?"

Grace shook her head. "It's a little sore, but nothing I can't handle."

"It doesn't appear that you have any broken bones. Still, you might want to follow up with your doctor, especially if your discomfort worsens."

"Thanks," she said. The EMT packed up his med kit.

A barricade, a wooden sawhorse painted yellow with GGPD stenciled in black, had been set up at each end of the block. From where she stood, Grace could see that the group of onlookers had grown to more than one hundred. Beyond protesters and gawkers, there was also a TV crew from nearby Kendall.

Melissa approached as the EMT left. She wore a blue windbreaker with a badge embroidered on the chest. She also wore jeans and a T-shirt. Her brown hair hung loose around her shoulders. Just seeing Melissa calmed Grace.

Grace knew the truth. Melissa wasn't at the scene to offer personal support. Rather, the other woman was the chief of police, and it was her job to be on the scene of a shooting.

"How's the wrist?" Melissa asked.

"Nothing's broken."

Melissa nodded. "Can you tell me what happened?"

Brett approached with Ember and waited as Grace began to speak.

Grace had already repeated the story several times. Still, she said, "I saw the suspect, Mr. Grimaldi, at a window. I identified myself as a police officer. It was then that he ran. In the alleyway, he threw his backpack at me. It struck me in the wrist when I batted it away." She drew in a deep breath, trying to slow her racing pulse. "He exited the alley, which is where I lost sight of him. As it turns out, he ducked into a doorway," she continued, pointing to the spot. "As I approached, he ran again. It was then that he drew his weapon. I fired. He went down. There was a couple, a man and woman, at the end of the street. They approached Mr. Grimaldi. I told them to back away. They didn't at first but left as I approached. I placed Mr. Grimaldi in custody and called for backup and medical care." Looking at Brett, she concluded, "That's when Detective Shea arrived."

Melissa turned. "Brett?"

"It all went down as Grace said. She pursued the suspect on foot while I brought my SUV around the block. There were protesters in the street, and it slowed my response. By the time I arrived, Grimaldi was down."

"What about the couple?"

"I saw a man and woman running down the street."

"So you arrived after Mr. Grimaldi was shot?"

"That's correct," said Brett.

Melissa continued. "You didn't see his gun? Or Grace firing?"

Dropping his eyes to the pavement, Brett ran his fingers through the fur on Ember's head. "I did not."

Melissa tensed her jaw. "Anything else?"

"We recovered the backpack." Brett continued, meeting Grace's gaze. "Grimaldi's driver's license was inside, as well as two laptop computers, a smartphone, jewelry—watches, rings, a diamond bracelet—and lots of cash. My guess, Mr. Grimaldi was routinely looking for open windows and letting himself into people's homes. We've already gotten calls about some of the missing items."

"Tell me about Grimaldi," said Melissa.

Brett held Ember's lead with one hand and his phone in the other. Using his thumb to navigate, he held up a screen. It was filled with a rap sheet. "He has a pretty long arrest record. Robbery. Larceny. Selling a controlled substance."

"What about his gun?" Melissa asked. "Have you found that yet?"

Brett shook his head. "No."

"You have Grimaldi's criminal history. Has he ever been arrested with a gun before? Are there any weapons charges in his file?"

Brett glanced at the screen and then wordlessly, shook his head.

Grace's knees threatened to buckle. No gun? What was going on? Was this all some ploy to make the department look bad? Could this be another attack on the police by Randall Bowe? Or maybe it was one of those Bowe sent to jail. The witnesses had been more than a little hostile. Had this whole incident been a setup from the beginning?

At the same time, Grace had another thought—worse than the first. What if she'd been mistaken? What if Grimaldi never had a weapon to begin with?

She drew a shaking breath and recalled those seconds

before she pulled the trigger. "He was armed," she said, her voice a croak.

"What's that?" Melissa drew her brows together.

Grace cleared her throat. "Grimaldi was armed. He had a gun. He pointed it at me." She paused. "I know what I saw."

"Get a CSI team down here for a thorough search. If the gun is out here, we'll find it," said Melissa. Her green eyes held an unmistakable look of concern.

If? "It's out here," said Grace, her voice stronger than she felt. She scanned the street. It was overflowing with cops. "Somewhere."

"And if it's not?" Brett asked.

Were Brett and Melissa really questioning what she saw? "Grimaldi had a gun."

"Let's just keep looking, okay?" said Melissa.

"Sure thing, boss," said Brett. He clicked his tongue, signaling Ember to follow.

"Before you go, I need you to do something else," said Melissa.

Brett stopped. "Whatever you need."

"This investigation has to be done by the book," said Melissa. "Officer Colton's firearm has to be examined by Forensics. Can I ask you to place it in an evidence bag? The body camera, too?"

Brett removed two evidence bags tucked into a pocket of his utility belt.

At the academy, every cadet had been warned that this day could come. If a gun was ever fired in the line of duty, that firearm would have to be analyzed and compared to the bullet. It made no difference if the officer admitted to firing or not.

Her throat tightened around a hard kernel of indignation. She was being wronged, but she knew her job and was determined to remain professional. Saying nothing, she handed over both her gun and her camera.

"For now," Melissa continued, "let's get back to headquarters. From there, we'll evaluate the body-cam footage you caught. That'll at least prove that Grimaldi was armed. Grace, you ride with me. Brett, we'll meet you there."

Despite the heat, Grace started to shiver. She followed Melissa to the car. Her cousin slipped into the driver's seat of an SUV, Grace into the passenger seat. Melissa maneuvered to the end of the block, where a police officer lifted the crossbeam of a barricade.

A light shone through, blinding Grace with the glare.

A reporter pressed her face next to the glass. "I'm Harper Sullivan from Kendall, I have some questions for you." A man stood behind her. A camera, along with the light, was perched on his shoulder.

Melissa said nothing.

The reporter continued. "Chief Colton, do you have any comment about what happened tonight? Is this case related to the Len Davison case? Or Randall Bowe? There was an officer-involved shooting. Is this the officer? Does she have any comment?"

Gripping the steering wheel with white knuckles, Melissa stared through the windshield. "Just look ahead," she whispered. "And don't say a word."

Tense, Grace faced forward and looked at nothing. The crowd parted as the SUV nosed forward. It took only a minute before they were on an empty street. Grace glanced in the side-view mirror. All the protesters and onlookers were behind her. She exhaled. "What in the hell was all that?"

"It'll be okay." Melissa smiled, but her brows were drawn together in concern.

"Thanks for saying so, but…" Grace shook her head.

"But what?"

"Just never mind," said Grace. "It's not important."

"I might be the chief of police and your boss, but I'm also your cousin. Don't tell me to 'never mind.'"

Just moments before, Grace had had too many thoughts to even know what to think. Now, her mind was blank. What was she supposed to say?

"I don't think this problem will be over soon." Grace's hands started to tremble. Tucking her palms under her thighs, she continued, "I think that the GGPD is about to be hit by the full force of this town's anger. It's all because…" Her words faltered. She cleared her throat. "It's all because of me."

Without speaking, Melissa drove. Turning a corner, she pulled into a lot at the back of the police department. A spot near the door was empty. A white sign on a post read *Reserved for Chief of Police*. She turned to Grace.

"I'm not going to lie to you," Melissa began. "You're going to have to be strong. The public doesn't like to see police shoot anyone."

"Of course not," she said, interrupting. "Nobody wants to have force used."

Melissa started again. "There's going to be questions you'll need to answer. My guess, there will be an investigation. Be honest, but don't answer a question until it's asked. You don't want to provide the IA investigator with details they can use against you."

Grace tried to swallow, but her throat was closed. "Don't give any information unless asked."

"Once we see what's on your body camera, a lot of

the furor will die down, I'm sure." She turned off the motor. The silence was total. Grace could hear her own breath and the resonance of her own heart.

Melissa continued. "I called Ellie. She'll be waiting to download the camera footage." Ellie Bloomberg was the IT expert for the GGPD and one of the hardest working people on the force.

Grace reached for the door handle. "I can't wait to get all of this behind me. Let's go."

Melissa reached out, placing her palm on Grace's shoulder. "One last thing. You did turn on your body cam, right?"

Grace recalled those few seconds as she raced through the alley. She could feel the pressure of her fingers on the Record button. "I'm positive," she said.

"All right, then." Melissa smiled again. This time the expression was real. "Let's go."

Despite what he'd said to Arielle, Camden worked later than he intended. As he finally parked his car in front of his town house, he glanced at the dashboard clock: 10:42 p.m. No wonder he was tired.

While loosening his tie, he walked slowly to the front door. Stepping into the townhome, his mind was already on a cold beer and a soft sofa.

He twisted off the cap and took a long drink. He sighed. Home, finally. Dropping onto the sofa, he turned on the TV. As the set flickered to life, he wondered about dinner—specifically if the leftover pizza in the fridge was still fresh enough to eat.

A sitcom was interrupted by a breaking-news alert.

A newscaster from a station in Kendall stood near a police barricade.

Camden recognized the street at once. It was in downtown Grave Gulch, about a block from the city park. Blue and red emergency lights flashed in the background. The reporter wore a yellow blazer. Holding her microphone, she looked into the camera and began speaking. "This is Harper Sullivan. I'm in downtown Grave Gulch, where a department beset by scandal can add another disgrace to the list. A police-officer-involved shooting."

The screen filled with footage of a man on a stretcher. His shoulder was encased in a white bandage, and his arm rested in a sling.

The chyron at the bottom of the screen read *Robert Grimaldi shot by Grave Gulch Police Officer.* "She just shot me for no reason," said Grimaldi, speaking into the camera. "The girl cop said I had a gun, but I don't got no gun."

The newscaster appeared in profile. "Why would the police officer think that you were armed if you weren't?"

"I dunno," said Grimaldi. "She's inexperienced, I guess. That, or maybe she's a liar…just like the rest of them."

Then, the victim was wheeled out of the camera's shot and into the back of a waiting ambulance.

The picture on the screen changed once more. This time, there was footage of two women in an SUV. Camden recognized one. It was the chief of police, Melissa Colton. The other was younger, blonde, pretty, in uniform. He'd never seen her before; still, he bet that she was the girl cop Grimaldi had mentioned.

The video in the car continued, as did the voice of the reporter. "Do you have any comment about what happened tonight? Is this case related to the Len Davison case? Or Randall Bowe? There was an officer-involved shooting. Is this the officer? Does she have a comment?"

Neither of the women in the police vehicle flinched.

The camera cut back to the reporter for a live shot. "There you have it. A citizen of Grave Gulch, Robert Grimaldi, shot by the police without warning or reason. And the police have nothing to say. This is Harper Sullivan, sending you back to your regularly scheduled program."

Setting his beer on a side table, Camden cursed with frustration. An officer-involved shooting would be his case, for sure. It was more than his interrupted night. He reached for his cell phone at the same moment it began to ring. The caller ID read *Arielle Parks*.

"Why am I not surprised," he muttered to himself before accepting the call. Without a greeting he said, "I saw it on the news."

"Good god, Camden. This is the last thing we need in Grave Gulch." He agreed with the DA, but knew she'd called to do more than complain. She continued, "I just got off the phone with the mayor. He wants you on the case."

"Understood. I'll head over to police headquarters now." Camden paused a beat and waited for Arielle to say more. "Everything okay?"

She gave a tight laugh. "The mayor's furious at everyone. It's not even my department and he chewed me out." He could well imagine Mayor Abels yelling at Arielle. The picture wasn't pleasant. "What are we supposed to do now?" Her tone was sharp. "*Someone...*" she drew out the word "...has to be held publicly accountable once and for all. It's for the public good."

Camden's neck and shoulders tightened. "I'm not interested in public accountability," he said tersely. "What I want is the truth."

"Well, the truth is that a man was shot. Was it caused by bad policing or bad training? That's what the people of Grave Gulch deserve to know."

Picking up his messenger bag, he slipped the strap over his shoulder. "What d'you know about the incident? The officer?"

"Her name is Grace Colton. Right now, she's on the way to police headquarters."

Camden turned off his TV and threw the remote onto the sofa. "Colton? As in she's Chief Colton's—what, sister?"

"I think they're cousins."

Detective Troy Colton was assigned to the Randall Bowe case, and Camden had worked with him more than once. Troy was a good guy. Still, Camden had to ask, "Is everyone in that police department related to one another?"

"Not quite. But there are a whole lot of them," said Arielle.

Camden stepped out of his town house and pulled the door closed behind him. The night air was oppressive, and he began to sweat. Yet, it was more than the heat and humidity of a summer holding on too long. Two things bothered him. The first was obvious. Camden was worried that with all the family relations in the GGPD, Chief Colton would want to protect her officer. Randall Bowe had tried to frame several members of the GGPD, as well. He had to assume that they'd be wary of anyone not named Colton—or an employee of the police department. What kind of cooperation could he expect?

The second problem was more oblique. An officer-involved shooting was too close to the one that had changed his father's life. Hell, it was the case that had made Camden who and what he was today. A sharp pain gripped his chest along with a memory of his father. Accused of a crime he hadn't committed, his pop had been found guilty, nevertheless. He'd been removed from the force. It was a disgrace that became a part of his father—like a tattoo on his soul.

The aftermath of those events had shaped the rest of Camden's life. In the span of a heartbeat, he saw his father as he was the night he'd been let go from the force. Sitting at the kitchen table, head down, hands resting on a placemat.

A headache started in his temple. Camden didn't have the luxury of wallowing in pity or doubt. He had a job to do and turned his thoughts to the news report and the female police officer in the passenger seat of the SUV. At first, it appeared that her gaze was impassive and without any emotion. But Camden had been wrong. There had been tension around Grace Colton's eyes. Her jaw had been tight. She was worried, perhaps even afraid.

That left Camden wondering: What did she have to fear?

Was she simply overwhelmed?

Or was she afraid of someone finding out what had really happened?

Camden's fists clenched. It was then that he realized he still held the phone to his ear. The DA was on the other end of the call, still waiting for his reply.

"I'm on my way to the police department now. I don't know what happened on that street tonight. Until I get the facts I'm not going to speculate. But there's one thing Grave Gulch will get from my investigation, Arielle."

"Oh, yeah? What's that?"

"The truth."

Ellie Bloomberg sat in front of a bank of computer monitors. She looked up as Melissa and Grace entered.

"Rough night," said Ellie. Her wavy brown hair was tied into a bun at the top of her head. She wore jeans, a T-shirt and a pair of flip-flops.

Grace ignored the comment about her rough night. Instead, she said, "Sorry for making you come into work." She continued, mentioning Ellie's longtime boyfriend. "Mick must be peeved."

Ellie waved away the comment. "He's fine. When I left, he was still in his office on a call with Tokyo or London or something." Sitting taller, she held up a plastic bag. Inside was the camera. "Brett dropped this off and said he was taking the gun for forensic analysis." A yellow-and-black *Evidence* banner ran along the top of the translucent bag. There were also several lines for signatures in the chain of custody. Brett Shea's name was first. Then, Melissa Colton's.

Ellie stood, pen in hand, and wrote her name on the third line.

The camera was small and black and had plastic casing. The lens was smaller than a dime. Recorded footage needed to be uploaded to a computer in order to be viewed. Sure, some of the newer cameras had a built-in screen. But the GGPD's budget hadn't allowed for an upgrade in years.

Ellie studied the bag and chewed on her bottom lip.

Grace didn't like the expression, and her stomach churned. "What's the matter?"

"It looks like this has been damaged." Holding up the camera for Grace to see, Ellie used the end of her pen and pointed. "See this? The Record button is cracked."

Grace sucked in a breath as her heart started racing. "That's impossible. I examined that camera myself before we left for patrol. It was in perfectly good condition then."

"Well, it's not now," said Ellie. "Let me see what I can do, and I'll get back to you."

Grace stood next to Melissa. The older woman placed a reassuring hand on her shoulder. "Let's go to my office. I'll get you a cup of coffee. Tonight's going to be a long night."

Grace's stomach still roiled. Her hands still trembled. She was already jittery. She'd paid attention to all of the academy lectures on what would happen if a cop ever shot a civilian. It's just that in those moments, Grace never imagined she'd be the one to pull the trigger. It didn't help that the gun hadn't been found or that the camera was now broken. What was going on? Could she be the victim of sabotage? It seemed far-fetched, but nothing that happened tonight made any sense.

"Let's get some coffee," Melissa said.

"I don't want any."

"Yeah? Well, I do. Besides, Ellie won't get her job done any faster if we're watching over her shoulder." Melissa tugged Grace. "C'mon."

Grace relented. They used a set of stairs that led to the main level.

The squad room was filled with more than a dozen desks. In short, there was always someone in there. At night, the GGPD headquarters wasn't nearly as busy as it was during the day. All the same, it didn't mean that it was ever empty. Yet, tonight was different. Every desk was vacant. The silence was total—not even interrupted by the ringing of a phone.

"Where is everyone?" Grace asked. "This place is like a tomb."

"Everyone's out." Melissa's answer was vague—yet not so ambiguous that Grace couldn't figure out what she meant.

"They're looking for the gun," said Grace grimly.

"Among other things."

"What if this is all a setup?" Grace asked.

"Setup?" Melissa echoed.

"Maybe it's someone who wants to make the department look bad." Once Grace began to speak, words flowed out of her like water from a firehose. "Maybe it's Bowe. He hates the department enough. He could have paid all those people…"

Melissa stopped in the middle of the squad room. "Ask yourself one question. Even if this whole scenario could be orchestrated, Grimaldi would never know which cop would find him. How could he be sure that he was shot in the shoulder and not the chest or the head?" She walked to her office and opened the door. "That's a hell of risk to take. For what? Money? Revenge?"

"I guess you're right," Grace grumbled.

"For now, we're going to follow the facts. First, coffee."

Melissa's office was tucked into the back corner of the squad room, a light turned on as soon as Grace crossed the threshold. A large desk sat in the middle of the room, a pile of manila folders filled one corner. One wall was filled with pictures of Randall Bowe. A whiteboard had been tacked to the wall. The names of all his victims had been written in blue marker. Beneath the names were the words *Don't stop until the job is done.*

Grace lifted a smaller picture from the table. It was a selfie of Melissa and her new fiancé, Antonio Ruiz. Melissa smiled at the camera, Antonio looking at her. It was impossible to miss the look of tenderness and dedication on Antonio's face. "This one's new."

"I figured I needed a picture of the two of us."

Grace handed the photograph back to Melissa. More than having movie-star good looks, Antonio was rich. "He's a catch. Plus, he looks like he's completely in love with you."

"I am lucky." Melissa stroked her finger over the picture before setting the photograph on the table.

Grace couldn't help but wonder how two people could find each other and fall in love. Obviously, she knew how Melissa and Antonio met. It was during the investigation into the kidnapping of Grace's nephew, Danny. Danny had been found and returned to his family, so the story had a happy ending all the way around.

But why had they met and fallen in love? Was it luck?

And moreover, why was Grace caught up in this and not in love? Was that luck, too? Good luck for Melissa and bad luck for Grace?

Gesturing to one of two chairs that sat near her desk, Melissa said, "Have a seat. I'll get a coffee started for you."

Melissa started her single-cup brewer. For a moment, the hiss of coffee brewing was the only sound in the room. What was Melissa thinking? What should Grace say? She was usually bubbling over with words, and now, well…

Glancing over her shoulder, Melissa asked, "How are you?"

Slipping her hands under her thighs, Grace said, "Fine. Not great, you know. But I'm fine." She nodded vigorously.

"I've known you your whole life. You're far from fine."

Grace's eyes burned, but she'd be damned before she'd cry—even in front of Melissa. She bit the inside of her lip hard. Still, she couldn't help but say, "I'm worried that I've made things worse for the department. I'm worried that I'm a failure as a cop." She stopped and drew a breath. "I'm worried that I've done the wrong thing or disappointed you."

Melissa stirred in a packet of sugar. She handed Grace a mug filled with steaming coffee. "Drink that."

Grace took a sip. The liquid scalded a raw spot on her lip, and she winced. *Damn, when had she hurt her mouth?*

"For the record, I'll never be disappointed in you, Grace. There's a lot of us Coltons, you know. But you're my favorite little cousin."

Grace smiled. "Thanks."

"Now, really, drink the coffee. Once the adrenaline wears off, you're going to have a hell of a headache. Besides, you aren't going home anytime soon. Someone from Internal Affairs will be here soon. You'll want the caffeine to keep you sharp."

Grace took another drink. At least she could always count on her cousin. "Yes, ma'am."

Melissa's cell phone rang. She glanced at the screen. "It's Ellie," she said, before swiping the call open and turning on the Speaker feature. "Hey." Melissa set the phone on her desk. "I have Grace here, and you're on Speaker."

"I'm glad she's with you. I was able to access the footage. Come down to the lab. I'll have everything set up for you to review."

"On our way," said Melissa and ended the call. She exhaled and smiled. "If all goes well, then we'll have Mr. Grimaldi on video, pointing a gun at you. This incident will be resolved tonight. By tomorrow morning, your life will be back to normal."

"If all goes well," Grace echoed, trying to summon her cousin's optimism.

Why did Grace feel as if it wasn't going to *go well* at all? And that things wouldn't be *normal* for a long time?

Chapter 3

Grace sat at one of the computer workstations, complete with three monitors. Melissa stood behind her, Ellie on Grace's right.

Clacking on her keyboard, Ellie spoke. "I've got good news and bad news."

More bad news? As if she was in free fall, Grace's stomach dropped.

"Start with the good news," urged Melissa.

"I was able to get footage from the camera." The center screen winked to life and an up-close image of a hand filled the screen. "This is where the video starts. It looks like you got a little over a minute and a half."

"Ninety seconds?" Grace folded her arms over her chest. "I'd swear that the incident took longer." Then she recalled those moments on the street when time seemed to bend. Maybe the recording was right, after all.

"All right," said Melissa, sliding into a chair next to Grace. "Let's see what we have."

Grace held her breath and watched the monitor.

"Is that the body-cam footage?" a male voice asked from behind.

Grace turned, her heart racing. A tall man, nearly six feet with dark short hair and dark eyes, stood on the threshold. Grace's heart continued to thunder—and it wasn't entirely from the start he'd given her.

"What are you doing here?" Melissa asked, rising from her seat. Her tone was less than friendly. Grace sat up taller. It wasn't like her cousin to be rude.

"I stopped by your office. You weren't there. I figured the next best place to find you was here." The man pointed to the monitor. "You never answered my question. Is that the footage from the body cam of tonight's shooting?"

"It is, and I suppose you want to watch with us," said Melissa.

"It's my job to see everything that you have on this case," said the man. "You know that."

Melissa gestured to the chair she'd just vacated. "Have a seat."

He slid in next to Grace. His hand brushed her wrist as he sat. A jolt of electricity shot up her arm. Was it just nerves? Or had there been something else—something more?

"Camden Kingsley," he said, holding out his hand. "Internal Affairs. You must be Grace Colton."

Grace stared at his palm. "Internal Affairs?" Her voice sounded small in the cavernous room.

"My being here is entirely procedural," he said, rubbing fingertips and thumb together before dropping his palm to the table. "You don't have to worry. I'm only looking for the truth."

Melissa gave a derisive snort.

Yet, Grace thought there was something trustworthy about Camden Kingsley. What was it? And how could she tell after only a few seconds?

He was confident and calm. Without him saying a word, his demeanor spoke of being in charge; even better, he was fair. She rubbed the back of her neck, loosening her tight shoulders. Maybe now, things would turn in Grace's favor.

"Can we see the video now?" Camden asked.

"Sure thing," said Ellie, typing.

The video began to play. There was footage of a man running. The image jostled, as the camera attached to Grace's chest recorded her in the middle of the pursuit. Her labored breath along with the staccato of her footfalls on the pavement were the only sounds in the room.

Mr. Grimaldi turned toward the camera. His eyes were wide.

"You captured a perfect video of his face, Grace. Good job," said Melissa.

"He's going to throw his backpack." Her wrist ached with the memory. "After that, I lost sight of him."

In a few more seconds, they'd all see what happened. Then, there'd be no more questions. No more slights about her professionalism. Better yet, her actions wouldn't stain the police force.

Just as she said, the suspect slipped the bag from his shoulder. Like an Olympic discus athlete, he threw the pack. It whirled through the air.

The camera's audio recorded a curse that Grace didn't remember uttering. The aspect of the picture changed.

There was a flash of brick wall. The side of her arm. The black bag, the nylon fibers visible.

The image was nothing but static as the timer on the camera continued counting off the seconds. Then, the screen went black—with no sight of a gun.

As if he'd been sucker punched, Camden's jaw ached. He stared at the computer screen, willing the video to start again. It didn't.

What would follow was a simple mathematical equation. No video equaled more civil unrest. The protests would grow. The calls for reform or defunding the police would become a constant chant. Politics would become paramount.

In the end, the truth wouldn't matter at all. And the truth was that Grace Colton had shot someone, apparently unprovoked.

Moreover, Grace Colton's career with the Grave Gulch police force would be over.

The dull ache became a stabbing pain.

Despite what he'd just seen on the camera, though, there was something about Grace. What was it?

Honestly, he didn't know.

All the same, he knew that this case was worth his time.

In the blackened screen of the monitor, Camden refocused his gaze to the reflection of Grace's face. Her complexion was pale. Her eyes were wide. What was she thinking? How did she feel?

Stricken was the word that came to mind.

Clearing his throat, he turned in his seat and looked at Ellie. "Is there any way you can recover more of the footage?"

She ran a thumbnail between the keys of her keyboard. "I'll see what I can do." Her tone had said much more than her words. Camden knew there was no way in hell she'd find any more of the video.

But he was far from being done for the night.

He really only needed to spend a little time with anyone before he knew if they were telling the truth—or not. Everyone had a tell when lying. A shifting of the eyes. A tapping of the foot.

Grace Colton would be no different.

He said, "Officer Colton, we need to talk about what happened. Obviously, the video isn't going to help us right now."

Grace stared at her folded hands. There were two red dots—hot coals of color—on her cheeks. "I'm not sure what else to say."

Melissa interrupted. "You don't have to say anything, Grace. You're entitled to counsel. Ask your union legal rep to come in."

Camden spoke slowly. "I'd like to talk to you now, while your memories are still fresh." She turned her gaze to him. Camden could look at nothing other than Grace's eyes. They were a soft blue, like the sky on the first warm day of spring.

"There was a couple at the end of the block," said Grace.

Melissa placed her hand on Grace's shoulder. "You don't have to talk to IA right now, without your rep."

Grace shook her head. "I don't have anything to hide. Besides, Mr. Kingsley's right. Now, my memories are fresh."

"Are you *sure*?" Melissa asked, stretching out the last word. "You haven't even had time to file a report."

Grace nodded. "I'm positive."

"Then, we should make this an official interview," said Camden. "I'd like to use a conference room."

Melissa glared. He sensed an argument. She wanted to protect the rookie cop. But was it as the chief of police or as a cousin? Moving toward the door, she said, "This way."

Camden was used to terse treatment from officers being investigated. Nobody liked oversight or having their professionalism questioned. But without oversight, there was no professionalism to be had. He stood and waited for Grace Colton to get to her feet. Then, they both followed Melissa Colton down a narrow hallway.

The chief a few steps ahead, Camden walked shoulder to shoulder with Grace. His wrist brushed the back of her hand. He searched for something reassuring to say.

What was he thinking? *It isn't my job to be reassuring.*

He had to admit that Grace was affecting him in ways he dared not examine. It was more than her looks, though she was beyond attractive. It was her reaction to the video. Her shock that the entire incident hadn't been recorded was sincere. In short, Grace needed his protection.

First, reassurance. Now, protection? It wasn't like Camden to get personally involved. All he could hope is that the case was resolved quickly. He needed to get away from Grace before he did something really stupid.

Melissa pulled a door open. "You can use this room."

Stepping across the threshold, an automatic light buzzed to life. A conference table stood in the middle of the floor. Two sets of chairs sat on each side of the table, leaving only enough room to slide into a seat.

"Let me know if you need anything," said Melissa, her hand resting on the handle. "And Grace?"

"Yeah?"

"I'll be right outside."

Grace gave a small nod. "Thanks."

Staying on his feet, Camden waited until Chief Colton pulled the door shut. "Please," he said, gesturing to a chair. "Sit." Grace pulled the seat out from under the table and dropped down with a sigh.

"Long night," he said, lowering into his own chair.

"You wouldn't believe, Mr. Kingsley."

"Call me Camden."

"Okay," she said. "Camden."

"I know you're nervous. Tired. Overwhelmed. I also know that I'm the last person in the world you want to be talking to right now. I want to assure you that I'm only interested in the facts." It was how he began each interview—and every word spoken was true.

"I appreciate it."

Camden kept a small tape recorder tucked into a side pocket of his messenger bag. It was with him at all times for moments just like this. He laid it on the table. The recorder was followed by a pad of paper and pen. "I'd like to record this interview—if that's okay with you?"

"A tape recorder. You don't see those often."

"It was my father's. Since it worked for my pop, I figure it'll work for me." He paused, not bothering to add that each time Camden used the recorder he felt as if he honored his father. Or that it was almost like the old man was in the room with him. "Do I have your permission to record this interview?" He pressed a button, and the Record light glowed red.

Grace nodded.

"Is that a yes?"

"Yes," she said. "You have my permission to record the interview."

"This is Camden Kingsley, Internal Affairs investigator with the Grave Gulch District Attorney's office." He also gave the date and time. "For the record," he said, continuing his well-practiced lines, "can you state your name?"

Leaning forward, she projected her voice toward the tiny tape recorder. "Grace Colton. Officer with the Grave Gulch Police Department."

"There was an officer-involved shooting this evening," he said. "Were you present?"

She nodded. "I was."

"Can you tell me, in your own words, what happened?" What she had to say was important, but Camden was also interested in how she told her story. Was it robotic, like she'd memorized details? Or was it disjointed, with details changing from one version to the next? Moreover, what were her mannerisms? Could she maintain eye contact? Did her breathing pattern change when answering specific questions? Were the facts of her story consistent? In short, Camden was looking for a lie.

She spent a few minutes recounting what he already knew. Camden took notes on it all. She'd witnessed a person trying to open a window. After she identified herself as a police officer, the person ran and she gave chase. Detective Brett Shea, still in the patrol vehicle, had circled the block in order to stop the suspect at the end of the alleyway. According to Grace, Robert Grimaldi had a gun. He'd aimed at her. She ordered him to drop his weapon, and when he didn't, she fired her own. The bullet had struck Grimaldi in the shoulder. Two individuals had been at the end of the block. They'd approached Mr. Grimaldi as he lay on the sidewalk.

Camden's pen quit moving. "I want to come back to the witnesses. What'd they look like?" he asked, interrupting.

Grace inhaled. "It was a man and woman. Caucasian. Late teens maybe or early twenties. The guy had longish hair and a thin beard. The woman was wearing a T-shirt with a concert schedule, cut-off jeans and sneakers."

"Are you sure they witnessed the shooting?"

Grace nodded again. "After Mr. Grimaldi was shot, they approached him. I told them to back up." She paused. Her eyes glistened with unshed tears. She blinked hard. Inhaled. Exhaled. "They did, but not at first. I got closer, and they ran off."

Camden looked at Grace. "Can Detective Shea verify the part about the couple?"

"He saw them running away," she said.

That brought up another important point. "Why'd they run?"

"I don't think they liked the police. The guy said something about cops being bad."

"Did Shea hear the remark?"

Grace shrugged. Then she seemed to remember the recorder. Leaning toward the small microphone, she said, "I don't know what he witnessed. You can talk to him, too. He also confiscated my gun for a ballistics review at the scene."

"I'll get to him soon." Camden leaned back in the chair. So far he thought she was telling the truth. "Could you identify again the people you saw?" Without body-cam footage, the witnesses would be the key to finding out what happened. "I need to talk to them, as well."

"Honestly, I've never seen those two before in my life."

"Would you recognize a picture?"

"Maybe." She touched her bottom lip with her tongue. "Probably."

Camden rose from his seat and opened the door. Melissa stood across the hall. She looked up as he stepped into the corridor.

"You need something?" she asked.

"Can I get a set of mug shots?" he asked. "Male, late teens or early twenties. Caucasian. Long hair. Thin beard."

Melissa rolled her eyes. "That guy sounds like a good bit of Grave Gulch," she said. "You have anything more specific?"

"Someone matching that description witnessed the shooting." Camden couldn't help it. He was sincerely relieved that there'd been witnesses. "Grace thinks she can identify him."

Melissa pushed off the wall. "I'll pull some files and be right back."

Camden returned to the room and closed the door. "Your cousin is going to get some photos for you to look through." He slid into the chair and rested his hands on the table. Grace traced a whorl in the faux wood. "If you can identify the witnesses, then we'll track them down and get their statements."

Grace pressed her palms together, as if in prayer, and rested her forehead on her hands. "That'd be great," she said. "If we can find them."

"While we wait," he said, "tell me about the gun."

"What do you want to know?"

"What kind of firearm did Grimaldi have?"

"A handgun."

"Was it an automatic or a revolver?"

She shook her head. "I think it was a revolver."

"Anything else?"

Grace closed her eyes. "It was silver. I remember the metallic glint on the barrel."

"What do you think happened to the gun?"

Opening her eyes, Grace folded her arms over her chest—a definite defensive move. She shook her head. "I don't know. Grimaldi must've dropped it when he went down. Maybe it skittered under a car or something."

Camden's phone pinged. He glanced at the screen. It was a message from Arielle.

Report on missing gun. Document attached.

He hit the link with his thumb. An official Grave Gulch police report filled the screen. The text was small, but its content was unmistakable. More than a dozen officers had searched for a weapon. Several canine units had been employed. They'd all come up empty.

It meant only one thing. There had never been a gun.

It brought up a new set of questions. Had Grace Colton been mistaken? Or was she lying?

As far as he could tell, she'd been truthful until now. Was she the kind of person who'd get angry and lash out? True, he didn't know her well but still, he couldn't see being anything other than careful and forthright.

His mouth felt as if it'd been filled with ash.

"The street was dark," he said, trying a new tactic. "How do you know that the suspect had a gun?"

"There was a streetlamp near the corner," she said.

"Mr. Grimaldi was standing in a pool of light. I know what I saw." She paused. "What's on your phone?"

The room was suddenly hot, and he began to sweat. Shoving the cell into his bag, he mumbled, "A report."

"About me? About the gun?"

Camden twirled the pen between his fingers and back again. He tried to collect his thoughts and decide what needed to be said. "Thing is," he said, deciding on the unvarnished truth, "the police officers searched. Canine units were used. Nothing was found. There is no gun."

Sitting back hard, she sucked in a breath. "That's wrong. I know what I saw…" Her words trailed off as the door opened. Melissa stepped into the room. She held a digital tablet, and a sheen of perspiration covered her brow.

"I created a file on everyone in the system with a description that matches the male witness." Chief Colton set the computer on the table before sliding into the seat next to Grace.

"You saw the report," said Grace. "The one about the gun."

It wasn't quite a question. Not really a statement, either.

Melissa swallowed. Nodded. She tapped on the computer, filling the screen with several pictures. Sliding the device over to Grace, she said, "Let's get a look at these mug shots."

"I know what you both are thinking." Grace leaned forward in her seat. "I'm young. Inexperienced. It's hard to see in the dark. Maybe you even think that I was mad at Mr. Grimaldi. After all, he threw a backpack at me. He damn near broke my wrist." She wrapped a hand around her injured arm. Her skin was mottled by a purple bruise. "The thing is, I saw what I saw. I might be young. I might not have worked many cases. But I'm not wrong."

"I know," said Melissa. Her voice was small. For the first time, Camden noticed worry lines creasing her forehead. "But without that gun, or any video from your body cam, it's your word against Grimaldi's. I don't have to tell you this, but public opinion isn't going to be in your favor."

Camden reached across the table and pushed the tablet closer to Grace. "Look at the mug shots. See if you can find the witness."

She let go of her wrist and picked up the tablet. She said nothing while flipping through screen after screen. After several minutes, Grace shook her head. "He's not here."

"Are you sure?" Melissa took the computer from her younger cousin and flipped back through the photographs. "What about him? He lives near the park. Matches the description perfectly. Or—" she tapped on the screen "—we can look for his girlfriend. She might be in the system."

Grace took the tablet from the other woman's hand. Placing it on the table, screen down, she shook her head. "The guy I saw isn't in any of the photographs."

"You have to keep looking, Grace." Melissa's voice was getting close to shrill. "What if this couple did more than witness the shooting, but they're actually the ones who took the gun? They had opportunity."

Camden connected the dots. "Not too long ago, a co-worker of mine was placed as a witness to a crime. The evidence had been fabricated. You think this is happening again? Is someone setting you up?"

Melissa and Grace exchanged a look. What had he missed?

"You're asking the same question I did," said Grace. "I know Evangeline. She and my brother, Troy, are an item." She continued. "I did wonder if this whole incident was a setup." She shook her head. "Like Melissa pointed out, the only way for this to work is for the police officer—that's me—to shoot Grimaldi. Even if he's desperate enough to take a bullet, he could've been killed."

Camden nodded. The theory made sense.

Melissa said, "I think that the witnesses may have taken the gun."

It was an interesting theory. "If the couple picked up the gun, it's doubtful they have it still. In fact, we have to assume they might've already dropped it into Lake Michigan."

"Until we find those witnesses, we won't know." Melissa pinched the bridge of her nose. "But if they don't have arrest records, how're we supposed to find them?"

Camden already had an answer to that question. "We use a sketch artist. See if we can get a likeness. Then ask the public for help."

"Help from the public," Melissa scoffed. "Not damn likely. Right now, the whole town hates the police department."

"Do you have any other ideas?" Grace asked.

"No," said Melissa. "None."

"Then, I say we try and get a sketch," said Grace.

Melissa asked, "Did you get a good-enough look for a drawing?"

"I can give a description, sure."

Melissa let out a long exhale. "I hope you know what you're doing, Kingsley. There's a lot riding on finding these witnesses and figuring out what happened to the gun."

Unbidden, the image of his father sitting at the kitchen table came to mind. It filled Camden with a steely resolve to find the truth.

Chief Colton drew in a deep breath yet kept her gaze on the table.

Camden knew what she was going to say. What she had to do. His chest tightened.

"I hate to do this, Grace," she said. "Really, I do. I need to put you on administrative leave for possible use of unlawful force."

"You what?" Grace asked, her voice tight.

"Until we find those witnesses, you can't come back to work. I'll need your badge."

Camden had witnessed this awkward moment too many times to count. He hated each and every episode. Each cop reacted differently. Some cursed. Others cried. A few even threatened lawsuits or violence. All the same, Camden couldn't help but wonder—how had his dad reacted? How would Grace react?

Without a word, Grace stood. She unclipped the badge that was hooked to her belt and set it on the table. Melissa scooped it up, holding it in the palm of her hand as if trying to gauge its weight. Or maybe she was weighing her own words.

"Well, then," the chief said. She cleared her throat. "Before you come back, you'll need to talk to one of the counselors. It's department policy after an officer is involved in a shooting." She pulled a business card from the pocket of her pants and slid it toward Grace. Had she been holding it the whole time? "Give them a call."

She paused. "I'll contact Desiree and let you get back to the interview."

Grace stared forward, said nothing. Without a word, Melissa Colton left the interview room.

Camden's throat was tight. Sure, he was affected by the heartbreaking moment between family members. Still, he knew there was more.

If the truth was what he valued most, then Camden needed to be honest with himself. The facts were not in Grace's favor.

He also knew something else. If he felt drawn to help Grace, then this case was the most dangerous of Camden's career.

Chapter 4

Since being hired by the GGPD, Grace had never given the interview room much thought. As she sat across from Camden Kingsley, she mentally christened it the Torture Chamber.

There was nothing here that could hurt her physically. But the tiny room trapped Grace with her thoughts.

She'd shot a civilian.

Her body camera hadn't captured the moment, though, when the suspect had brandished his own firearm.

The gun in question was missing.

There were witnesses, yet their identities were unknown. What was worse, the couple had certainly seen the incident, but they weren't bothering to come forward.

The population of Grave Gulch had turned against the police force, too, and this incident was certainly going to make matters worse.

So, on a day when she had little to make her thankful, she inexplicably counted the Internal Affairs investigator as a blessing.

He'd questioned her for nearly a half an hour. So far, she'd gone over the shooting three times. Grace started off hoping that this was all a mistake or that she'd somehow been framed. There was no evidence to prove either scenario. It meant one thing: she was in serious trouble.

With each telling, the IA investigator said nothing, only watched her with his dark eyes. At the end, he'd ask her to clarify a point or two. Compare her words from one story to the words used in another.

Obviously, the guy was looking for inconsistencies— a way to trip her up. Grace should feel threatened, yet she didn't. Ironically, she admired his methodical and patient questioning.

In the short thirty minutes with Camden, she'd learned a lot about interrogation. One day, she planned to use the techniques herself—that was, if she didn't get fired.

"Let's spend a little time talking about you," he said.

"What do you want to know?"

"When did you eat last?" he asked.

"At dinner, right before my shift."

"Which was?"

"Around half past five, I guess," she said.

"You guess?"

She tried to reign in her annoyance, but Grace couldn't keep the peevish tone from her voice. "Why does any of this matter?"

"I'm trying to establish your state of mind prior to the shooting. A good bit of how you feel is physical.

Were you hungry? Hungover? Mad about a fight with your boyfriend?"

"I haven't had a drink since last weekend. That was a single glass of wine. I was with my sister, Annalise, and cousin Madison. We spent the evening looking at wedding dresses online." She paused before saying, "My cousin is getting married in the spring."

Camden scribbled a note. Grace couldn't help but wonder what she'd said that was so noteworthy. "And your boyfriend?"

"I don't have one."

"Good." For a moment, they stared at each other. Camden dropped his gaze to his notepad.

Was it her imagination, or had Camden Kingsley sat taller when she'd told him she was single?

After clearing his throat, he spoke again. "I mean, it's good that you didn't come to work upset."

Grace tried to remember her day—a time before the shooting. It had only been a few hours ago, yet the memories were lost in a fog. To her, it seemed as if everything had happened years earlier. A flash came to her. She started again. "I broiled a piece of chicken and had leftover rice pilaf. The bagged salad I planned to eat was wilted, so I had an apple with my meal. I finished eating, put my dishes in the sink. Since I was already in my uniform, I left for work. My shift runs from six o'clock in the evening until two o'clock in the morning. I sleep from about three in the morning until ten o'clock. Get up. Run. Breakfast. Errands. You know, the grind."

"Do you find life to be a grind?"

Damn. Grace had been given a single piece of advice for talking to the IA investigator: don't give any information that's not asked for. What had she done? She'd broken the sole rule. Now, Camden had reason to think she was malcontent—or, worse, angry.

"It's just an expression." And then, "What other questions can I answer?"

Camden gazed at Grace. She wanted to look away. Yet, she couldn't. He asked, "Is there anything else you want to add?"

Grace paused. Was there? Sitting in the tiny room it was easy to question everything. Had she been mistaken? Had Robert Grimaldi actually been holding a gun—or not? She brought back those moments in the alleyway. The air, heavy and humid. She'd been damp with sweat, and her uniform clung to her skin. The street was silent, save for the slapping of her footfalls on the pavement and Grace's own labored breathing.

Then, Mr. Grimaldi had seemed to come from nowhere. He sprinted down the street. He slowed and turned. There was a glint of silver in his hand as light reflected off his sidearm.

"I know what I saw," she said. "The suspect had a gun. I wasn't tired. Or angry. Or distracted."

After hitting the Stop button on his recorder, Camden asked, "You okay?"

"Yes," she said. Then, "No, not really."

"You and Chief Colton are related, right?"

He already knew the answer, so why ask? Still, she answered his question. "She's my cousin."

"Must be tough, to have your cousin take your badge."

Was Camden trying to set Grace up? Were his kindness and professionalism actually just an act? "Probably not half as tough as it was for her to take my badge."

"Listen," he murmured and leaned forward. "The investigation will follow the evidence. We will find out what happened." He stopped and swallowed. "One day soon, you will be okay. I promise."

After just a few minutes, she knew she somehow trusted Camden to be honest and uphold justice. Was that wise, especially since Melissa had warned her to be wary? Or was Grace so keenly vulnerable that she wanted him to be trustworthy?

"How long have you been doing this?" she asked. "Working for IA?"

"A while," he said.

"So you've seen a lot, then?"

Smiling, he shook his head. "I've seen more than enough."

His smile stirred her blood, creating a fluttering in her belly. She disregarded the sensation. "Has there ever been a case like mine in Grave Gulch? A shooting with a missing gun? Witnesses who won't come forward?"

Camden tapped the pen on the table. "No," he said. "I can't think of any."

"Anything close?" she pressed, hoping for a crumb of good news.

"There have been times when police officers have fired their guns and the civilian's weapon wasn't found at the scene." He pinned Grace in place with his gaze. "In the end, it was determined that the officer was mistaken. Maybe the suspect did have something in their hand. Because of the angle or the lighting, it looked like a firearm." He paused again, lining up his pen with the pad of paper. "Despite training and experience, mistakes happen."

"What about those police officers?" Her hands were cold. Grace couldn't help it. She was worried. Would Camden believe the Grimaldi had a gun? And if he didn't, what did that mean for her career? "What about their jobs?"

Why had she even bothered with the question? She could guess the answer—and knew it wouldn't be good. Then again, maybe hope was all she had left.

With a shake of his head, Camden exhaled. "The department had to let them go. You can't hold the public's trust if someone on the force shoots an unarmed person. It doesn't matter if it was an accident. Or a mistake."

Was that what he thought? And would he be right? Had she been mistaken? Dear God, Grace never would have fired if she hadn't been certain. Now, she wasn't sure of anything.

Suddenly, Grace was exhausted. She wished like hell that she still had the cup of coffee Melissa had made. Camden was waiting for her to say something. But what?

The door opened, saving her from having to say anything.

Desiree, Grace's half sister, stepped into the room.

Her curly dark hair was wound into a bun at the nape of her neck. She was casually dressed in a pair of jeans and a hoodie. A leather-bound sketch pad was tucked under her arm. She also carried a metal tin filled with pencils. "Hey, honey. I heard what happened on the news. Stavros sends his love. Danny would have, too. But he's asleep," Desiree said, mentioning the new man in her life and with her two-year-old son.

Desiree was only at police headquarters as the department's part-time sketch artist. Still, emotions—relief and regret—washed over Grace in a wave. She felt her lip start to quiver.

Desiree rushed forward. Pulling Grace from the chair, she wrapped her into a big hug. Enveloped in her sister's embrace, Grace's throat closed. Her eyes burned. She fought with everything in her to keep from crying.

"How ya doing?"

"Ya know." Even Grace heard the tremor of emotion in her voice. "Lousy."

"I'm here for you. You know that, right?"

Grace nodded, not trusting her own voice.

Desiree released her younger sibling. "I got a call from Melissa. She said there were some witnesses to the incident. You need me to do a sketch…" Her voice trailed off as her eyes moved across the table.

"This is Camden Kingsley," said Grace, answering the unasked question of *Who's that guy?*

"Nice to meet you, Camden," said Desiree, offering her hand to shake. "I'm Desiree. Sketch artist. Grace's eldest sister."

"I'm from Internal Affairs," he said.

Desiree's spine went rigid. "IA?" she echoed, still shaking his hand. "Why's IA here?"

"He's doing his job," said Grace. She stopped speaking.

Why was she defending the man who had the power to ruin her career? Heck, he could ruin her life. But she knew his goal was to seek out the truth, even if he didn't believe her. Not yet, anyway.

"I guess we all have a job to do," said Desiree. "Before I get started, do you need anything? A water, maybe?"

Grace slipped back into her seat. Her back ached. Her head hurt. Her eyes were heavy, and she wanted to sleep for two weeks straight. "Coffee," said Grace. "With sugar, no milk."

"I know how my baby sister drinks her coffee," said Desiree with mock indignation. Her phone pinged with an incoming text. She glanced at the screen and drew her brows together.

Grace's chest tightened. "What's wrong? Is it something with Danny?" she asked. "I can't handle more bad news."

"Nothing's wrong." She smiled. "It's Stavros. I'll call him back when we're done."

Camden rose to his feet. "I could use a coffee, too. You two get started. I'll be back in a minute." He pointed to Desiree. "What do you want?"

"I'm good for now." She set her pad and pencil box on the table. "Thanks for asking, though."

Desiree stood by the table and waited until Camden left the room. "He's really easy to look at. Too bad he's IA."

"Camden's not a bad guy. He's just got a difficult job, that's all."

"A cop getting other people to tattle on cops." Desiree dropped into the chair next to Grace's. She opened the sketch pad to a fresh sheet. "That sounds like a whole lot to me."

"Or he's keeping us all honest," said Grace.

Desiree lifted one brow. "Right. Honest."

"What?" Grace asked. She knew, though. Her cheeks warmed, just thinking about Camden and his eyes.

"What do you mean, *what?*"

"What's up with the look?" Lifting a single brow, she mirrored her sister's expression mockingly.

Desiree swatted Grace's arm. "You know what your mom says. Your face will freeze that way."

"My face," said Grace. "What about yours?"

"You want to see a face?" Desiree asked. She rested

her chin on her hands and batted her eyelashes. "That's you looking at the IA guy."

Had her appreciation of Camden—his smile, his broad shoulders, his honesty—been that obvious? Or did Desiree know Grace better than Grace knew herself? "Is not."

"Is too! But don't worry, he is hot."

"Really? I hadn't noticed," Grace lied to her sister. As far as she was concerned, Camden Kingsley was more than good-looking; he might actually be a good person. What was she thinking? She couldn't have a crush on the IA investigator.

"Aren't you worried that your pants will catch on fire for telling lies like that?"

Grace let out a peal of laughter. It felt good to do so and yet the timing was all wrong. Desiree and Grace weren't at home, joking around. She was in an interrogation room at the police station. What was more, *she* was the one being questioned.

"Hey," said Desiree, rubbing the back of Grace's arm. "It'll be okay. I promise."

"You have to tell me the truth. How bad is the media coverage?"

Desiree exhaled and shook her head. "It's bad. That's what Stavros said when he texted me. Even at this hour, the protests are getting worse. People are calling on Melissa to resign."

"No. Melissa can't leave the department. She's the chief of police! Whether Grave Gulch wants to admit it or not, the town needs Melissa."

"The problem is that she's your cousin," said Desiree. "There are a lot of Coltons who work for the GGPD. People are complaining about nepotism."

Bile rose in the back of Grace's throat. Not only had the shooting put Grace's career in jeopardy, but it had further threatened Melissa's, as well.

Grabbing Grace by the wrist, Desiree said, "We will get through this—together, as a family—like always." Patting her arm again, she continued, "Now, let's get this sketch done. The sooner we can get a picture out to the public, the quicker we can find your witnesses."

Camden walked down the empty hallway of the police station. True, he'd left to get a cup of coffee, but what he really needed was time. Time to think. Time to regroup. Time to figure out why he was so damn affected by Grace Colton. For starters, she was pretty. No, that wasn't exactly right. Flowers were pretty. Sunsets were pretty. Every time he glanced at Grace it was like seeing the ocean or the Grand Canyon for the first time. In a word, she was breathtaking.

If he was lucky, he'd run into Brett Shea. Then he could ask about the witnesses. Who knew, maybe he'd get lucky twice, and Brett would have something more to add that exonerated Grace.

His phone began to shimmy, and he fished it from the pocket of his coat.

Damn. Maybe his luck had just run out.

"Hey, Arielle. What's up?"

"So what have you learned?"

Above, fluorescent lights buzzed and cast a jaundiced glow. But no coffeepot. What'd a guy have to do to find a cup around here? "There were witnesses."

"What'd they say?" Arielle asked.

"They ran off." He opened the metal door that led to a set of stairs and paused. He did have information for his boss. "Chief Colton put her on administrative leave pending the outcome of my investigation and an evaluation with a counselor."

"As she should," said Arielle. "What else can you tell me?"

"Officer Colton is with a sketch artist now. We hope to have a likeness to share with the public soon."

"*We*?" Arielle scoffed. "Remember whose team you're on, Camden."

"I'm on whichever team is looking for the facts." He owed it to his father to not let politics or public outcry get in the way of the truth. "I'm on the team that won't jump to conclusions."

Arielle spoke. "It's like what the mayor said, the GGPD has messed up. A serial killer is on the loose because their forensic investigator tampered with evidence. Innocent people went to jail because the police failed to do their jobs. Guilty people are on the street."

Camden leaned against the open door. There was no denying that Arielle and Mayor Abels were right. "Sure, but none of that has anything to do with what happened tonight."

"Or maybe it has everything to do with what happened. Is it bad leadership?"

Camden closed his eyes. Hadn't he been wondering the same thing just hours before? Then, he'd met Grace Colton. Had he forgotten about the other facts—focusing only on her blue eyes, her smile, her tight rear and strong legs, and, well, how damned attractive she was?

Which meant what?

For starters, he'd never be able to remain professional and impartial.

"I might not be the guy for this case," he began.

"You're kidding, right?"

"It's just…" He paused. Camden needed to choose his words with extreme care. "Grace Colton has integrity. It's hard to see her as being anything other than honest."

Above, the clang of footsteps drew Camden's attention. He looked up the winding stairwell. Chief Colton was descending.

"I have to go. I'll stay here until the sketch artist is done. We'll regroup in the morning."

"The mayor wants you on this case. Get used to it."

Before Camden could respond, the line went dead.

Melissa stopped on the bottom step. "Everything okay?"

While tucking the phone back into his suit coat, Camden said, "It's Arielle. She's looking for an update."

After a beat, she asked, "How's the sketch coming?"

"I don't know. It seemed like the sisters needed a moment. So, I took the opportunity to come looking for coffee."

"That's something I can help you out with," said Melissa, pivoting on the step. "There's always a pot brewed in the squad room, but you have to be pretty generous to call that stuff coffee. I have a single-serve in my office. I can make you something fresher."

"And a cup for Grace," said Camden. Damn. Even he heard the eagerness in his tone. Clearing his throat, he followed the police chief up the stairs.

"She's been through a lot," said Melissa, stopping to open a door.

Camden stepped onto the main floor. "Officer Colton seems to be holding up well under all the pressure."

"Don't let the cool exterior fool you. Usually, my cousin is quite chatty."

An image of Grace laughing and talking came to mind—and brought a smile to Camden's lips. He had to get this case reassigned.

As she started brewing a cup, Melissa asked, "How do you take your coffee?"

"Just black," he said. "Grace takes her with sugar. No milk."

Openmouthed, Melissa stared at Camden. He immediately understood his mistake. Knowing how Grace Colton liked her coffee made him look like a lovesick schoolboy. His chest was hot with embarrassment. He needed to fix the problem—and now.

He cleared his throat. "Downstairs, Grace and Desiree were talking. She mentioned it. I guess I just remembered."

Damn. Had he just made matters worse? Now he looked like a lovesick schoolboy who'd also memorized the class schedule of his crush. Clamping his jaw shut, Camden swore to say nothing more.

What was wrong with Camden? It's not like he'd never met a good-looking woman before. It's just that Grace was different. Hell, it felt like he'd been waiting for her to show up for his entire life.

With a smile, Melissa handed him a steaming cup of coffee. "Sugar. No milk."

He took the cup. Yet, he couldn't help but wonder—why the smile? Had he already let on that his interest in Grace Colton went beyond professional?

Chapter 5

"Here you go." Desiree held up her sketch pad for Grace to see.

The rendering was in black-and-white. Yet, her sister had drawn a close likeness to the woman she'd seen on the street. "That's her." Grace sighed with relief. "Maybe the case will start moving in a positive direction."

"That's why I'm here." She flipped to a clean page. "Let's get started on the male witness, and I can get home to my baby."

"Is Mom taking care of Danny?"

"No, Stavros is home with him," said Desiree. "Danny was asleep when I left," she continued. "He should be okay. But I don't like to leave Danny alone for long."

Grace didn't blame her sister. True, she was a protective mother, but there was more. At the beginning of the year, Danny had been kidnapped at a wedding. Then over the summer, a woman had stalked Grace's nephew and tried to steal him, as well. It was a huge blessing that Danny was physically unharmed. Still, the incidents had left their mark on the child.

"How's he doing?"

"Nights are the worst, to be honest. He has nightmares. He doesn't like the dark."

Grace's chest tightened with a pang of guilt. "You've done too much for me already. Go home. Take care of your family. We can finish up in the morning."

"Like it or not, you're part of my family, baby sister. I'm here for the long haul."

Opening her mouth, Grace was ready to argue. The door opened, and whatever she might've said was forgotten. Camden stood on the threshold with a cup of coffee in each hand. He'd loosened his tie, and a narrow strip of flesh was exposed at his neck. Grace couldn't look away.

"Sorry it took so long," he said, setting the cups on the table. "Your cousin had to help me find the coffee." He pushed a cup toward Grace. "Sugar, no milk."

The same fluttering from before filled her middle. "Desiree did a likeness of the female witness." She reached for the coffee. "She was just about to go home and see my adorable nephew."

"I'm not leaving until we're done, Grace," Desiree said. "Besides, I'll stay till you're done, too. After that, you can stay with me."

"No way to both," said Grace, suddenly feeling very young. "I don't need a babysitter. I'll be fine." She took a sip of coffee, as if that somehow proved her point. The caffeine hit her system, and her head began to buzz. Now, she'd never get to sleep tonight. Not that she really thought she'd get much rest—even without drinking the coffee.

She was worried about her job, her reputation, and in a small way the health of Robert Grimaldi.

"I don't think you need a babysitter, either. But here's what we do need to do—finish the second sketch."

Grace sipped her coffee to hide a smile.

"What's that for?" Desiree asked.

"You."

"Me?"

"You sound like you did when we were younger, and Mom left you in charge."

"Are you saying that I'm using my bossy-older-sister voice?"

Grace measured a distance between finger and thumb. "Maybe a little."

"Good. Then, let's get this done."

"Honestly, you can go home." Grace was almost positive that Danny was fine. Yet, she hated that Desiree was worried. And it was all because of her.

Camden sat on the edge of the table, lifting his own cup of coffee to his lips. "Your sister is right, finishing the sketch. Do it now. You'll forget details later."

He was right, she knew. Yet, with him so near she could think of nothing else than, well, him. His dark eyes. His full lips. His thick hair. His features, somehow both strong and refined. In fact, he looked so damned perfect that she'd swear he was an artist's rendering of what a man should be—not simply flesh and blood.

Grace swiveled in the cramped seat to face her sister. "Where do you want to start?"

"The eyes," said Desiree. "After all, they're the windows to the soul, right?"

Grace closed her own eyes. Inhaled. Exhaled. She pictured the street and the young man with a thin beard. She focused on only the man. His face. His eyes.

They were dark brown. Full lashes. Beautifully shaped.

Full lips.

No, damn it. In her mind's eye, she saw Camden.

With a sigh, Grace slumped back in her seat. Would she ever be able to prove her innocence? Especially since there was one thing she knew for certain. Grace was drawn to the guy who'd been sent to find out if she was guilty.

What was her problem? Was it because almost everyone in her family had found a person to love? Or was it because Grace hadn't been on a date worth mentioning since joining the force?

"Can I see the sketch you did of the woman?" he asked, interrupting her thoughts.

Desiree handed over a sheet of paper. For a moment, Camden studied the likeness. "I don't recognize her, but someone must. I'll take this to Melissa. At least she can get the picture to the local reporters. They can splash it all over social media. Then I'm going back to my office. We should meet in the morning, Grace. Here. Nine o'clock."

"Nine o'clock," she echoed. "I'll be here."

He took another sip of coffee before rising from the table. Then he was gone.

Grace had been warned about the IA investigator. Yet, that was before she'd met Camden Kingsley. She couldn't help it: she trusted him to do the right thing. Did that make her a fool?

* * *

For once in his life, Camden had not been a man of his word. He had not returned to his office. Instead, he'd stayed at the police department and commandeered a small conference room on the first floor—courtesy of Chief Colton.

It had been more than an hour since he'd left Grace Colton with her sister, the sketch artist. The time was now 1:45 a.m. And still he couldn't bring himself to go home.

The metal door that led to the stairs opened and closed with a clang. Camden looked up just as Grace strode past. Desiree was at her side.

The two women couldn't look more different. Desiree, several years older, had dark curly hair that matched her curvy figure. Grace, blond-haired and blue-eyed, was tall and lithe. She glanced into the room as she passed.

Camden's mouth went dry with desire.

"Hey," she said, slowing to a stop. "I thought you were going back to your office. Did you find anything new? Did the gun turn up? Was Ellie able to recover any more of the body-cam footage?"

It was impossible to miss her hopeful tone. He had nothing to offer, unfortunately. Instinctively, his shoulder blades pinched together. Rubbing the back of his neck, he said, "Your cousin offered me this conference room to use. For now, it seemed better to stay put." His words trailed off. What else was there to say? He couldn't admit the truth—that he'd waited around for more than an hour hoping to catch another glimpse of Grace.

Nodding slowly, she exhaled. "Okay, then."

"If there's nothing new, then I'm going to go," said

Desiree. "I don't like to leave Danny at home, even with Stavros on duty."

"You know, you're the only mom I know who isn't even satisfied with a physician watching their child." Grace pulled her sister in for a hug.

"I think a lot of moms are like me. You sure you're okay?"

With a nod, Grace released her sister.

Desiree continued. "You know I'm always here for you, right? You can stay at my place if you want. My kid would love to see you in the morning."

"I'm tempted, but I'm good." Grace gave her sister a wan smile. "Honestly."

"All right, then, I am finally going home." Desiree flicked her fingertips with a small wave.

He'd been charged with finding the truth about Grace Colton. Was there more to the family than what he'd seen so far? Or were they simply a kind and loving family?

Redirecting his gaze back at his open laptop, Camden saw nothing. Was he a heel for staying on the case? Or was he just a guy doing his job?

Grace loosened her hair, shaking her tresses out of the bun she'd worn at the nape of her neck. Golden locks flowed over her shoulders. His fingers itched with the need to touch her. Good Lord! What was the matter with him? *Focus, damn it. Focus.*

"Do you need to speak to me about anything else?" she asked, bringing him back to the tiny conference room.

"It's been a long evening. Go home. Sleep if you can."

"Sleep?" she echoed. "I doubt I'll get much rest."

"You might surprise yourself. We'll get back together in the morning."

She placed her hand on the doorjamb and drew her bottom lip between her teeth. He waited, wondering what she wanted to say. Or ask.

She exhaled and met his gaze. "Well, good night."

"Yeah," he said. The heavy weight of fatigue dropped to his shoulders. "G'night."

She turned and walked away. He waited until the sound of her footfalls faded to nothing. Camden glanced back at his computer. The monitor was now asleep, and his reflection wavered in the dark screen.

"You have to get off this case," he said to his shadowy self. "There's no two ways about it. If you keep working on this investigation, you're going to ruin her career as well as yours."

He gave a short laugh. He could definitely get the case assigned to someone else if he admitted to Arielle that he'd developed a crush on the subject of the latest IA investigation.

After packing up his computer, Camden stood. Stretched. For the first time in hours, his stomach grumbled with a reminder that he'd skipped his late dinner.

He made his way through the squad room. The waiting room of the police station was empty. Not even a duty sergeant sat behind the front desk.

He walked into the holding area and stopped short. Beyond the glass doors, the street was filled with more than two dozen protesters.

Some held signs that read:
Fire the Chief.
Others read:
Grave Gulch Deserves Better.
Or others:
Police Reform NOW!

A line of cops—all in uniform—stood in front of the doors. No doubt, they were blocking people from entering the building.

Despite the different signs they held, the protesters were all unified in their message. "What do we want?" one person called out.

A crowd of more than two dozen answered in unison. "To fire Grace Colton!"

"When do we want it?" the leader on a bullhorn asked.

Everyone called back with a single word. "Now!"

The sound of a gasp caught his attention. On the opposite side of the lobby, Grace stood near a corner. She'd changed out of her police uniform and now wore a light blue T-shirt and jeans. A duffel bag was slung over her shoulder.

The change in Grace from just a few minutes earlier was remarkable. Yet, it was more than the way her jeans hugged her rear and thighs. Or that the delicate blue of her shirt matched her eyes perfectly. Her complexion was pale.

She looked at him, her eyes wide and her voice small. "What do I do now?" she asked.

The last thing Camden needed was to spend more time with Grace. Was he going to leave her to face that mob alone?

"Obviously, you can't go out those doors." He hustled to her side. God, it felt good to stand next to her. He held out his hand. "Come with me. I'll take you out the back."

She looked from his palm to his face and back again. Without a word, she slipped her fingers through his. In taking her hand, Camden had crossed a line. He'd become personally involved with the subject of an investigation. From here, would he ever be able to go back?

He really didn't care how much damage he might be doing to his career. In the moment, there was only one thing that mattered to Camden: it was Grace.

Head buzzing, Grace walked down the hallway. Was there really a mob outside the police station? Were they all calling for her resignation? It was almost two in the morning. Good god, they really must hate her. Each fact was a punch to her gut, painful and surprising, and left her ready to retch.

Obviously, you can't go out those doors, Camden had said.

Come with me, he'd offered. *I'll take you out the back*.

Then, he'd grabbed her hand, and now, she was being led through the police station. This whole situation had been nothing short of a nightmare. From the time she'd fired her gun, Grace felt as if she'd been walking in a fog.

She was young, and a rookie to boot. But if Grace wanted to prove her innocence, it was time to wake up. She needed to act, not be led around and told what to do.

She pulled her hand from Camden's grip and stopped in the middle of the corridor.

He strode on for a step or two, before turning to face her.

"You okay?" he asked.

"I'm not sneaking out the back door like a criminal. It makes me look guilty." She pivoted. "I'm going outside. I'll explain to that crowd what happened."

"What? No way. That crowd is peaceful now. What will you do if that changes?" He didn't wait for an answer. "There's a lot of police officers standing in front of the building. What happens to them if things get violent?"

"I…" Grace began. Maybe her plan wasn't as solid as she thought.

"There's a time and place for you to tell your story. Now's not it."

He was right, she knew. Yet, she couldn't think of anything to say.

"Do you trust me?" he asked.

Did she? Melissa had warned her about the IA investigator. Yet, Camden was so different than the man she'd imagined. Maybe she did trust him—at least a little.

She shrugged.

"Come with me. I'll get you out of the building and get home safe." He paused. "Where do you live?"

"I have an apartment a few blocks from here."

"Car?" he asked.

She shook her head. "I walked to work today."

"C'mon," he said. He didn't reach for her hand a second time. "Let's go."

Was he really going to walk her home? Honestly, Grave Gulch was a fairly safe town—or had been, until recently. She'd be fine on her own.

But would she?

She'd seen the protesters at the front door. There was no telling what would happen if they found Grace. "Thanks," she said. "I appreciate the offer."

He opened the back door. The air was still hot and heavy, and sweat gathered at the nape of her neck.

The chanting from the protesters was clear even at the back of the building.

"What do we want?"

"To fire Grace Colton!"

"When do we want it?"

"Now!"

The police station's parking lot had more than a dozen vehicles—both police cruisers and personal cars—parked inside the perimeter. Thankfully, the street was empty. After pulling the door open, Camden said, "Ladies first."

Grace paused before stepping through. "I know you don't have to do this," she said. "You know, help me out." Her eyes rested on his hand. His fingers were long, his nails neatly trimmed. For a moment, she recalled the feeling of his palm in hers. She liked the memory a little too much. Returning her gaze to his face, she continued, "Anyway, I want to thank you."

He accepted her gratitude with a nod. "Let's go before someone comes around the building and sees you."

She slid through the door and paused on the side street.

"This way," said Camden. He led her away from the police station and the waiting mob.

The lights from police headquarters were the only ones on the block. Within a few yards, the shadows moved in, surrounding Grace with darkness. The voices of the protesters faded.

Camden stayed at her side yet said nothing.

She didn't mind the quiet. It gave her time to think. Too much had happened for her to actually have a thought.

Ahead, the light from Mae's Diner spilled onto the sidewalk. Camden's pace slowed as they passed. He stared at the door.

"What is it?" she asked.

He gave a small smile. "I was thinking that I haven't eaten since lunch. That was—what, twelve—" he looked at his watch, an old-school timepiece with a leather band "—make that fourteen hours ago."

"We can stop and grab a bite." Had she just invited herself to have a midnight snack with Camden Kingsley? What was the matter with her? Grace had to get a grip. "I mean, I can get myself home from here. It's just a few blocks away. You get something to eat."

He'd already turned back to Mae's Diner. "Or we can both stop."

The pull to be with Camden was strong—maybe too strong. "Really, I shouldn't." She hooked her thumb over her shoulder. "I have an early meeting in the morning."

"Yeah," he said, pulling the door open. "With me. We can move back the time if you want. Come in and at least keep me company. Eating alone—and in the middle of the night, no less—is just sad."

There were about a million reasons for Grace to say no. She could recite them all without thinking. It was late. She was tired. She'd had the worst day of her life, and she just wanted it to end. She shouldn't be hanging out with the man in charge of her investigation—especially since she found him so damned handsome.

Yet, her mouth didn't listen to her mind. Grace found herself walking through the door. "I guess I could stay for a little bit…"

A man with sparse hair and a round middle stood behind a long counter. He wore a white apron and a blue shirt. A name tag read *Mike*. "Evening, folks," he said as they walked through the door. "Heck of a night to be out."

"You mean, all the people at the police station?" asked

Camden, not letting on that they'd just been inside the building. "Heck of a night."

"Have a seat anywhere you'd like. I'm the only one here, so the menu's pretty limited."

Aside from the counter, the room was ringed with booths, the seats covered in red and gray vinyl. A dozen tables, with chairs set on top, sat in the middle of the room.

Camden slid onto a stool near where the man stood. Grace took a stool beside him. She dropped her duffel bag at her feet. "What d'you recommend?" Camden asked.

"The apple pie's fresh this morning," Mike said. "Not many people ordered, so I'd give you a big slice."

Camden gestured to Grace, allowing her to order first. "I'll take pie and a coffee. Decaf."

"Make that two," said Camden.

"Two pies and two decaf coffees, coming right up," said Mike. "You want that pie heated?"

"Sure," said Camden. And then, "You got vanilla ice cream?"

"Any other way to eat apple pie?" Mike asked.

"Not that I know of," said Camden, slipping his messenger bag over the chair back.

Grace enjoyed listening to the easy banter. It was a nice break from the chaos of the evening. "Same," she said.

"Give me a minute, and I'll be right back," Mike said, before disappearing through a set of doors marked *Kitchen*.

Grace picked up a set of silverware wrapped in a paper napkin. She twirled it between her fingers. "So," she began, not knowing what to say next, "how'd you end up working for IA?"

"I was a cop first," he said. "State police. I worked a lot with Arielle, and when a position opened up, she helped me get the job."

Grace nodded. She wasn't sure where the conversation was going. Was it right to chat up Camden? No, she decided, she definitely shouldn't try to get chummy with the guy from Internal Affairs.

If it was wrong, why had she even asked about his life?

"My dad was a beat cop in Detroit," he continued. "I grew up admiring him and wanting to be just like my pop. Probably the same reason that you joined the force. I mean, there certainly are a lot of Coltons working for the GGPD."

It was definitely part of the reason why Grace had become a police officer. "There's that aspect," she said. "I admire the hell out of Melissa. Annalise, my other sister, works for GGPD as a canine instructor. You met Desiree, who's a part-time sketch artist. I have a brother who's a detective."

"I know Troy."

"There's a cousin who's with the FBI."

"I've never met Bryce, but I've heard the name."

"So you know that we're very heavy into law enforcement. But…"

"But what?" he asked.

"There's more to the story." She drew in a deep breath, not completely certain why she was sharing her family's history. "Desiree and I are half sisters. Her mother, Amanda, was murdered decades ago. The killer was never found."

"Wow," said Camden. "That's rough." He paused. "I know how a family's history can influence everyone."

She waited a beat. And then another. Was there something else he wanted to say? Camden stayed silent.

"Anyway," she sighed. How long had it been since Grace had told this story? It had been years, and still she knew all the details. Smoothing a seam on the rolled napkin, she spoke. "My dad was heartbroken. A few years later, he met and married my mom. She was a preschool teacher at the time. Amanda's memory looms large in our house. In our entire family, really. We all want to make sure that justice is done for everybody—even if it never happened for Amanda."

She looked up and met Camden's gaze. He opened his mouth, ready to speak. Before he said a word, the kitchen door opened. Mike emerged, holding a tray with two huge slices of pie and two steaming cups of coffee.

"I made a new pot of coffee for you folks," he said, setting the tray on the counter. "The other one had gotten old." He set a cup in front of Grace. "How'd you both take your poison? Milk? Sugar? Straight black?"

"She'll take sugar, no milk. I like my coffee black."

Mike placed a dish filled with sugar packets next to Grace's cup. Then he set down the plates of pie. "Enjoy."

Grace unwrapped her utensils. Using the side of her fork, she cut off a piece of pie before swirling it through the melting ice cream. She took a bite and chewed slowly, savoring the flaky crust, the spicy cinnamon and the sweet-tart apples.

Swallowing down her bite with a sip of coffee, she couldn't shake the feeling that Camden had been ready to tell her something but changed his mind. It left her wondering about what he'd been about to say…and why she was so eager to hear more about him.

Chapter 6

Camden scraped the last bit of pie off his plate and took the final bite. He hummed with satisfaction. "Delicious."

Grace sat beside him and nodded. "Good idea to stop. I didn't know that I needed a break, but I did." She pushed her plate back with a finger.

A clock above the kitchen doors read 2:37 a.m. Without a doubt, this had been one of the longest workdays in recent memory. Camden was comfortably full and ready for several uninterrupted hours of sleep. Yet, he didn't want the night to end.

"Can I get you folks anything else?" Mike asked. "A top-up on your coffee?"

"I'm good," said Grace, placing her hand over the cup. "It's late. I better get going."

"We'll just take the check," said Camden.

"Two checks." Grace held up two fingers.

"I'll make it easy on you both. You each owe five dollars," said Mike. "And you can figure it out on your own. I never interfere in anyone's love life."

Grace's cheeks reddened. "Oh, we're not a couple."

"Yeah, right." Mike drew out his words.

The last thing Camden wanted was to let things get uncomfortable for Grace. Despite the fact that he'd had a better time with Grace than on his last three dates combined, they weren't involved. What's more—they never would be in a relationship.

Pulling his wallet from his back pocket, Camden found a twenty-dollar bill. He threw it on the counter. To Mike he said, "Thanks for the pie and coffee." He stood. "C'mon. You're right, Grace. It's late. Let's go."

Grace stood and picked up the duffel she'd stowed on the floor. "You don't have to pay for me," she said. "I'm completely capable. I have a job…" She blanched. He could only guess what she was thinking—*at least, she used to have a job.*

Camden didn't want anything to get weird. "I was the one who invited you. I can cover the tab for coffee and pie." He walked to the door and held it open as she passed. The street was silent. The heat from the day had finally broken, yet the air was heavy with humidity. "It feels like rain," he said.

"Maybe the storm will chase away the protesters tomorrow." She started walking down the sidewalk. "I believe that everyone should exercise their First Amendment rights. Still, it's a little different when a group is calling for me to be fired."

Camden jogged to her side. He wanted to offer her some kind of comfort, to tell her everything would be okay. But would it? Besides, he worked for Internal Affairs. In stopping at Mae's Diner, he'd come dangerously close to crossing a professional line.

They walked the next few blocks in silence. Grace stopped in front of a brick apartment building. Narrow with four stories, it was much like all the other buildings on the block. A set of steps led to a security door. "This is my place." While retrieving a set of keys from her black duffel bag, Grace climbed the short flight of stairs.

"You're okay to get into your place yourself?"

Sliding a key into a security-door lock, she said, "I'll be fine. See you in the morning."

And now what? Did he follow her up the steps? Shake her hand? Hug her? God help him, in a flash he imagined Grace's lips on his own. "Well," he said stepping backward, "I have to get my car from the police department." A rumble of thunder sounded, and a far-off flash of lighting glowed at the horizon.

Grace turned her gaze to the sky. "I think that's the storm you predicted."

Without a backward glance, Grace slid into the foyer. He only caught a glimpse of the cramped space—just a tiled area, with a bank of mailboxes set into the wall. The door closed, the lock engaging with a click.

Remaining on the sidewalk, Camden watched the building. A moment later, a window glowed as a light inside a room was illuminated. It was Grace's apartment—second floor, unit on the left.

A breeze blew, sending leaves skittering down the street. There was the hint of a chill in the wind. Had he been right? Was a storm coming?

Camden turned toward the police station. As he walked, he tried to think of everything he knew about Grace and her case. Yet, his mind continued to wander to another time and another cop who hadn't been given the benefit of a fair investigation.

At the diner, he'd been tempted to share what had happened to his father. He never spoke about his pop anymore. So why now? Why with her?

It's not that Camden lived like a monk. He dated but nobody had created a spark of excitement for a long time. Grace had definitely awakened feelings that he dared not examine too closely.

Lights over the parking lot of GGPD's headquarters still blazed bright. Fewer cars filled spaces now than before. The protesters at the front of the building were gone. The only sound was the slapping of Camden's shoes on the pavement. He crossed the lot to his car. Using a fob, he unlocked the door. As he slid behind the passenger seat, the first raindrop fell. The storm had finally come.

As Grace woke the next morning, she felt her head throb. Her tongue was thick, and her mouth was dry. Was she hungover? What had she done the night before? The alarm on her phone continued to blare the opening chords of a pop song. With a groan, she rolled over and silenced her phone.

Then it hit like a wave crashing on the shore. Everything from last night came back in an instant. The break-in. The chase. The shooting. And, worst of all, the missing gun and damaged body camera. A cramp gripped Grace's middle. With a moan, she curled into a ball.

Breathe, she told herself. *In through the nose. Out through the mouth.* Just like the yoga teacher had instructed when she, Annalise, Desiree, and her mom had taken that class in the spring.

The controlled breathing, along with the happy memory, settled her stomach. Flopping to her back, Grace stared at the ceiling. Her curtains were pulled tight. Outside, rain tapped against her window.

In a flash, she recalled standing next to Camden Kingsley on the sidewalk. He had held out his hand and looked to the sky. "Feels like rain," he'd said.

She guessed that he'd been right.

Honestly, she didn't know what to make of Camden. They both knew he had to investigate her—never mind that he spoke only of finding the truth. It was the truth about *her* that he hoped to find. Yet, he'd been kind. Concerned. Almost caring.

He wasn't at all what she'd expected. And it had nothing to do with the fact that he was good-looking. He was distractingly handsome, in fact.

Was Camden really as good a guy as he seemed?

Or was it all an act—like Melissa warned it might have been? Was he trying to get Grace to share incriminating evidence?

There were other worries, as well. Had she really shot someone? Her palm ached with the recoil from her gun and her chest tightened. There was a part of Grace that hoped it was all a bad dream. She knew it wasn't. Being the cop who shot a civilian was now a part of her new reality.

Sitting up, she stretched her arms above her head. There was no sense in lying in bed all day. She had to get up and face whatever came next.

As she set her feet on the floor, her phone began to ring.

Sitting on the edge of her bed, she swiped the call open. "Morning, Mom."

"Baby, how are you? I saw what happened on the news and wanted to call you last night. Your father said to wait. He said that you'd call us when you wanted to talk. But I haven't slept."

Grace's stomach cramped again, this time with guilt, not anxiety. She knew her parents—especially her mother—would be upset. She should've reached out before now. "Sorry for not calling earlier. I didn't get home until after two o'clock this morning. Then it was too late."

"You can call me anytime, you know that."

"Yeah, I do."

"Tell me everything," said her mother. "What happened?"

Grace had only given herself forty-five minutes to get ready. "I have a meeting with the guy from IA in less than an hour. I wish I could talk more, Mom…"

"IA? Why do you have to talk to someone from Internal Affairs? Are they saying that you're in the wrong?"

Rising from the bed, Grace walked down the short hallway to the kitchen. "Nobody is saying anything. Camden is trying to gather all the facts, which is what everyone wants."

"Camden, is it? Well, he's only after one thing—to make you guilty. Watch what you say to him, Grace. Don't let him ingratiate himself with you. I saw a movie on TV last week. Wait, no. It was last month. Or the month before that."

"Mom," she interrupted, "I really can't chat."

"It doesn't matter when I saw the movie. The point is that a police officer gets wrongly accused of stealing from the precinct. Then someone from Internal Affairs gets involved. It's almost like what happened with Evangeline. You remember that, right?"

"I remember, Mom. But really..." she began, trying to get off the phone.

"Oh, yes. The movie," her mother said. "After an investigation, the officer is found guilty. He's fired. His wife leaves him. He develops a drinking problem."

"I don't have a drinking problem, Mom." Grace set her phone on the counter and actuated the Speaker function. With both hands free, she scooped coffee grounds into a paper liner. "I'm running late, though."

"Well, I'll make this short. The guy knows something is wrong. So he launches his own investigation of the investigators. Guess what? It was the person from Internal Affairs who embezzled the money. The police officer had been set up from the beginning."

"That sounds like an interesting movie, but it has nothing to do with me. Internal Affairs didn't force Mr. Grimaldi to run when I told him to stop. Or to pull a gun on me in order to escape." She filled the coffee maker's reservoir with water and started a pot brewing. The nutty aroma filled her kitchen.

"I'm just saying," said her mother, "I don't think that people from Internal Affairs are to be trusted."

Wasn't that what Melissa had said already? And Desiree? "I appreciate your concern," said Grace. "You always look out for me."

"That's because you're my baby, even though you're twenty-five."

"I love you, Mom. But I really do have to go."

"Okay. I'll see you tonight."

"Tonight?" Grace echoed. What was happening tonight?

"Don't tell me you forgot," her mother began. "I know you got the invitation because I handed it to you myself."

"Umm…" Invitation?

Her mom sighed. "Remember? Your dad and I are hosting an engagement party for Palmer and Soledad. Six o'clock at the restaurant."

Grace's father, Geoff, owned the Grave Gulch Grille. It was one of the nicest restaurants in town. Her mom, Leanne, worked as the hostess—which was perfect for her mother's bubbly personality. More than that, it was a convenient place to celebrate all special occasions. That being said, she'd completely forgotten about the party for her brother and his fiancée.

"You wouldn't believe the outfit I found for Lyra," her mother gushed about Soledad's adopted daughter. "All pink and frills. It has these little bloomers. She'll be adorable."

"That baby could wear anything and be adorable," said Grace, smiling. Actually, the whole family was pretty darned cute.

It really did seem like everyone in the Colton clan was finding love. Of course, Grace knew she'd be the final one to settle down. As the baby of the family, she always was last.

It's just…

Unbidden, Camden's face came to mind.

"So, you'll come to the party tonight?" her mother asked.

While pouring a cup of coffee, Grace opened her mouth, ready to remind her mother that she wouldn't be able to attend. After all, she was supposed to work the night shift for the next month.

Then she remembered. Until further notice, Grace was on administrative leave. She wasn't expected at work tonight, or any other night. Disappointment, like a boot heel to the gut, hit her hard.

"I'll see what I can do about the party," she said, breathless. "But I really do have to go, Mom."

"Call me later."

"Okay."

"Promise?"

Grace stirred a spoonful of sugar into her coffee. "I promise."

"Love you, baby."

"Love you, too," she said, before ending the call.

After setting her phone aside, Grace picked up her mug and took a sip. Three times she'd been warned about Camden—well, not about him personally. But she'd been warned not to trust anyone from IA.

Did her family want her to be extra cautious?

Or was there something more to Camden Kingsley?

He was good-looking. What's more, he'd seemed like a decent person who was looking only for the truth.

She couldn't help but wonder, what if she was wrong?

What if he was only interested in finding a way to make Grace pay?

Chapter 7

Camden stepped out of the shower and grabbed his towel from the hook. Running it through his damp hair, he mentally prepared for what he needed to do next. He had to get taken off the Grace Colton case. There was no way he could be impartial, given his immediate attraction to her. Hell, Grace had even shown up in his dreams. She'd been in his arms. His lips had been on her neck. He'd woken hard with desire, something that never happened with an investigation's subject before. In the end, his biases would cost them both.

Wrapping the towel around his waist, he walked to his bedroom. Sitting on the edge of the bed, he lifted the phone from a charger on his nightstand.

After pulling up Arielle's contact, he placed the call.

"Hello. Camden? This is early, even for you. What happened?"

"We have to talk about Grace Colton," he said.

"Okay. Talk."

He paused. Where should he begin? "Last night, there were protesters outside the police station. They were calling for her to be fired. She was shaken by everything, and I offered to walk her home. We stopped at Mae's Diner and spent some time together. She trusts me." He paused. Be direct. Be professional. Be done with this case. "You have to talk to the mayor and reassign the Colton case. I can't work it—not anymore."

"Of course, you can. You've done a good job getting her to trust you. Now, let's see what she shares."

"I'm not setting up anyone." Camden's pulse rose with his temper.

"I'm not asking you to set up anyone. I'm asking for the truth," said Arielle.

Camden exhaled loudly. If he was going to get the case reassigned, he had to do it now. Rip off the bandage quick. Wasn't that the best way? "Someone else needs to take over."

"I can't call the mayor for no reason. Keep me posted throughout the day. We'll talk soon."

The line went dead.

Sitting on the edge of his bed, Camden stared at the phone. He hated that politics was part of his job.

Too much had happened recently for last night's shooting to be ignored. The public wouldn't allow it. Certainly, someone needed to be held responsible for the incident. After all, both the mayor and the DA relied on the voters to stay in office.

It meant only one thing. There was about to be a reckoning at the GGPD, courtesy of the DA's office—and his boss.

* * *

The weather app predicted scattered showers throughout the day. To Grace, it seemed like fall had arrived overnight. Yesterday's sweltering heat was replaced by cooler temperatures and a steady stream of rain.

Shoving her hands deeper into the pockets of her rain jacket, Grace hustled down the street. With the hood doing a decent job of hiding her face, she couldn't help but be thankful for the storm. To any member of the press who might be lurking around the police station, Grace would be almost invisible.

The station came into view, and she stumbled to a stop. A podium, covered by an awning emblazoned with the GGPD seal, stood on the steps. Satellites, flowers of metal, bloomed from several media trucks that were parked across the street. Half a dozen officers were setting up a microphone. Grace recognized Daniel Coleman and approached.

"Hey," she said. "What's up?"

Coleman had been on the force forever and was like an uncle to every rookie. "Hey, kid. I heard about what happened. Tough break."

"Yeah, tough break."

Did everyone on the force know what had happened?

It was a stupid question to ask. Of course the entire force had heard. Even if they hadn't been part of the investigation. Or assigned to stand on the steps of the station last night. Or if they'd missed the media coverage. They'd certainly heard the gossip.

Yet, Grace wasn't sure if she hated the fact that she hadn't been the one to share her side of the story. Or if she was relieved that she'd never have to tell people what happened. "So…" She rolled her wrist. The gesture took in the tent, the microphone, the press vans. "What's going on?"

"The chief's giving a press conference."

Did it have something to do with last night's shooting? Was there a development in her case? If so, why hadn't she heard already? And if not, what else was going on? For a moment, Grace felt dizzy. Holding onto the podium for support, she asked, "What's Melissa going to say?"

"You know how it goes. They don't tell us street cops nothing." Daniel hooked a thumb toward the front door. "Melissa's been locked in her office with Brett Shea for the last hour."

"I'll let you get back to work." Grace stepped from under the awning.

"See you later, kid. Don't get too down about all of this." He held his hand out to catch the rain. "Just like a storm, it'll blow over."

"If it doesn't?" she asked, pausing. "You know, blow over. What happens then?"

"Me, I've been around a long time. It always blows over."

"Thanks, Dan," she said. With the injection of the older cop's no-nonsense positivity, her spirits lifted. But by the time she walked through the front doors, the mental storm clouds had returned.

She didn't bother checking in with the duty sergeant. Why should she? She'd been put on administrative leave. Grace checked her watch. Nine o'clock. At this moment, she was supposed to be sitting down with Camden, reviewing anything that she'd forgotten or answering new questions. Yet, she couldn't help but wonder: What did Melissa plan to say at the press conference?

She bypassed the conference room commandeercd by Camden. Instead, she headed directly to Melissa's office. Who knew? Maybe she'd get lucky and catch her cousin as the meeting was ending.

Water dripped from her raincoat, hitting the floor and leaving a trail. The door to Melissa's office was stubbornly closed. Pausing, Grace lifted her hand, ready to knock. She stopped at the moment flesh connected with wood. With a sigh, she let her hand drop.

Could she really interrupt?

"Damn it," she muttered, softly kicking the door.

Her phone, tucked into the pocket of her jacket, began to ring. She fished it out and looked at the caller ID. Camden Kingsley.

Her pulse spiked. Why the reaction? Was she nervous about the investigation? Or was she excited to see Camden again?

Pivoting, she swiped the call open. "I'm here," she said, by way of a greeting. "I'm in the building. I'll be at the conference room in just a second."

"Good," he said. "You noticed the podium outside? Any idea what Melissa plans to say?"

"That's actually why I'm late," she said. "I stopped by her office to see if she'd share anything with me."

"And?" Camden asked.

Grace stood on the conference room's threshold, the phone to her ear. "I didn't bother," she said to both Camden on the phone and in person. His dark hair, still damp from a shower, curled slightly at the end. He wore black trousers, a pristine white shirt and a yellow tie. Even in business attire, Camden's strong shoulders and the muscles in his arms were hard to miss. What would it feel like to have him hold her? She swallowed. His dark brown eyes pinned Grace where she stood. She couldn't help it: at the sight of him, her pulse did a little stutter-step. She lowered the phone from her ear. "Melissa's door was shut."

"Damn it," he cursed, ending the call.

"Did any other evidence turn up? Any idea what happened to my body cam?" Grace asked. "Anything about my case?"

Camden shook his head. "No. Sorry."

"Oh." Grace's pulse, racing only moments ago, slowed to a sluggish beat. "I was hoping that Melissa learned something. Maybe she heard from one of the witnesses."

In the narrow corridor, several police officers passed Grace.

"You coming?" one of the cops asked.

"Where?"

"Melissa's press conference," he said, walking backward. "It's about to start."

Grace was supposed to be interviewed again by Camden Kingsley. Yet the IA investigator had already lifted his suit jacket from the back of a chair and slipped it on. "After you," he said.

Without speaking, they walked down the corridor. Several police officers—both those in uniform and those in plain clothes—gathered in the lobby. Grace and Camden took up a spot near the doors. Through the glass panels, they had a perfect view of Melissa, Brett Shea and others from the rear.

The local press stood at the bottom of the steps. Their spot had them sandwiched between the podium at the front and more than two dozen protesters at the back.

Many of the protesters carried signs. From where she stood, Grace could read them all. There was *Ditch the*

Chief. Or *Chief Colton Has Got to Go.* Or Grace's least favorite, *Jail to the Chief.*

"Is that Harper Sullivan?" Camden asked. "From the TV station in Kendall?"

Grace peered into the crowd. Sure enough, the dark-haired reporter stood in the drizzle.

She didn't have time to react before Melissa approached the podium.

She started speaking. "I'd like to thank you all for coming today, even though I ordered the rain special—hoping that it would keep the press away." Polite laughter rippled around the group of cops inside and reporters outside. "Let me begin by giving you an update on what happened last night. There was a police-officer-involved shooting in downtown Grave Gulch. While this incident is being investigated by both the District Attorney's office and the GGPD, we need the public's help."

Melissa held up two sheets of paper. They were the sketches Desiree had drawn based on Grace's description of the witnesses. "We have reason to believe that these two individuals witnessed the shooting. Obviously, we are interested in speaking to them immediately. We need to know what they know. The individuals fled the scene, so it's likely that they don't want to talk to the police. But someone knows these two. To let them disappear—all without making a statement—is a gross miscarriage of justice."

Lowering the pages to the podium, Melissa continued. "Copies of both sketches will be provided to anyone who wants them. Also, they have been emailed to all local newsrooms." She sighed. "If anyone sees these individuals, they should contact the police. Questions?"

Harper was the first to raise her hand. "Is it true

that the person who was shot, Robert Grimaldi, was unarmed?"

"I cannot comment on an ongoing investigation," said Melissa.

"Is it true that the officer's body cam wasn't used during the incident?" Harper asked.

The cramped vestibule grew warm. Grace started to sweat.

Outside, Melissa exhaled. "Again, I can't comment on an ongoing investigation."

"What's the status of the police officer who fired their gun?"

"She's been put on administrative leave," said Melissa. "Pending the outcome of the investigation."

Harper asked, "Is it true that the officer in question is also your cousin, Grace Colton?"

Grace wished the floor would open up and swallow her whole.

Melissa's voice was a low growl. "No comment."

Daniel Coleman stood in front of Grace. Peering over his shoulder, he whispered, "It'll all blow over, just like a storm. Remember that."

She wanted to believe him. Yet, nothing had been okay—not since she'd seen Robert Grimaldi in the alley last night.

"One last question, Chief Colton." Harper continued, the phone still in her hand. "A serial killer, Len Davison, is on the loose. A crime scene investigator—one who worked for your department—fabricated evidence that both implicated the innocent and exonerated the guilty. Why should the public trust you now?"

"*Well*." Melissa drew out the single word. "I have a second announcement to make. I can see that the citizens of Grave Gulch have lost confidence in the GGPD and in our ability to keep peace in the city. It's my responsibility to maintain a trust between the town and the police department. I haven't. Therefore, I'll be temporarily stepping down as chief of police."

Gasps rippled around the room.

Grace went numb.

No. No. No! She wanted to scream. This couldn't be happening. Melissa was Grace's cousin, her role model, her protector and champion on the force. How could she be stepping down now, at the exact time Grace needed her most? Melissa continued. "Beginning now, all my duties will be handled by Detective Brett Shea." She concluded, "It's been the honor of a lifetime to lead the fine men and women who make up the Grave Gulch Police Department. I will do anything—including releasing my position—to assure that they're able to do their job. Thank you for your time." Reporters yelled questions. Protesters began to cheer.

Without another word, Melissa stepped away from the microphone. One of the officers held the door as she crossed the threshold. All eyes, including Grace's, were on Melissa.

"You all heard what I said out there. I meant every word. Being chief of police has been an honor and a privilege. But I can't stay. I've become a distraction. Like I said, Brett Shea will be acting chief, and I expect you to keep acting in the same professional and caring manner you do every day. Whether the people out there realize this or not, they need the police."

She paused. "There are a lot of cases to work, but the top priority is to find the witnesses from last night's shooting."

"What about social media posts?" Officer Daniel Coleman asked. "Have the witnesses posted anything online?"

Grace knew it was a good question, but she also knew the answer. Neither one of them had recorded the incident with their phone or shared any information on social media.

"We feel that the witnesses didn't want proof of what happened," Melissa said. "But Ellie will continue to monitor what's being posted."

Brett added, "Our best hope is that someone will recognize the sketches and give us a call."

"On that note," said Melissa, "I'll let Brett take charge."

She walked forward, with Brett at her side. The crowd parted like the Red Sea, and she strode across the squad room, before disappearing inside her office.

Grace was many things—angry, scared, outraged—but confused wasn't one them. True, Melissa had said she wasn't stepping down because of a single case. But that had been a partial lie. She was stepping down because a single incident had proven to be the last straw. It was the police shooting that had happened last night.

It meant that Grace hadn't simply ruined her own life but Melissa's, as well.

Standing taller, her spine filled with a steely resolve. She had to make this all right. She had to find those witnesses.

But how?

Daniel Coleman held a stack of sketches. He walked through the crowd, handing them to police officers.

"Plaster the city with these things, folks. We need to find this couple and get a statement."

"Hey, Dan," said Camden. "Can I have a couple of those?"

"Sure thing." Dan held out two sets. "I hear that you're looking into last night's shooting."

Camden wasn't surprised that the entire force knew about his role. "You heard right," he said, taking the papers.

"Grace Colton is a good kid, you know."

"You make me sound like Santa Claus. It's not my job to decide who's good or bad. I'm here to find the facts. That's it."

Papers in hand, Camden scanned the entrance. Grace, huddled in a corner, chewed on her bottom lip. The need to reassure and protect Grace came on strong. Despite the fact that he should feel neither, he made his way to her. "That announcement was a shocker." Although he doubted that Arielle or the mayor would be upset.

Grace drew in a deep breath. "I wasn't expecting Melissa to step down, that's for sure."

"Like she said, it's just temporary." Camden didn't know what else to say—or do. Grace looked miserable. His fingers twitched with the need to reach out and touch her. Yet, giving her comfort would be beyond inappropriate.

He'd hoped that a decent night's sleep would rid him of his infatuation with Grace.

It hadn't.

He had to get this case reassigned to another IA investigator and soon. Until then, maybe he could both help Grace and do his job at the same time. "Come with me," he said, heading for the door.

She followed. "Where are we going? Don't you want to interview me some more?"

"We can talk," he said once they stood on the steps. The rain had stopped, but the sky was still gray and the air cool. "We can do more than two things at once." He held up the sketches. "I have an idea of where we can look for the witnesses. There's a neighborhood a few blocks from here where a lot of young adults live. Small apartments. Lots of coffee shops and restaurants. Let's walk the neighborhood and show these. Maybe someone will recognize them."

He handed Grace a set of sketches. Her fingertips brushed the back of his hand. His skin warmed, and his pulse raced.

"Thanks," she whispered, pulling her hand away.

Damn it. There had been something in their touch, something more than a simple attraction. Camden needed to ignore his reaction.

"It's this way," he said, striding down the sidewalk.

Grace jogged to catch up. "So what's next?"

"Hopefully, Ellie can pull something off your body camera after all. If not, it's old-fashioned police work. Let's start here."

He was supposed to find out what happened with the shooting and the couple was an integral part of the investigation. Find the witnesses and find the truth.

Several sidewalk cafés sat in a row. Tables were filled. Some people sat alone and stared at laptops. Others were crowded around a table meant for two. Dozens of people passed them on the street. Camden's blood buzzed in his veins. If the couple Grace saw was anywhere in Grave Gulch, it was in this neighborhood. And if they were here, he'd find them.

"It might be easier if we separate," Grace suggested. "I'll start across the street and at that end of the block." She pointed. "And you can work from here. We'll meet later and compare notes."

"Makes sense," said Camden with a nod. All the same, he hated not being at her side. Or maybe that was the best reason of all to split up.

"I'll see you in a bit," she said.

Camden watched as she called out to a duo—two men with beards and beanies.

"Excuse me." Grace held up the sheets of paper. "I'm wondering if you've seen these two."

"Sorry," said one. "Never seen 'em before in my life."

"Me, either," said the other.

Grace smiled. "Thanks for your time."

Camden felt a smile pull at his lips, as well. The young men didn't know the witnesses, but he liked watching Grace work. She was competent and professional and kind. She moved on to another group, farther away, and Camden could no longer hear what she was saying.

It was time he got to work.

Grave Gulch Coffee and Treats was on the corner. Half a dozen tables filled the sidewalk. At one of the tables, a lone woman wore noise-canceling headphones and stared at her phone.

"Excuse me." He waved to get her attention.

The customer looked up and smiled. "Hello?"

"Sorry to bother you, but I'm wondering if you've seen either one of these people." He held up the sketches.

"Oh, those two. Sure, I've seen them."

Camden had hoped it would be easy to locate the witnesses, but he'd never dreamed it would be *this* easy. "Really? Where?"

The woman held up her phone. The screen was filled with the same sketches he now held. "They're all over the place. Social media. The actual news."

Camden wanted to groan. He didn't. "Have you seen them in real life? Like, around here?"

Pursing her lips, she considered his question. "Not that I remember."

"Thanks for your time."

Camden worked his way up the block. Dozens of times he asked the same question. "Have you seen these two?"

Dozens of times, he got the same answer.

"No. Never."

It was as if these people had disappeared. Or maybe they didn't exist at all.

What if that were true? What did it mean? Was Grace guilty of framing a suspect and an unlawful shooting after all?

Pausing on the sidewalk, he searched for Grace. She walked down the opposite side of the street. He watched as she talked to another group of people, gathered around a bench. They all glanced at her sketches. They all shook their heads.

No luck, either.

She glanced across the street. Her gaze stopped on Camden. She waved.

He didn't want to feel anything. He didn't want his chest to get warm. Or for his pulse to race. He definitely didn't want his mouth to twitch up into a smile—and yet, they all did.

He waved back. She jogged across the street.

As her foot hit the curb, a few fat raindrops splattered

on the sidewalk. Camden glanced skyward. Black clouds roiled, and then a deluge began.

Holding the sketches overhead, Grace ducked into a recessed doorway. Camden followed. The space was just a small square of concrete beneath the building's brick overhang. They were both wedged in tight, her shoulders pressed against his chest.

"That rain came from nowhere," she said, water dripping from her nose. She wiped a hand down her face. The gesture was vulnerable, unpretentious and somehow sexy. "I'm soaked. The damn sketches are trash." She held them up. The paper was waterlogged and shredding. She turned her gaze to Camden. "And look at you. Your suit. It's ruined."

Camden glanced at the clothes. The jacket was stained with water, the hem of his trousers damp and dirty. "It's nothing that dry cleaning won't fix."

"So what do we do now?"

The cafés, busy only moments ago, were vacant. Coffee cups, forgotten in the rush, filled with rainwater.

Suddenly, he didn't care about the investigation.

He watched her lips and wondered what it would feel like to have her mouth on his. To taste her. To touch her. She was so close that he could feel the whisper of her breath on his neck. The floral scent of her shampoo surrounded him like a fog. From where he stood, he could see the swell of her breasts beneath her shirt.

It was then that Camden realized she was watching him, as well. Their gazes met and held. Her sleeve brushed against the tips of his fingers. He wanted to touch her. Hold her.

But he couldn't. Shouldn't.

He swallowed and shifted. The wall was at his back.

He was trapped, with no place else to go. Camden wouldn't try to escape—even if he had the chance. His hand brushed her waist.

She drew in a short breath.

"Sorry," he said. "I didn't mean to touch you."

"It's okay," she said, her gaze on the ground. She lifted her eyes. "I don't mind."

He moved closer. She didn't retreat. Camden bent toward her, then stopped.

What the hell was he doing?

It didn't matter that he was drawn to Grace Colton. Standing tall, he smothered a curse behind his hand.

She hitched her chin to the side. "Looks like the rain stopped."

It was a small torture to look at anything other than Grace. Puddles dotted the sidewalk and street. Sodden tablecloths hung limp. Awnings dripped. The downpour was over as soon as it had begun.

She stepped away, and his chest ached.

He'd stopped himself from kissing Grace this time. The question was: What would he do if he got another chance?

Chapter 8

Standing on the sidewalk, Grace's pulse raced. She was a rookie cop, albeit currently suspended. Yet, she'd had a life beyond the force—one that included her share of former boyfriends and flirtations. In short, she'd been kissed before today.

So, what had happened between her and Camden in the doorway? Why was she drawn to him like she'd never been to any other man?

Had he really been ready to kiss her?

Getting involved with this IA investigator would be career suicide.

Yet, she couldn't lie to herself—she'd thought about kissing him, too.

What was worse, she wouldn't have stopped him if he'd tried.

What did that make her? A horrible person? Desperate? Or was she inexplicably drawn to him because he was the one guy she shouldn't want?

It wasn't like her to make bad choices...well, until she pulled the trigger last night. Still, she knew better than to kiss the IA investigator. Never mind that he was intelligent, focused on finding justice and handsome.

Sun broke through the clouds, and mist clung to the ground as the puddles started to evaporate. She should say something to Camden. But what?

He still stood in the doorway. "Come on," he said, stepping toward her. "We should go."

She held the set of sketches, drenched and ruined. "These won't do me any good." A recycling bin sat at the curb. She tossed them inside.

He checked his watch. "It's already after eleven o'clock. Let's get something to eat. I skipped breakfast."

Did the guy never eat on time? Grace worked the night shift and still she made time to eat regularly. "You have to get on a better schedule for meals."

"I know. I know." He lifted his palms in surrender. "You're right. But don't keep me from my lunch now. Come on. I know a good pizza place."

Having lunch together was a decidedly bad idea.

Especially since Grace had to admit that she was attracted to Camden Kingsley. She was drawn to more than his good looks: his self-possession, as well. Camden was calm, collected and able to think on his feet. He was everything that Grace—passionate, reactive, talkative—was not.

Besides, they hadn't actually kissed. It was just a reaction to the moment, right?

Still, she needed to get away for her sake—and his.

Tell him you can't go out to lunch. Tell him you have to go.

She knew she was right. She opened her mouth, ready to decline the invite. Instead, her voice betrayed her. "Pizza sounds nice. Which way?"

"Left at the corner, then two blocks down."

"So," she began, as they walked.

"So, what?"

"So what comes next in the investigation? We've showed the sketches. No luck in finding the witnesses, though. The gun is missing. What do you do now?"

"I still have to do some more interviews," he said.

Was he being evasive? "And then?"

"I bother Ellie and see if she's gotten anything else from the body cam."

"What happens after that?"

"I'll look at all the evidence. If there's enough, I'll write a report with my findings. If I need more facts, I'll keep looking." He stopped in front of a restaurant. A green and red canvas awning hung over the doorway. Painted on the glass door in gold and black were the words *Paola's Pizzeria: New York Style Pizza.* Beneath was a similar gold and black skyline of Manhattan. "You ever eat here?"

Grace had grown up in Grave Gulch, but whenever she ate out, she ate at her father's restaurant.

"Never," she said.

"You'll like it." Camden pulled the door open. He smiled as she passed. "Trust me."

Maybe that was another problem. Grace *did* trust Camden.

A counter stood between the dining area and the kitchen. A glass hood covered a long line of prepared pizzas, ready to be reheated by the slice. A large dome brick oven was attached to the back wall.

"Hey, Camden. Good to see you, buddy." A man with dark hair and a graying mustache stood behind the counter. He smiled as they approached.

"How's it going, Stu?" Camden asked.

"Busy. Lots of protesters downtown, and they get hungry. But I'm not doing as good as you. Are you going to introduce me to your lunch date, or what?"

"I'm not his date. We're, um…" How could she categorize their relationship—especially since she didn't want to admit that *she* was one of the reasons protesters had been out in force?

"This is my colleague. Grace."

"Nice to meet you, Grace."

"Likewise."

"So what'll it be?" Stu asked.

She scanned the line of pizza choices. Buffalo chicken. Margherita. Cheese. Hawaiian. Veggie. She wasn't hungry, but there was something comforting in the idea of sitting down with a hot, saucy and greasy slice of pizza.

"I'll take the lunch special." A slice of pizza, a side salad and a drink. "Cheese."

"Make that two," said Camden.

"But you'll want sausage and pepperoni on your slice, am I right?"

"You are," said Camden.

Stu handed over two empty plastic cups. A drink fountain stood in the corner. "Your order will be up in a minute."

The restaurant had seating for two dozen. Round tables, covered with a checkered vinyl cloth in red and white, filled in the middle of the room. Three booths, all in a row, were placed along the window.

Grace and Camden were the only patrons. Since the shooting, Grace had felt as if everyone knew exactly who she was and what she'd done. What's worse, they hated her for her actions.

She didn't feel judged by Camden, despite the fact that his job was to investigate her guilt.

"Is here good?" Camden pointed to the booth in the middle.

Grace looked up from where she stood, filling her cup with unsweetened iced tea from a metal dispenser. "Works for me."

She approached the table and set her cup down. After stripping out of her sodden jacket, she hung it on the corner of the bench. Sliding onto the seat opposite from Camden, she took a sip from her drink.

Usually, she had an easy time with chitchat. But what was she supposed to talk about with Camden? The restaurant was empty save for the two of them and Stu at the counter. Maybe now was the perfect time to have a candid conversation.

"Last night you said you were only interested in the truth," she began, then felt not entirely certain where to go after such a bold statement.

He'd gotten himself a soda and sipped before nodding. "I am. The truth. The facts. Those are the only things that matter."

"But they're different, aren't they? The truth and facts."

Camden shook his head. "Not to me, they aren't."

"Facts are like a math problem. Two plus two is always four. The truth is what you can convince people to believe."

He took another drink, seeming to consider her words. "I guess you're right, although I never thought of it quite that way."

"Tell me this, then. What's the truth about my case?" Staring out the window, she watched a car drive by. "Right now, it's my word against Grimaldi's. I say he had a gun. He says he didn't. The gun hasn't turned up, so those facts prove Grimaldi's truth—not mine."

"Basically," he said.

She waited for him to say something. Anything.

He didn't.

Grace continued, "My body cam was broken, so there's no video evidence. There are witnesses, but they haven't come forward. There's a lot of anti-police feeling in the community." She paused and met his gaze. "I'm a cop. I know what kind of narrative those facts create. It makes me look guilty as hell. But here are the facts. I'm innocent. Grimaldi had a gun, and he pointed it at me. If I hadn't fired first, he would've shot me."

Camden wiped a bead of sweat from the side of his glass. He opened his mouth, ready to speak. But Stu approached with a tray of food, and Camden snapped his jaw shut.

The other man set down two salads in bowls, along with two gravy boats filled with dressing—creamy ranch and tangy Italian. He also had two wedges of pizza, bigger than the plates, and he set those down, as well. "How's that look?" Stu asked, tucking the tray under his arm. "Can I get you anything else?" He quickly removed two sets of silverware rolled in paper napkins from the pocket of his apron and set them on the table. "Aside from these," he added.

"It looks great," said Grace. Her stomach clenched in a hard knot of anxiety. She'd never be able to eat much more than a few bites.

"All righty, then. Enjoy."

Stu retreated behind the counter as Camden unrolled his silverware. With the other man out of earshot, he turned back to Grace. "If there's evidence that proves your story, I'll find it."

"And if you don't?"

"I will."

"Do you swear that you won't give up on the case?" Grace asked. "On *me*?" She shoved a bite of salad in her mouth and chewed. Had she really just pressured him to make a personal promise? That was a bad move. "Never mind what I asked. It was wrong." She washed down her salad with a swallow of tea.

"Grace, listen," he began. "I need to tell you something from when I was a kid…"

His phone started to ring, and he quietly cursed. He'd already told her that his dad was a cop. Was there more? Fishing the cell from his pocket, he glanced at the screen. "It's Ellie."

"Ellie?" Her chest was tight. Had the IT expert recovered the missing footage? Was this nightmare about to end? Wiping her mouth with the napkin, she leaned forward. "Let's hope she has good news."

Camden swiped the call open and put it on Speaker. Setting the phone on the table, he said, "Hey, Ellie. I'm here with Grace. What have you got for us?"

"Nothing," she said, her voice flat. "I tried everything I know. But there's nothing more to get off the body camera. I'm sorry."

"Can you tell if anyone tampered with the camera?" Camden asked.

The chain of evidence was well-established. The camera went from Grace to Brett to Ellie. But weirder things had happened recently. Holding her breath, she waited for Ellie's answer.

"The video and physical evidence suggest that the camera broke when Grace was hit with the bag."

Grace's pulse went sluggish. Having footage of Grimaldi pointing a gun at Grace was the only sure way to clear her name. Without it, would Grace have to live with a stain on her reputation forever? A wave of despair washed over her, and she began to sweat. "Sure," she said. "Thanks for trying."

"What else can be done?" Camden asked. "There has to be something."

He was definitely trying to exonerate Grace. She knew that she should be pleased. Yet Melissa's warning not to trust anyone from IA was still fresh.

What did Camden really want? Before Grace could wonder anything more, Ellie spoke.

"I've done all I can." She paused. "I am sorry." She ended the call.

The single bite of salad now sat like a rock in Grace's gut. The phone, screen blank, lay on the table. Camden picked it up and tucked it into his pocket.

Grace pushed the bowl away. Finding more footage on the camera had been her final hope. Now, that was gone. She knew one thing for certain—she'd been defeated. Her eyes stung, yet she refused to cry in front of Camden. "Well, that's a dead end."

"I know that you're disappointed," he began. "But you need to consider some other facts."

She held up her hand, stopping Camden before he got started. "I appreciate whatever you plan to say. But I'm not in the mood for a pep talk."

In fact, there was really only one person Grace wanted to talk to right now: Melissa. She'd know what Grace should do.

Just because Melissa had stepped down from being the chief of police didn't mean that she'd lost any knowledge. Her jacket hung on the corner of the bench. Standing, Grace patted down the pockets until she found her phone. "Give me a second. I need to make a call."

Striding through the restaurant, Grace opened her contacts. She pushed out of the restaurant. After the morning rain, the sun had come out, and the sky was now a cloudless blue.

Melissa answered the call on the third ring. "Grace, where are you? I just heard from Ellie. She wasn't able to get anything else off the body camera."

"Yeah. I heard that, too. Where are you?"

"I'm still at headquarters, cleaning out some personal stuff from my office. I looked for you after the presser, but Coleman said you were gone."

There was a lot more to talk about than just last night's shooting and the lack of evidence. Her cousin had stepped down from being Grave Gulch's chief of police, and it was in part because of Grace. "I took a set of the sketches and canvased a few blocks. I was hoping that someone would recognize the witnesses."

"That's a smart idea," said Melissa. She chuckled quietly. "You always were smart."

"I wasn't the one who thought it up. It was Camden."

"Camden? As in Camden Kingsley? You're working with him? Are you serious?"

Grace bristled at Melissa's incredulous tone. "He's looking for the truth," she said, paraphrasing what Camden had told her earlier.

"He's looking for someone to hold accountable, and don't forget it."

Grace glanced at Camden through the window. He sat at the table, slice of pizza in hand. He took a bite and looked up. Wiping his mouth with a paper napkin, he nodded at her.

Her heart skipped a beat. Despite herself, she smiled. "I haven't forgotten anything." Grace changed the subject. "How are you? You must be devastated about having to step down."

"Actually, I'm not. Antonio and I had a long talk last night after I got home. Even before now, we've been talking about getting married and starting a family. It'd be hard to be chief of police and a new mom all at the same time."

A hard kernel of disappointment lodged in Grace's throat. "Is that it? You're quitting?"

"I'm not *quitting*." Melissa drew out the last word. "I'm taking time to evaluate what I really want."

Grace knew what she wanted. She wanted to clear her name and get back to work. But would the GGPD be the same without Melissa around, even if Grace was eventually exonerated? Would Grace ever find a guy she loved enough to stop being a cop? She thought not, and yet she felt Camden's gaze on the back of her neck. She tried to think of something else to say but had nothing. "I need to get off the phone."

"Chin up, okay? You'll get through this."

"That's what everyone keeps saying."

"Because it's true," said Melissa. "Will I see you to-night?"

Oh, yeah. The party for Palmer and Soledad. She had no place else to go. "I'll be there."

Grace ended the call and folded her arms across her chest. She should go back into the restaurant. But her life was falling apart, and worse, she didn't know how to put it back together.

Camden tried not to watch Grace as she stood on the sidewalk. Or to appreciate how her jeans hugged her hips and rear. Or that the sun, just beginning to peek through the clouds, turned her hair into a golden halo. He also tried not to wonder what she was telling Melissa—or what advice Melissa was sharing in return.

On all accounts, he failed miserably.

Maybe now was the time to ask Arielle to inter-vene and get him taken off the case once and for all. He looked around the restaurant, still empty, and removed his phone. Arielle answered his call on the first ring.

"I've got a meeting in two minutes," she said. "What have you got for me?"

"The body camera was damaged. The IT expert can't get any more video off the device."

"That's convenient, isn't it?" said Arielle, her voice dripping with sarcasm. "Chief Colton's cousin shoots a civilian. At the time, she claims that the person had a gun. Then, the camera is so damaged that they can't get any video of the incident."

"Melissa Colton stepped down temporarily," said Camden. His jaw tightened. "She's not able to manipu-late the investigation, if that's what you're suggesting."

"And she named Brett to replace her. Interesting, don't you think? Especially since I heard he's involved with Annalise Colton, Grace's older sister." Arielle sighed. "They're all a big family at GGPD. Literally. You have to find out more about what's happening."

"Here's what happening, Arielle. There's a conflict of interest."

"A what?" And then, "You're right, we do have to talk, but not now. My meeting is starting. Stay on the case, and I'll call this evening."

"Arielle," he said, his teeth gritted. "Do not hang up the phone. This is important."

Whatever he was about to say was for naught. She'd already ended the call. Camden muttered a curse in frustration.

Grace opened the door to the small restaurant. She came back to the booth and sat.

He said, "Your pizza's gotten cold. Stu can throw it back in the oven if you'd like."

Grace shook her head. "I'm not really hungry."

"You want to take it to go? We can canvas a few blocks from here…"

"Listen," she began. Grace tightened her jaw. From the resolute look on her face, Camden knew that he wasn't going to like whatever she had to say next. "I appreciate what you're trying to do, really. More than that, I understand you're going beyond what's expected of someone from IA. But…" She exhaled, her breath ruffling her hair. "I should probably just go. There's not much more that can be accomplished by us walking around, you know."

He'd just been asking to be taken off the case. Maybe

now was the best time to part ways. Why was his chest suddenly tight?

She asked, "What do I owe for lunch?"

Camden waved away her offer to pay. "I've got this." He held out her plate and bowl. "Take this with you. You don't want to waste food. Besides, what'd you tell me? To get on a regular meal schedule?"

"I guess I did say something like that." Taking both salad and pizza, she stood. "Thanks."

At the counter, Stu wrapped up Grace's lunch and tried to get her to buy a cannoli. Then, without another word, she was gone. He should be happy, or at least pleased, that she'd left. His attraction to her was more than a distraction; it was the best way to ruin his career.

But Camden pushed his salad through a pool of dressing. He took a bite and swallowed, despite the fact that his throat was closed like a fist. Working his jaw back and forth, he wondered if he'd ever see Grace again. Or was she gone from his life for good?

Chastity Shoals lay on the sofa and scrolled through her newsfeed. She glanced at a post and clicked on the link. The headline read *Police Chief Steps Down Amid Scandal, Police Shooting.*

Her heart pounding, she opened the article and read.

Once again, the Grave Gulch Police Department is forced to investigate one of their own. This time, the scandal has cost Chief Melissa Colton her position—at least temporarily. In a press conference at GGPD headquarters, Melissa Colton spoke to reporters and the public. In her statement, she took responsibility for the police's mishandling of sev-

eral investigations, including last night's police-involved shooting. Detective Brett Shea will take over the role of police chief until Colton's return.

The officer in question, Grace Colton, has given a statement that Robert Grimaldi, 29, of Grave Gulch, brandished a firearm while she was trying to apprehend him. Officer Colton fired her weapon first. No weapon of Grimaldi's has been located, despite an extensive search of the area. Grimaldi claims that he was unarmed at the time of the shooting. Officer Colton has been placed on administrative leave.

The police report that there were witnesses to the incident. They are asking the public for their help in identifying the couple. If you know those pictured below, contact the Grave Gulch Police Department.

Two sketches accompanied the article. Her nose was a little bigger, and Thad's eyes were farther apart. But without question, the pictures were of Chastity and Thad.

"Thad." She stood. For a moment, the floor seemed to tilt. Dark spots danced in front of her eyes. Holding onto the side of the sofa, she waited for the dizziness to pass. "You have to come here and see this."

Thad sat at a table. He was huddled over a laptop, where he worked on his newest project as a game designer. "What is it?" he asked, without looking up.

She crossed the small living room and shoved her phone in his face. "See?"

He focused his vision on her hand and the phone. "What is it?" he asked, again. This time, his voice was sharp with alarm.

"Us," she said. "Our pictures. We witnessed that shooting. Now the cops want to talk to us…"

"We aren't saying anything to cops," said Thad. He returned his gaze to his computer.

"We shouldn't have split last night. I told you that."

"Yeah, you told me after we got home, and you drank like half a bottle of wine. It wasn't helpful in that moment."

"Maybe we should call," Chastity began.

"Maybe we shouldn't, and you should let me get back to work."

"No need to be nasty."

"Listen, Chas, I'm sorry. It's just that I'm on a deadline, and you know how that makes me stressed."

She did know that deadlines left Thad stressed. He had a degree in computer programming, but he did so much more than write the codes. In fact, he was more of an artist. And like he always said, *Art can't be forced. It has to be found.*

Still, she didn't like that the police were looking for them.

"What should we do?"

"Well." Thad lifted his arms over head. His shirt rode up, exposing his stomach and his abs. "Do you have classwork?" he asked. "Or you could find a workout video on the internet. Get a head start on the weight you wanted to lose."

She pulled her T-shirt lower over her leggings. "I'm not asking what I should do right now. I'm asking what we should do about the police."

"Oh, that." Thad turned back to his work. "I say we do nothing."

"Nothing?" she echoed. "Where's your civic duty?"

"How many times have you told me that you hate the cops? Or how often have you said that cops are just schoolyard bullies but with badges?"

The single time she'd dealt with the cops came back to Chastity with a sharp clarity. The memory stabbed her in the chest. She *had* said that before. "A lot."

"Yeah, a lot. So, why aren't you happy that we took the gun? It sounds like the lady cop is up crap creek without a paddle."

"They know about the gun, though." Annoyance, hot and sticky, bubbled up from Chastity's gut. Did Thad really not care about the truth? Or maybe he didn't understand what kind of trouble they'd be in if the police found them and the weapon they'd taken from the scene of a crime. For Thad, everything was like the games he designed. There was always a secret work-around for any problem. Only this time, there wasn't.

Sighing, Thad turned toward her. "They don't know jack. Obviously, we have the gun. The guy—" he glanced at the article on her screen once more "—Robert Grimaldi isn't going to say anything. If he admitted to pointing a gun at a police officer, he'd be in deep, deep trouble. There's no video of the incident—or us. All we have to do is lay low for a few weeks. And also, we have to get rid of the gun."

"Lay low? Get rid of the gun? How're we supposed to do both?"

"We stay in the apartment for a few weeks and keep the gun here. When this story blows over—and it will blow over—we dump the gun in Lake Michigan. Or we ditch it at the town dump."

Chastity could feel the walls of the small apartment

closing in on her. "Have you thought about food? How're we going to eat if we're stuck in here?"

"What's the matter with you? Order groceries for delivery. Order food from restaurants online, too. My work is online. Your classes are online. We just moved here at the beginning of the month. The only person we've spoken to more than once is the old man who lives downstairs. I don't know if he remembers us all that well to begin with."

Thad was right. He always was. Chastity slunk back to the sofa and flopped onto the cushions. It's just that she had hoped Grave Gulch would be more than a place to live, that the town would become their home.

For a moment, she let her favorite daydream swirl around her. She pictured the apartment filled with smiling faces of friends they hadn't yet made. Laughter. Light. Happiness. Chastity would stand in the galley kitchen. A glass of wine would sit on the counter, as she mashed avocado for her soon-to-be-famous guacamole.

"Who's hungry?" she'd ask, bowl of chips in one hand, dish of guac in the other.

Thad, while taking both from her, would kiss her cheek. "My girlfriend," he'd announce. "Pretty. Smart. Talented."

The party disappeared as the last tendrils of Chastity's fantasy faded to nothing.

Of course, Thad was right. They only had to stay inside for a few weeks. By then, the whole story would be forgotten.

Still, Chastity couldn't keep from asking a single question. If Thad was right, why did all of this feel so wrong?

Chapter 9

It was barely past noon. Already Grace was exhausted. It was more than the exhausting night and the fruitless search for the witnesses this morning. Striding down the street from the pizza parlor, she wanted nothing more than a nap, a cup of tea and to see her mother.

Folding her arms against the chill, she knew that she could get the tea and the nap in her apartment. Seeing her mother would have to wait for tonight's party.

Ugh. The party.

Grace unlocked the door to her building and trudged up to the second floor. From there, she entered her apartment.

Pushing the door shut with her heel, she wondered if there was any way to get out of going tonight. Surely, her brother would understand if she needed an evening at home and alone. Yet, while Palmer might understand, her parents would not. She was a Colton—and expected to attend.

After setting her phone and her keys on the counter, she placed her leftover pizza and salad in the fridge. Automatically, she moved to the closet. Hand resting on the knob, she stopped.

Damn. She'd had a jacket on when she left this morning. Now, it was gone.

Obviously, she'd left it somewhere.

In a flash, she remembered hooking it over the back of the bench at the pizza place. With a sigh, Grace knew she'd have to turn around and go back to the restaurant. To her, it seemed like the tea and nap would have to wait forever.

Still, there was something she needed to do. Something she'd been avoiding, until now.

Leaning on the closet door, she searched through the apps until she found the one for the TV station in Kendall. Grace opened the app. The most recent headline hit her like a slap to the face: *Police Chief Steps Down Amid Scandal, Police Shooting.*

Holding her breath, Grace scanned the article. It was short, precise, and while not flattering, nothing had been misleading, either.

A video clip of the news conference, posted by a subscriber, accompanied the article. A white arrow was superimposed on the footage. Grace played the video.

Melissa stood behind the podium. To her left was Brett Shea. At her right was the mayor. Melissa began speaking. *"I'd like to thank you all for coming today, even though I ordered the rain special—hoping that it would keep the press away."* She paused. Chuckles could be heard in the background. *"Let me begin by giving you an update on what happened last night."*

The camera panned the gathered crowd. Those in the back, with their signs. A group of reporters, huddled together, in the rain. Then, the aspect zoomed to the front of police headquarters. Shadowy figures could be seen inside. Grace would have been one of those forms. It was odd to watch the scene unfold. After all, she'd already lived these moments once. Yet Grace was driven by the need to know what was being presented in the media.

Melissa continued to speak, her voice in the background. *"There was a police-officer-involved shooting in downtown Grave Gulch. While this incident is being investigated by both the District Attorney's office and the GGPD, we need the public's help."*

The camera focused in on a person—but it wasn't just anyone. They'd caught Camden in profile. His eyes. His jaw. His hair. His face was as familiar to Grace as her own. Yet, she'd only known him for less than a day.

True, Grace had never been one to believe in luck. She saw success—or failure—as the result of a person's work ethic. Yet, as she watched the video of Camden, it was easy to think that luck—and bad luck, at that—was in control of her life.

How else could it be that she'd met a nice guy, only to have him be the totally wrong person?

Her phone rang, interrupting the pity party for one. She glanced at the caller ID. It was her cousin, Madison. "Hey," she said, after accepting the call. "How are you?"

Madison's voice was full of concern. "I should be asking you the same thing. I saw what happened on the news."

Madison was more than another Colton cousin. She

was also one of Grace's best friends. "I can't believe this is happening. I mean," she said and dropped onto her sofa, "I'm always so careful. The guy definitely had a gun."

"Of course he did. It'll just take some time to pull all the evidence together."

"I don't know." Grace sighed as her stomach began to grumble. Maybe she should have eaten something for lunch. "There's no video from my body camera of the incident. Both Brett and I saw two witnesses, but they ran away. Melissa's circulated a set of sketches, but so far...nothing."

"Yet," said Madison.

"I know what you're trying to do. Lift my spirits. I love you for trying, but I need more than positive thinking."

"You might be surprised—" Madison began.

"Hey," Grace interrupted, "how can you be calling me, anyway? Don't you have a classroom full of kids?" Madison, a kindergarten teacher at Grave Gulch Elementary School, lived a charmed life. Aside from having a job she loved, she was also engaged to one of the teachers at her school, Alec Lash.

"It's my planning period," said Madison. "The kids are in lunch, then they have music."

"I'm sure you have more to do than just chat with me."

"There's always something to take care of as a teacher, that's for certain. But right now, you're my top priority."

"I'm just happy to hear your voice." Grace paused. "Let's talk about something that's not me. Have you found a dress yet?"

"Actually—" Madison let out a squeal "—I think I have. I saw it in *Lake Country* magazine this morning."

"Really?" Grace couldn't keep the amazement out of her voice. Madison had been engaged for months yet refused to do anything for the wedding. She claimed that planning began with finding the perfect dress. Until now, nothing had been good enough. All the same, Grace suspected that Madison might not just want a fairy-tale gown but a different Prince Charming altogether. Clearing her throat, Grace forced her voice to be upbeat. "Really! That's so great. Pictures?"

"Hold on a sec, and I'll text you."

"Tell me all about it," said Grace, while switching to Speaker.

"Well, it's white and fancy…"

Grace laughed. "I bet it's both." Her phone pinged with a text, and she opened the picture. With a lace bodice and full train, the gown was stunning. For some reason, the image of Camden wearing a tuxedo came to mind. "That's the most beautiful dress ever. You'll look stunning."

"There's only one problem."

"Uh-oh," said Grace, not surprised at all. There was always a problem with wedding dresses. "What's that?"

"The dress is only available at a boutique that's all the way in Kendall."

"All the way in Kendall?" Grace echoed teasingly. "Kendall's only two hours away. You took me shopping for a prom dress there, remember? You can certainly take that drive to try on a wedding gown."

"I guess you're right…" Madison began, before letting her words fade to nothing.

"Unless there's something wrong with the dress."

Grace paused. Should she bring up Madison's constant hesitation? "Or the wedding."

"It's not that…"

"I'll tell you what, tomorrow is Saturday. Why don't we go and look at the dress? It'll be fun. We can make a day out of the trip. We'll wear cute outfits and have lunch in one of the swanky bistros afterward. What do you say?"

"You'd go with me? Really?"

"Of course I'll go. I'm on administrative leave. What else am I going to do? Besides," Grace continued, feeling happy for the first time all day, "it'll do me good to get out of town and have something to do other than worry about the investigation."

"It's a date." And then, "Listen, I have to go and actually do some prep work. I'll see you tonight, all right? Can you believe that your brother's actually getting married?"

Grace still didn't want to go to the party, but maybe being around her family would help. Besides, Madison was right. Palmer was her brother, and she needed to be there for him—if not for herself. "See you tonight."

Madison ended the call. Grace rose from the sofa. In the kitchen, she filled the kettle. As she set it on the stove to boil, fat drops of water began pelting her kitchen window. Damn. She'd never gone back to get her jacket.

Did she really want to walk in the rain?

Absolutely not.

Opening a search engine on her phone, she found the number for the pizza parlor and called.

"Paola's Pizzeria. This is Stu. What can I get started for you?"

"Hi, Stu. This is Grace. I was in your restaurant with

my, um, colleague Camden Kingsley. I think I left my coat. Can you grab it for me? I'll get it later this afternoon, if that's okay."

"Your coat?" he echoed. "I don't see your coat."

"I draped it over the side of the booth where I was sitting."

"I'm looking at that spot, and it's not there."

"Are you sure?" Even she heard that her voice was an octave higher. It wasn't as if the jacket were extremely valuable, or even one of Grace's favorites. But the loss of something personal typified this day: rotten and unfair.

He paused. "I've had some customers since you left, but they all did takeout. Plus, I think I would've noticed a coat just lying around. Maybe Camden grabbed it when he left. Have you called him?"

The kettle began to whistle. She took it from the burner. One-handed, she filled a mug with boiling water. *Camden Kingsley.* Her mind repeated his name as if it was a wish or a prayer. "I'll give him a call. Thanks."

"If it turns up, I'll let you know. The number on caller ID good?"

"It is," said Grace. "And thanks."

The call ended, and she dropped a tea bag into the steaming water. As the tea began to turn the liquid to a dark bronze, Grace set the phone on the counter.

Should she bother Camden about her jacket?

After all, it was just a coat. She had others.

Why the hesitancy to make the call, though?

In truth, Grace knew the answer, even without asking.

The prudent thing would be to avoid him at all costs.

In a short time, her physical attraction to Camden had taken on a decidedly emotional turn. Developing a deeper attraction for the man who was tasked with investigating her was dangerous, dumb and reckless. Despite it all, Grace couldn't deny it: she was drawn to the man investigating her.

Tucking Grace's jacket over his messenger bag, Camden walked back to police headquarters and made a mental list of everything he needed to do. First on the agenda was to drop off Grace's jacket with Mary Suzuki, the GGPD desk clerk. Second, he needed to talk to Brett Shea. Finally, he had to visit with Robert Grimaldi.

True, Camden was supposed to be neutral. All the same, he couldn't help it: he wanted Shea or Grimaldi to give him something that would exonerate Grace.

Turning the corner, the GGPD building came into view. Brett Shea jogged down the steps.

"Interim Chief Shea," Camden called. "Hold on."

Brett stood on the sidewalk and waited for Camden. "What's up?"

"I'm trying to piece together what happened last night with Officer Colton. You got a minute to chat?"

"Actually," said Brett with a sigh. "I don't. I'm headed to the hospital to interview Robert Grimaldi."

"Sounds like it's my lucky day. I need to speak to him, too. Care if I tag along?"

"I'll drive, and you can talk." Brett's car was parked in front of the building. "Ready to go?"

Brett still had Grace's jacket. He should take it to Mary and move on. Then again, he didn't want to miss his chance to interview Brett and Grimaldi. Shoving the jacket into his bag, he approached the auto. "Let's go."

Camden said nothing as Brett pulled away from the curb. As the SUV rolled down the street, he began by asking, "What do you remember about last night?"

Brett recounted a story that Camden knew well. The figure in the alley. Grace's chase on foot. Brett coming around the block but being delayed by protesters in the street. He described seeing the witnesses—a man and woman—running away from the scene. Brett ended with "When I pulled up, Grace was providing first aid to Grimaldi. Ember and I looked for the gun, but…" he exhaled and shook his head "…we didn't find anything."

So far, Camden had learned nothing new.

"You know Grace, um, Officer Colton pretty well, right? I heard that you're engaged to her sister."

"Annalise," Brett offered. "She's a canine instructor for the police department."

"What about Grace?"

"Grace is a good person and a great cop in the making."

"In the making?" Camden repeated. The hospital was only a few minutes away from GGPD's headquarters. If Camden was going to learn anything, he didn't have much time. "What do you mean by that?"

"It's just a phrase. But she is young."

"Inexperienced?"

"No, I wouldn't call her that."

"What *would* you call her?" Camden asked. His palms itched. It felt like the truth was so close that he could reach out and grab it.

"Enthusiastic."

"How so?"

"She's very loyal to the police force, for starters. I mean, of course she is. Most of the family works for the GGPD. Plus," said Brett, turning into the hospital's parking lot, "she adores Melissa."

"From what I've seen, the feeling is pretty mutual."

"They're all protective of one another, I'll give you that."

Protective? Protective enough to lie? "Give me an example."

There was a space in front of the hospital's main entrance reserved for law enforcement. Brett maneuvered the big SUV into the spot. He turned off the engine. "I don't know that I have an example, it's just a feeling I get."

"Why?"

"Well, last night Grace was upset by all the protesters."

"When they were standing in front of the building and calling for her to be fired? I'd think anyone would be upset."

"No," said Brett. "Not then. Earlier. Right before she saw Grimaldi. We were driving near the park and the protesters were calling for Melissa to be fired. Grace took it personally. That's what I mean." Looking at his watch, Brett said, "We can talk on the way back, but I made arrangements with the hospital to speak to Grimaldi now."

"Sure. Right." Camden opened the door and stepped from the SUV. He walked next to Brett, his messenger bag over his shoulder. Camden had just gotten his first glimpse into Grace's state of mind moments before the shooting.

Last night, he'd asked if she was upset—specifically, about a boyfriend. She'd told him she was single. Honestly, he'd been satisfied with the answer. Now he knew it'd been a stupid mistake made because of his attraction to Grace.

Yet, what did it mean for the case?

Was there more that he'd missed?

Brett and Camden approached the front doors of the hospital. They opened automatically. A water feature of copper and brass was attached to the lobby's far wall. A semicircular desk stood in the middle of the room. A woman, in a purple shirt with the word *Volunteer* embroidered on her pocket, looked up and smiled.

Despite the pleasant surroundings, Camden knew he was in a hospital. It was unnaturally quiet, and the pungent smell of disinfectant hung in the air.

"May I help you?" the woman asked, her voice as soft and soothing as the bubbling water.

"I'm Detective Shea with the GGPD, also acting chief. This is Camden Kingsley from Internal Affairs. I'm here to talk to Robert Grimaldi. I spoke to his doctor. She's expecting us."

A computer terminal sat below the lip of the desk, and the volunteer tapped on the keys. "Mr. Grimaldi's in East Seventeen. Take the elevators to the second floor. The East wing is the third door on the right. I've sent a message, and the doctor will be waiting for you."

Brett and Camden thanked the woman. The directions they'd been given were perfect, and soon they were shaking hands with Grimaldi's attending physician. Dr. Murielle Shah was a woman who Camden estimated to be in her late fifties. Her dark hair was streaked with gray, and she wore a silk blouse under her lab coat.

Dr. Shah greeted them. "I wasn't expecting two police officers."

Camden held up his official ID. "I'm with Internal Affairs, investigating the shooting last night."

The doctor studied the ID before nodding her approval. "Obviously, Robert Grimaldi's injuries aren't life-threatening. Still, I want to know where my patient will be taken if I release him."

"Dr. Shah," said Brett, "as soon as you say Mr. Grimaldi is healthy enough to leave the hospital, he'll be brought before a judge. From there, it's up to the courts to decide what happens and where he goes. Until then, I need to speak to him about what he was doing last night."

"What about the shooting?" she asked.

Camden bristled at the sharp edges of her tone. "What about it?"

"I can't release a man who's been shot by the police for no reason. What if there's retribution?"

"That's why I'm here," said Camden. He understood the pressure from the public. Still, he refused to be bullied into turning Grace into a scapegoat, even if it'd make a lot of people happier. "It's my job to figure out what happened."

Dr. Shah shook her head. "I don't like this, but I'll let you both speak to him. Fifteen minutes only. I'm keeping him in the hospital until Monday morning. With his history of abusing controlled substances, I want to monitor his pain medication until he's healed enough for only OTC meds. Then, you can take him to court. Fair enough?"

"You're the doctor. We'll do whatever you say."

Because Grimaldi was viewed as a flight risk, police protection had been assigned to the room 24-7. A patrol officer sat on a chair and scrolled through his phone. He looked up as Brett and Camden approached. Shoving the phone into his pocket, he swallowed. "Everything okay, Chief?"

"We're here to talk to Grimaldi. You can take a break

if you want. The doc says we only have fifteen minutes, so don't go far."

"Thanks," said the officer as he stood. "I'll be right back."

Even though a police officer was outside his room, Grimaldi was handcuffed to the rail of his bed. A TV hung on the wall. The screen was filled with a sitcom from the '70s.

Grimaldi looked up as Camden and Brett crossed the threshold. The room was little more than a closet—big enough for the bed, the TV and nothing else. The suspect wore a hospital gown. His cheeks and chin were covered with stubble, and his shoulder was immobilized with a sling.

"Get out of here. My attorney told me I don't have to say anything to you."

Attorney? Had Grimaldi already lawyered up? Once a suspect had a lawyer and had invoked their right to remain silent, there was little more for the police to do or say. Luckily, Camden wasn't exactly a cop. "What kind of counsel did you retain?"

"The kind that will sue the ass off the police department. My lawyer came to me. I don't have to pay him nothing, unless we win big." Grimaldi pointed to himself with his thumb. "Did you know that girl cop who shot me was the police chief's cousin? Don't that seem like a crime to you?"

"How's that criminal?" Brett folded his arms.

"Too much of one family working together ain't right. It's…oh, what's the word?"

"*Nepotism?*" Camden offered.

"Yeah, *nepotism.*"

"I'm with Internal Affairs." Camden held up his ID

again. "And investigating the shooting. I know you said that you don't want to speak to Shea, but would you talk to me?"

"About what?"

"I'm looking into Officer Grace Colton's actions."

Grimaldi said, "I was shot for no reason."

"That must be tragic." Camden kept his tone neutral and reminded himself that he was still after one thing. The truth.

"Tragic, yeah. It was."

"So." Camden paused. "Can we talk?"

"Who'd you say you worked for, again?"

"Internal Affairs."

"You're looking into the girl cop who shot me?" Grimaldi asked. Had his voice cracked? Was it nerves? Pain? Both?

Camden nodded. "I am."

"Okay. I guess I can talk to you. But only if the other cop ain't here."

Brett stepped toward the door. "I'll wait outside."

Camden removed the tape recorder from his messenger bag. He set it on the edge of the bed.

Grimaldi eyed the recorder. "What's that for?"

"To be certain I get an accurate record. Mind if I record what you say?"

"I guess you can use that thing."

Camden hit the record button. "Can you state your name?"

"Robert Grimaldi."

"Tell me what happened last night."

"Like I told you, I was shot for no reason."

"No reason?" Camden echoed.

"I was running. But running ain't a crime."

"Why were you running?"

Grimaldi turned his gaze back to the TV. His left eye fluttered. "Exercise."

"Do you recall if Officer Colton told you to stop?"

Grimaldi kept his eyes on the TV. "No."

"No, you don't recall? Or no, she didn't tell you to stop?"

"I don't recall."

Camden nodded. "Can we talk about the gun?"

"I didn't have a gun."

"Do you own a gun?"

Grimaldi looked back at the TV. His left eye twitched. "No."

"Tell me about the witnesses."

"What witnesses?"

"A man and woman approached you after you were shot. According to Officer Colton, the man spoke to you. What did he say?"

"I don't remember." Grimaldi once again glanced at the TV. Slightly, but unmistakably, his left eye twitched again.

Looking at the TV and the eye twitch: Were those Grimaldi's tells? There was only one way for Camden to find out. "How many homes did you break into last night?"

He looked at the TV. His left eye twitched. "None."

"Can I ask you one more question?"

"I guess."

"Why did you point your gun at Officer Colton? Did you intend to shoot her?"

"I think we're done here." His gaze was trained on the TV. His left eye spasmed. "You take your recorder, and get the hell out of my room."

Those were his tells—and everything that Camden needed to see.

Scooping up his recorder, he left the room.

He strode down the hallway.

Brett caught up with Camden. "How'd it go?"

"Everything that guy just said was a lie. He had a gun. He pointed it at Grace. He spoke to the witnesses."

"So what if he is lying?" They stood in front of a bank of elevators and waited for the car to come up from the lobby. "Can you prove that any of his story is false?"

Camden shook his head. "But he said something else. He said he doesn't own a gun. That's a lie, too."

The elevator doors slid open, and the two men stepped inside. "How do you even know?"

"Everyone has a reaction to their lying. It's their tell. For Grimaldi, he looks away, and his eye twitches."

"Everyone has a tell?"

"Everyone." The elevator doors opened, and the two men stepped into the lobby.

Brett whistled. "Remind me never to play poker with you. How's this going to help Grace?"

"Grimaldi made one more statement, also a lie, but this one should be easy to disprove."

"What's that?" Brett asked as they crossed the lobby.

"He said he doesn't own a gun, but I can tell he does. If I can prove that, then I have him on making a false statement. Also, I can ask him to produce the gun, which he won't be able to do. It might not be a perfect solution, but at least it'll help get Grace out of the jam."

Brett used the fob to start the police SUV. "It'll work in theory."

Now all Camden needed to do was prove it.

Chapter 10

Camden had spent a fruitless afternoon. First, he called one of his buddies with the state police and asked if Robert Grimaldi had registered a gun in Michigan.

No matches were found.

For Camden, there was no doubt. Grimaldi had lied about owning a gun. Being able to prove that fact could be the difference between showing that Grace had acted appropriately to a threat or having the world believe that she'd misused force.

In order to find the gun, Camden needed to request information from forty-nine other states. So far, he'd contacted three. He glanced at his watch.

It was 6:25 p.m.

Correction: it had been a very long afternoon—and part of an evening.

After powering down his computer, he rose from

the conference table. His gaze was drawn to Grace's jacket—the same one she'd forgotten at the pizza parlor. The garment held her floral scent.

He really should just drop off the coat on his way out.

Why, then, was he tucking it into his bag?

He knew the answer to that question without even thinking.

Camden wanted to see Grace again. Still, it was a bad idea—horrible, really. He strode through the squad room and toward the front door.

Mary Suzuki stood at the front desk. Looking up with a smile as he approached, she said, "Evening, Camden. You done for the weekend?"

"Define *done*," he said jokingly.

She laughed. "Always something, right?"

"Right."

"Can I do anything for you?" she offered.

Camden paused. This was the moment. He could give Mary the jacket. Certainly, one of the many Coltons who worked at the department could pick up the coat. From now on, he could put Grace Colton behind him. Shaking his head, he said, "I'm good for now. See you Monday." He pushed the door open.

"See you Monday," she called after him.

The streets were wet, glistening in the light that spilled from the windows of downtown businesses. It was dusk, yet roiling dark clouds blocked out whatever sunset there might've been. The lack of color left the world awash in shades of gray. Camden, in his black suit and white shirt, felt as if he'd just stepped into an old-time movie.

He rounded the building and found his car in the back lot. Slipping behind the steering wheel, he started the engine. Indecision lay heavy, like a rock in his gut. For Camden, it was a foreign feeling. After inhaling deeply, he emptied his lungs in a single exhale. His mind, organized as ever, filled with dozens of ways to remedy the situation. Top of the list: return to the station and leave the coat with Mary. It's what he should have done from the beginning.

Instead, he put the gearshift into Drive and pulled out of the parking lot. Grace's apartment was only a few blocks from the police station. In less than five minutes, he was parked in front of her building. Leaning forward, he stared at her apartment window. The curtains were drawn, yet the glow of a lamp inside turned the fabric golden.

She was home.

Now he had to wonder: Was he really going to stop by, unannounced?

All the same, if he wasn't going to see her, why had he come at all?

After turning off the engine, he pulled Grace's jacket from his bag and stepped onto the sidewalk. At the same moment the door to the apartment building opened. Grace stood on the stoop. Their eyes met. She froze, her hand resting on the door.

She wore a dress in cream and pink. The bodice fitted her breasts perfectly, and the fabric skimmed over her body to the waist. The skirt was full and flowing. He recalled the feeling—only moments ago—that he'd been plunked into a black-and-white movie.

Then there was Grace. The Technicolor wonder on the screen. Her entrance onto the set was the magic that propelled the story forward.

It also made Camden wonder if he'd needed a bit of color in his own life.

"Hey," she said.

Camden shut his mouth. Swallowed. "Hey."

"What are you doing here? I was just heading out."

Damn. "A date?" he asked, his jaw tight.

"It's a family party. I'm waiting for my rideshare." Glancing at her phone, she sighed. "I ordered the car over half an hour ago, and still nothing." She paused. "Did you hear anything about the case? Have the witnesses shown up?"

Camden shook his head. "Sorry. No." He held up her jacket. "You left this at lunch."

"Oh, thanks." She came down the short flight of steps. The skirt flowed around her as she walked. "I appreciate you bringing it by."

She reached for the coat. Her fingertips brushed the back of his hand. Her touch was electric, and Camden's skin warmed. "You look great, by the way."

Grace rotated at the waist, sending the skirt twirling around her legs. "I'm usually a jeans and T-shirt kind of girl. The party is at the Grave Gulch Grill and kind of swanky. So I thought, what the hell? I can dress up for an evening, right?"

His gaze was drawn to the deep neckline of her dress. An image of his mouth on her skin flooded his mind. "Right."

Grace slipped her arms into the coat. "Well, thanks again. I probably should order another rideshare. I don't think my first one will ever show."

Walk away. Just say "Good night" and walk away.

Yet, he couldn't. Camden inclined his head toward his car. "I can give you a lift."

"Thanks for the offer, but I can't be a bother. You were nice enough to drop off my jacket. So already I've taken up too much of your time."

The little voice in his head returned. This time it was accompanied by an alarm that wailed.

After all, he'd offered Grace a ride. She'd declined. He should just leave well enough alone—but he couldn't. "Dropping you off wouldn't be a bother. Besides, I can't leave you on the street. Alone. It's getting dark."

She lifted a brow. "You think I can't take care of myself?"

"Oh, I know you can. It's just that giving a lady a ride is part of the gentleman's code."

"You're a gentleman?" she asked, lifting her eyebrow yet again. "I didn't know."

Was she flirting? God, he hoped so. Straightening his tie, Camden asked, "Don't I look dapper?"

She laughed. The sound went straight to his soul. "You do look nice." Pausing, she chewed on her bottom lip. "Are you sure that dropping me off won't be a problem?"

"Positive," he said.

He hadn't bothered to lock his car and moved to the auto, opening the passenger door as Grace approached. "Wow," she teased. "You really are a gentleman."

"You sound surprised," he joked in return. Rounding to the driver's side, he slid behind the steering wheel.

"You know the way?" she asked, as he started the engine.

"I do." He pulled onto the nearly empty street and began to drive toward the restaurant.

"Your parents own the Grave Gulch Grill, right?"

"You read that in my file?" She winked to show that she was teasing him, at least a little.

Truth was, he had read her file. But there was more. "I've worked with your brother, Troy. He mentioned it."

She nodded but said nothing. He drove, wondering what she was thinking.

He glanced at Grace. "What's the occasion?"

"My brother, Palmer, got engaged. Mom and Dad wanted to celebrate and welcome his fiancée, Soledad, and their baby girl, Lyra, to the family."

"Sounds nice. Your family seems pretty tight."

Grace lifted a shoulder and let it drop. "I guess."

"You don't seem convinced. You aren't a close crew, or it isn't good?"

"We are definitely very close. It's just…" She exhaled and looked out the window.

"It's just what?"

Before she could answer, his phone began to ring. The caller ID showed on the entertainment screen. Arielle Parks. *Crap.* He sent the call to voice mail.

"You aren't going to answer that?"

Camden tightened his grip on the wheel. "I'll call her once I get home. It'll just be a minute."

"Home?" she echoed. "You mean you don't have plans for a Friday night?"

With a shake of his head, he turned off Grave Gulch Boulevard. "Just work."

A long drive led to the Grave Gulch Grill. Tall trees, the leaves starting to turn from green to golden, lined both sides of the road. Then, the restaurant came into view. It was a large stone building. Inside, lights spilled onto the walkway and the adjacent parking lot.

What would it feel like to show up at a place like this,

with a girl like Grace Colton as his date? True, Camden had never suffered from a lack of female companionship. It's just that he hadn't met anyone interesting for several months.

Correction: he hadn't met anyone interesting until he'd met Grace.

Pulling into a space near the door, he put the gearshift into Park. "I'll call you if we get any leads on the witnesses." He knew well enough that Brett Shea would hear first. The Colton grapevine would deliver the message to Grace before Camden was even notified.

"Thanks," she said.

Camden tried to look only at the windshield. Yet his gaze was drawn to her face. Her eyes. Her neck. Her lips.

"I hate to think of you home all alone and bored."

"I won't be bored," he said.

Tilting her head toward the door, she smiled. "You want to join me?"

What in the world had Grace just done? Obviously, she'd invited Camden to attend the family party. But why?

He began, "I really don't think I'm your cousin's favorite person."

Now was the moment she could demur. Grace had done the polite thing in inviting Camden inside. It's what her mother—always classy and gracious—would do. He'd declined. She should just go. Why was she still sitting in the car? Why did she feel compelled to ask "Which one?"

True, there were a lot of Coltons. Camden chuckled. His eyes crinkled with his smile. His teeth were white.

His jaw was chiseled, and his lips looked strong. Her own lips tingled.

"I was thinking of Melissa," he said. "I guess any of the others might not like me, either."

"Because you're an IA investigator?"

"It's because I'm investigating you."

He wasn't wrong—and they both knew it. "One drink." She held up a single finger.

Camden shook his head. Relief and disappointment washed over Grace until she felt as if she might drown in her emotions.

And then he said, "Okay. Sure. One drink. It's Friday night, after all."

She couldn't help but smile. "C'mon, then. Let's go."

Opening the car door, she headed to the restaurant. The main dining room was one large space. Tables, covered in pristine white cloths, filled the room. Almost every table was filled with customers. The din of conversations was the background music. "I worked here as a kid," said Grace, circumventing the dining area.

"What'd you do?" Camden asked. He walked at her side.

"What didn't I do? I washed dishes. Bused tables. Worked as a server. Hostess. Hell, I did everything but cook."

"You didn't like the restaurant business? You weren't tempted to stay and help your folks run this place?"

"Not for a minute," said Grace with a laugh. "The restaurant has been good to my family. It's put a roof over our head, food on our own table and all of us kids through school. But it's a hard life. Early mornings. Late nights."

"Sounds like being a cop," said Camden.

Grace stopped at the door to the private-party room. She gripped the handle. "Running a restaurant makes being a cop look easy."

He laughed as she pulled the door open. The private-party room was filled with people. High-top tables, covered in blue and burgundy cloths, circumvented the room. Waiters in tuxedos maneuvered through the crowd while holding trays of tapas. A long bar was set against the far wall, and overhead a set of crystal chandeliers glowed. The first person who Grace saw was Melissa. She stood with Antonio and Grace's parents—of all people.

Melissa's gaze fell on Camden with a look that could only be described as frosty.

Then, the two women made eye contact. Grace lifted her brow—not quite a challenge, not quite a threat.

Whatever it was that she meant to communicate, Melissa understood. The scowl was replaced with a smile as she approached. Antonio Ruiz, Melissa's fiancé, stood at her side.

"Grace. Camden. It's good to see you both." She then introduced Camden to Antonio. The men shook hands.

"Camden gave me a ride here tonight," Grace said. "I invited him in for a drink."

"Oh, really?" Melissa drew her brows together. "How kind of him."

For a second, nobody spoke.

"And speaking of that drink…" Camden said, filling the silence. "I'll go grab one from the bar. What'll you have?"

"Draft beer. Thanks."

Grace watched as Camden moved through the crowd, admiring his tight rear with every step.

"Grace Colton," said Melissa. "What are you thinking by bringing an IA investigator to the party?"

"Whoa," said Antonio, interrupting. "I might let you two have a private conversation. I'm going to the bar, too. What can I get you, Melissa?"

She sighed, looking tired. "Just water."

"Water it is," he said, before slipping away.

As soon as Antonio was out of earshot, Melissa leaned in close. "An IA investigator. Really? He's investigating *you*."

"It's his job," said Grace, not entirely sure why she was defending the person tasked with establishing her culpability. "It's not his entire being." She paused. "Besides, I trust him to do right by me. I've thought this through…"

Folding her arms across her chest, Melissa said, "I don't know what part of your anatomy you're thinking with, Grace, but it's not your head."

"Excuse me?" asked Grace, feeling her face burning hot. "You don't need to be rude. Or crude."

Holding up her hands in surrender, Melissa took a step back. "You're right. That was out of line, but I'm worried."

Grace was still upset, but she wasn't going to deny the obvious. "Maybe he is a good-looking guy. What of it?" She paused. "You've been on the force for a long time. Have you heard something about Camden? Has he used his looks and charm to implicate someone before?"

Melissa let out a long exhale and moved closer to Grace. "The only time Kingsley gets brought up, it's to mention his honesty."

"So why are you questioning his character now?"

"That's easy. I want to protect you."

"I appreciate that you're always looking out for me." Grace reached for Melissa's hand and gave it a squeeze. "If I can trust him, you can, too. Or is the problem that you don't trust me?"

Camden stood at the bar, elbow on the wooden top, as he waited for drinks. He glanced at Grace. Smiled.

Just looking at him warmed Grace to her toes. She smiled back.

"I trust you," Melissa said, letting her hand slip from Grace's grasp. "I just want to make sure that you're safe. I can see the way you look at him. Getting involved with Camden can cost you more than your career. Your heart, as well."

"So what if I look? He's a handsome man."

"I'll give you that. Camden is easy on the eyes." Melissa's words trailed off.

"I hear a distinct *but* waiting to come out."

She shook her head. "I don't want to ruin the evening."

"Not saying anything is what's going to ruin the evening. Spill."

Melissa sighed again. "Just be careful, that's all."

It was then that Grace noticed the dark circles around Melissa's eyes. The color in her cheeks looked more feverish than the flush of excitement. Her cousin had made a huge sacrifice in stepping down from her job.

No wonder Melissa was in a foul mood. "I'm sorry about what happened. All of it. You might still be police chief if it wasn't for me."

Shaking her head, Melissa said, "There's so much going on at the department. Me having to step aside was inevitable. I just wanted it to be on my own terms, you know?"

Grace did know. "You look tired."

"I'm definitely fatigued. All the stress, I guess. But, c'mon. Tonight's not the night to dwell on the bad." Melissa linked her arm through Grace's, maneuvering them so they faced the bar. "It's a celebration. Lots of us Coltons are getting married—not just Palmer and Soledad. Tell me the truth, what do you think of Antonio?"

"He's amazing, honestly."

Melissa smiled, all of the weariness in her face melting away. Grace recognized the expression on her cousin's face: it was pure love and joy. "He is kind of amazing."

Grace searched the room for Camden. He was still at the bar. As she watched him, she couldn't help but wonder if she would ever find a love of her own like that.

Camden scanned the private room. The space was packed, just a sea of people. Typically, a crowded party wouldn't have been his thing. He preferred more intimate settings for his socializing, such that it was. Yet, he had to admit, as the music of animated conversations and the peals of laughter swirled around him, the Colton family was a happy crew.

It was totally opposite from his family. Camden was the only child of a father who'd died too soon. His mother, all these years later, was still wrapped in a cocoon of grief. A pang of jealousy filled his chest, gone as quick as it came. Still, Camden couldn't help but wonder what it would be like to be a part of such a large and boisterous clan.

His gaze was drawn to Grace. She stood with her cousin, Melissa, and a group of other women. They all favored each other—hair, eyes, nose—and he assumed they were more of the Coltons.

"Hey, my man," said a familiar voice. "I didn't expect to see you here."

Camden turned toward the greeting. It was Troy Colton, Grace's brother. He was almost as tall as Camden but had broader shoulders. From the looks of his rumpled suit and loose tie, Camden guessed that the other man had come to the party right after work. Then again, Camden had on a suit, worn all day, as well.

"Troy," he said, holding out his hand to shake. The two men had worked on the Randall Bowe case, Troy trying to find the forensic scientist, Camden trying to find out why he got away with so much. "I gave Grace a ride over to the party. She invited me to stay.

"I'm glad she did."

"How's Evangeline?" Camden asked, mentioning the former ADA and Troy's love.

"Busy. She'll be here later and will be happy to see you."

"It'll be great to see her, too."

Then, the conversation moved, as it always did with cops, to work. Troy asked, "What're you working on?"

"Aside from Bowe?" Did the GGPD detective not know that Camden was looking into last night's shooting? Or was he trying to gauge what Camden would say? "I'm working on what happened with Grace."

Troy glanced over his shoulder. He watched Grace for a moment, before turning back to Camden. "How's she doing?"

"Your sister's tough and smart." Camden pressed his lips together before he said anything that might give away his true feelings.

"Any leads on those witnesses?"

"None at all." The bartender slid two beers across the bar, and Camden picked up the glasses. "And what about you? What're you working on these days?"

"All my time is spent on the Bowe case. You know Randall texted Melissa a while back."

Camden did. He nodded and took a sip of beer. "He wants to talk to his brother."

"It's been my job to find him."

"Any luck?"

"None at all," he said, echoing Camden's words. "I've talked to my cousin Bryce. He's with the FBI. Bryce put out feelers with the US Marshals for Randall's brother, Baldwin. So far, nothing's turned up. It's like Baldwin's a ghost or something."

"Who's a ghost?" Another guy dressed in a suit and tie approached the bar. He had sandy-brown hair and blue eyes and looked fit. He was taller than Camden. Was this another Colton? "You know I always love a scary story."

"Camden Kingsley, let me introduce you to my cousin, Bryce." Troy draped his arm over Bryce's shoulder. "Bryce is with the FBI, but don't let the fancy job fool you. He's still an okay guy."

So this was Special Agent Colton? Camden nodded his greetings. "Nice to meet you."

"Same," said Bryce. "Really, what're you two talking about?"

"What else is there to talk about?" Troy asked. "Work. Camden's with the DA's office. Internal Affairs. He's looking into the Bowe fiasco, among other things."

Camden stepped to the side so the other men could order their drinks.

"What else are you working on?" Bryce asked, leaning an elbow on the bar.

"Last night's shooting, for one."

"Grace?" Bryce asked.

Camden nodded. He should've known that he'd be persona non grata before he ever walked through the door, although the Coltons hadn't really treated him like that.

"What've you found out?" Bryce asked.

"Not much more than has been reported to the media." He paused. No, that wasn't right. "Today I interviewed the guy who was shot. Robert Grimaldi's his name and he's still in the hospital. The guy has a tell. When he lies, he looks away, and there's a twitch in the left eye."

"Impressive that you figured it out," said Troy.

"Just a bit of paying attention to his response. Plus, I asked him a question that I already knew the answer to. He lied, and again there was the tell."

"What's all of this mean for Grace?" Bryce asked. "Were you able to figure anything?"

"For starters, I think he's lying about owning a gun. It's not registered in Michigan, but until we find the firearm, we got nothing."

"For the record, I'm glad you're the one looking into last night's shooting," said Bryce. "You're doing the right thing by Grace."

"I'm not sure Melissa agrees with you. She gave me quite a look when I arrived."

Bryce shrugged. "All us Coltons are pretty protective of Grace, Melissa especially. Plus, she must feel some extra responsibility because she's chief of police. Or was until this morning."

"I have to get this beer to your cousin before it gets warm."

"Go. Let me know if you need anything."

Stopping short, Camden turned. "What'd you say?"

The bartender handed Bryce a glass filled with amber liquid and ice. "What'd I say about what?"

"If I need help."

"Oh, sure, let me know if you need help. The bureau has resources. We can help with local cases, but only if the authorities ask."

"What about the gun?" Camden's pulse started to race. "Could you get into the database for other states?"

"I can, but only for a reason."

"Today, I talked to Robert Grimaldi—the guy who was shot. I asked him if he had a gun. He said he didn't own one, but he's lying. I checked Michigan's firearm registry." Camden shook his head. "Nada."

"But he might've bought one in another state. Is that what you're thinking?"

"More like hoping, but yeah."

"You have to come to my office," said Bryce. "Can you meet at eight o'clock tomorrow morning?"

"Got it," said Camden, his head buzzing with excitement.

"I'll text if anything changes."

Grace still stood in the middle of a group of women. Some he recognized—like Melissa, Desiree and Annalise, the K-9 instructor. Others he could only guess were members of the family.

He approached the group, drink in hand.

Grace excused herself from the knot of women. "Thanks," she said, taking the offered beer.

"Nice party. I spoke to Troy and Bryce."

"About?" she asked, taking a sip.

"Work. Randall Bowe. You." He took a drink from his beer. "I think Bryce might be able to help."

Grabbing Camden by his elbow, she pulled him away from the group of women. "Help me? How?"

"The FBI has access to firearm databases for different states. It might be able to tell me if Robert Grimaldi purchased a gun. If he owns a firearm—but can't produce it—it would prove a bit of your story."

"You think that'll work?"

"It's a long shot, sure. Mostly because there are states that don't keep track of gun sales. Or Grimaldi might've stolen a gun or bought a stolen gun."

"Let's hope that, for once, he followed the rules."

"Hello, dear. Who's your friend?" An older woman stepped away from the group of chatting women. She stood right behind Grace. "Are you going to introduce me?"

"Mom, this is Camden Kingsley. He works for the DA's office and gave me a ride to the party." Grace paused. "Camden, this is my mom, Leanne Colton."

"Mrs. Colton, it's a pleasure to meet you. I can see the resemblance between you and your daughter," said Camden, shaking the other woman's hand.

"It's nice to meet a friend of Grace's. But please, call me Leanne."

Camden immediately liked her. She was gracious and kind and obviously cared about her daughter.

Leanne continued. "I'm glad you could join us to celebrate. We are a tight family, but we love our friends, too. Eat lots. I picked out the menu personally."

"Mom does all the customer relations here. Dad is in charge of the kitchen and the business." Grace paused

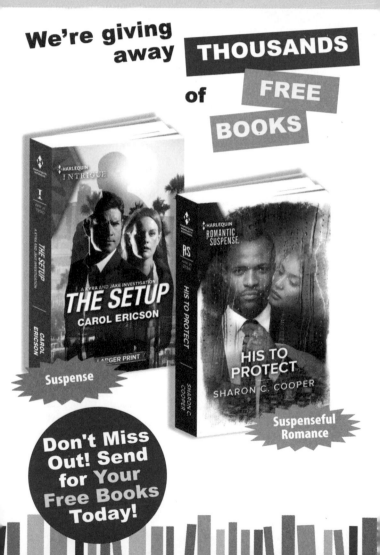

Get up to 4 FREE FABULOUS BOOKS You Love!

To thank you for being a loyal reader we'd like to send you up to 4 FREE BOOKS, absolutely free.

Just write "YES" on the Loyal Reader Voucher and we'll send you up to 4 Free Books and Free Mystery Gifts, altogether worth over $20, as a way of saying thank you for being a loyal reader.

Try **Harlequin® Romantic Suspense** books featuring heart-racing page-turners with unexpected plot twists and irresistible chemistry that will keep you guessing to the very end.

Try **Harlequin Intrigue® Larger-Print** books featuring action-packed stories that will keep you on the edge of your seat. Solve the crime and deliver justice at all costs.

Or **TRY BOTH!**

We are so glad you love the books as much as we do and can't wait to send you great new books.

So don't miss out, return your Loyal Reader Voucher Today!

Pam Powers

LOYAL READER
FREE BOOKS VOUCHER

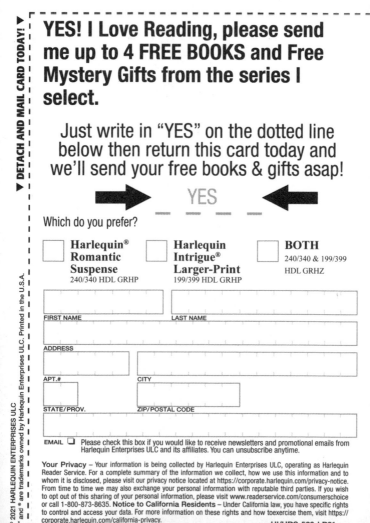

YES! I Love Reading, please send me up to 4 FREE BOOKS and Free Mystery Gifts from the series I select.

Just write in "YES" on the dotted line below then return this card today and we'll send your free books & gifts asap!

➡ YES ⬅
— — — —

Which do you prefer?

☐ **Harlequin® Romantic Suspense**
240/340 HDL GRHP

☐ **Harlequin Intrigue® Larger-Print**
199/399 HDL GRHP

☐ **BOTH**
240/340 & 199/399
HDL GRHZ

FIRST NAME	LAST NAME

ADDRESS

APT.#	CITY

STATE/PROV.	ZIP/POSTAL CODE

EMAIL ☐ Please check this box if you would like to receive newsletters and promotional emails from Harlequin Enterprises ULC and its affiliates. You can unsubscribe anytime.

HI/HRS-520-LR21

▲ If offer card is missing write to: Harlequin Reader Service, P.O. Box 1341, Buffalo, NY 14240-8531 or visit www.ReaderService.com ▲

BUSINESS REPLY MAIL

FIRST-CLASS MAIL   PERMIT NO. 717   BUFFALO, NY

POSTAGE WILL BE PAID BY ADDRESSEE

HARLEQUIN READER SERVICE

PO BOX 1341

BUFFALO NY 14240-8571

NO POSTAGE
NECESSARY
IF MAILED
IN THE
UNITED STATES

and scanned the room. Camden's gaze was drawn to the hollow of her neck, and his mind was filled with a single question: What would it feel like to kiss her throat? He looked away. "Where is Dad?"

Leanne laughed. "Guess."

"The kitchen," said Grace with a mock groan.

"You should see the cake we have, Camden. Soledad owns Dream Bakes. She and Grace's father have been working on the cake all day. The reveal itself will be an event. I hope you can stay for the whole party."

"Don't pressure, Mom. He was just nice enough to give me a ride. Nothing else."

"I'm not pressuring your friend. I'm *inviting*. There's a difference…"

Camden could tell that the two women had deep affection and admiration for each other. His phone rang. He fished it one-handed from the inner pocket of his suit coat. It was Arielle. Finally. "I have to take this, Mrs.—" he stopped to correct himself "—I mean, Leanne. It was nice meeting you."

Swiping the call open with his thumb, he pressed the phone to his ear. Making his way to a set of glass doors at the back of the room, he said, "Hold on a sec."

Beer in one hand and phone in the other, Camden used his hip to open the door. He stepped onto a patio of gray stone. A short wall, also of gray stone, surrounded the semicircular area. Glass globes, on wrought iron poles, cast pools of golden light. Several seating arrangements filled the space. Nobody from the party had ventured outside, leaving Camden completely alone. After the noisy room, he breathed in the silence.

Setting his beer on the ledge, he stared into the night.

"You still there, Arielle? I had to get outside so we could speak."

"It sounds like you were in the middle of quite a celebration. Where are you?"

"The Coltons are having an engagement party for Grace's brother."

"You got invited? How?" And then, "That's amazing, really. You're doing a heck of a job sticking close to Grace."

Now was the time. He could confess all to Arielle, and she'd have no choice but to remove him from the investigation. If he recused himself, would he still be able to work with Bryce Colton?

No. If he stepped away from Grace's case now, he walked away forever. Could he rely on someone else to follow up with the FBI agent and his offer to help? Or would it be seen as another Colton protecting a member of the family?

"There's more going on right now than me learning what I can about Grace and the rest of the Colton clan."

Like a whisper of pressure on his spine, Camden could feel a set of eyes on his back. Worse, he knew who was watching him.

Turning slowly, he faced Grace Colton. Had she heard what he'd said to Arielle?

Her complexion was pale, almost ashen. Her lips trembled. Yet, there was a fire in her eyes, and he knew: she'd heard. And she was pissed.

"Arielle, I have to go."

"Go?" his boss squawked. "Go where? You've been trying to talk to me all day."

"I'll call you back," he said, hanging up.

Camden let the phone slip from his ear. Standing in the dark, he stared at Grace. "Hey."

"Hey, yourself." She still held her drink. Her hand shook. Beer sloshed over the glass, leaving her sleeve soaked. She'd donned the jacket that he'd kept with him just to give him an excuse to see her again. Now, the coat was going to be his ruin.

Hell, he should have left the coat with Mary at police headquarters.

"Damn it," Grace cursed. After setting the beer on the wall, she wiped her hand on the tail of her coat.

Camden knew there was no way forward other than to tell the truth. "Listen, I know what you overheard, but I can explain…"

"Explain?" She snorted. "I heard plenty. You're spying on my family, trying to make sure that I'm guilty. That, somehow, we're all guilty. But that's where you're wrong. The Coltons might not be perfect, but we're good people…"

"I agree," he said.

"I don't care what you say. Robert Grimaldi had a gun."

"I agree," he said again.

"Wait. You *what*?"

"I agree. Your family isn't corrupt. Maybe a bit unlucky with everything that's happened recently."

"And me?"

"You? You're *really* unlucky. But that doesn't mean you're guilty of shooting an unarmed man."

Grace shook her head and muttered a curse.

Camden knew that she wasn't ready to forgive—or forget.

After a moment, she asked, "What's up, then? I heard what you said, so don't deny it."

"I'm not going to deny anything," said Camden. The truth always won in the end. Moreover, it was well past time that he was honest with Grace. "There are reservations about how the most recent cases have been handled in the GGPD. But I've been trying to talk to Arielle all day. There's something I need to tell her."

"Oh, really?" Grace's voice dripped with derision. "Why's that?"

"I need to be taken off the case."

"Really?" His confession appeared to blunt some of Grace's fury. She drew in a deep breath and sat on the stone wall. "Is it because you're going to have to find me at fault?"

What was Camden supposed to say? He could let Grace think that her case was hopeless—and in a lot of ways it was. But when had lying ever solved a problem?

He shook his head. "It's not that."

"What is it, then?"

Camden turned to face Grace. God, she was beautiful. And strong. And sincere. And kind. In short, she was everything he'd ever want in a woman—even if she'd never be the one for him. "I need to be taken off the case because the truth is…" he inhaled "…Grace Colton, I like you. A lot."

Chapter 11

Grace's pulse thundered in her ears. Her heart beat wildly against her chest, a trapped animal trying to break free. "You like me?" She echoed Camden's words.

She found him more than handsome. He was also stalwart, honest and determined. Suddenly, she was aware of how very secluded the patio was. Camden stood so close that she could feel his breath on her neck. The heat of his body warmed her flesh.

She didn't mind being alone or feeling his breath on her skin, like a lover's caress. Yet, what did she intend to do with this moment?

"Is that so hard to believe?" His whispered words disappeared in the dark night.

He sat next to her. His finger was so close to hers that she need only move a little and they would be touching. Was that what she wanted—to hold Camden's hand?

In truth, she wanted so much more. An image of Camden—his lips on hers, his hands on her body—flooded her thoughts. Her mouth tingled with the imagined kiss. Her skin burned with the fantasy of his touch.

She could lean in close and let the fiction become reality.

And then what?

Grace might be a rookie cop on leave, but she wasn't stupid. The best way to ruin her career would be to get involved with Camden.

Still, she sat in the darkness wanting nothing more than to give in to her longing.

No. She couldn't. She loved her job. Even after the last twenty-four hours, she wanted nothing more than to get back to work.

Scooting back, she picked up her beer and took a sip. Maybe the little bit of alcohol gave her some courage. Or maybe it just lessened her reservations. Or maybe it was as simple as the need to tell Grace the truth was paramount. She took another swallow of her beer. "I like you, too. But we can't. You know that."

Camden's head hung. He nodded slowly. "You're right, which is why I've been trying to get taken off the case all day. Until now, that is."

"Now you want to stay. Why?"

"It's what your cousin said about the FBI having tech that the GGPD doesn't. What if we can prove that Grimaldi owns a gun?" He still whispered, but his words tumbled out, a stream rushing over rocks. "I can't trust anyone else from the DA's office to do the right thing. After I see what Bryce can find, I'll recuse myself from the investigation."

"What happens then?" she asked, her gaze on his lips.

"Then we have to go our separate ways. There isn't anything else to do."

He was right. Yet a pain stabbed Grace in the chest.

"Sure." She paused a beat. "You're right."

He reached for her. His pinky stroked the side of her hand. The touch danced along her skin. She wanted to lean in to him, to feel his lips on hers just this once. That would be a step too far.

Camden must've known, too. He stood. "I better go. Thank your mom for letting me stop by the party."

"Should you get behind the wheel? You've had a beer."

He gestured to a glass, nearly full, that sat on the wall. "Only a sip or two. I'll be fine to drive home."

There was nothing else she could say or do to keep him with her even if she wanted. Grace rose, too. Her mouth was dry, and her throat raw. Still, she couldn't let him walk out of her life without saying goodbye. "It's only been a day, really less than twenty-four hours. I already know that I was lucky to have met you."

"Well." Camden stood taller and held out his hand for her to shake. "I guess that makes two of us."

She placed her palm in his. Her hand warmed as a golden glow crept up her arm and lodged in her heart.

They still held hands. "I better go."

"Drive safe." She closed the distance between them.

"I'll let you know if the FBI can find out anything about a gun." Closer still. His palm slipped from hers, and he traced the back of her hand. They were hidden from the party room by the shadows, and his touch was a delicious indulgence.

Was that the moment that Grace decided she didn't

care about expectations, propriety or even her career? Or had the decision been made long ago?

Slipping her arms around his neck, she pulled him to her. His mouth was on hers. Hungrily, he claimed her with his kiss. The desire was intense. It registered deep in her belly. Grace opened herself to him, wanting to be devoured.

Tongues. Mouths. Teeth. Camden and Grace embraced, tasted and explored.

Camden's touch trailed under her jacket. His fingertips were hot against the thin fabric of her dress. Her clothes were too tight. The cool night was suddenly too warm. The pain of desire built in her middle.

It was all hands and touch. Mouths and kisses. Longing and passion, at first ignored, had now ignited. She ran her fingers through his hair, pulling him closer. Yet he'd never be close enough.

His arms were around her as he claimed her hungrily with his mouth. Grace was drunk on the sensation. She pressed her body into his. He was already hard. She was wet, and her innermost muscles clenched.

"Camden," she breathed into the kiss. "Oh, Camden."

His touch branded her skin. But Grace didn't care if she got burned. He reached into the bodice of her dress. Inside her bra, he teased her nipple.

"Grace, you are so damned perfect."

"Perfect, huh?" Nipping his bottom lip, she teased. "Perfect how?"

"Perfect breasts," he whispered, rubbing his thumb over her taut nipple. "Perfect mouth." He claimed her once more with a kiss. "Perfect body." His touch moved lower, and he reached up the skirt of her dress and then into her panties.

She'd never wanted anyone the way she wanted Camden Kingsley. Could she take him as a lover after only knowing him for one day?

At the moment, she didn't care about any personal rules.

She ran her hands over his chest and torso. The muscles of his pecs and abs were unmistakable. What would it be like to have him hold her with his strong arms?

He slipped his finger between the folds of her sex. Grace lifted her leg, wrapping it over Camden's hip, and giving him complete access. He found the top of her sex already swollen and sensitive. He rubbed repeatedly, and Grace's world shattered into a million pieces. Crying out as she came, she knew the noise was captured by Camden's kisses.

Reckless, a small voice whispered from the back of her mind. *This is beyond reckless, and you know it. If you sleep with Camden now, then you'll have to live with the consequences for the rest of your life.*

Her pulse pounded in her ears, drowning out the little words of her conscience. Every inch of her body buzzed, as if she'd been electrified. Yet, it was more than the pleasure of Camden's touch. It was the man. She wanted him. No, she needed him inside her, the personal costs be damned.

Besides, in the darkened corner of the patio, nobody ever needed to know.

She reached for the front of his pants and her fingers trembled as she worked the top button free.

He kissed her again. "Grace, you're driving me wild."

Good. She wanted him to lose control. She wanted him to need her as much as she needed him. Tugging on his zipper, she pulled down. Grace glanced at Camden, he pressed against the fabric of his shorts. Her hand slipped inside the waistband and she slid her finger over the head of his penis. Collecting a bead of moisture, she gripped him and ran her palm over his length. Closing his eyes, he hissed as her movement took on a rhythm.

Camden held tight to her wrist, stopping Grace. "I'm about to lose it, but I want…" He kissed her lips softly. "I want to be inside you when I do."

"Do you have a condom?"

"I do," said Camden, reaching for his wallet.

He pulled out a foil packet and Grace's knees went weak with longing.

You don't want to live with the work-related consequences of this moment for the rest of your life, the voice in her head warned.

Yet, as Camden placed his lips on hers, she told the voice to shut up.

After rolling the condom down his length, Camden gripped Grace's rear. He lifted her and she let out squeal of surprise and delight. Wrapping her legs around his waist, she pulled aside her panties. The silk of her skirt cascaded down, and then he was inside her. They moved together, hot and frantic. His fingers dug into her flesh and as he thrust into her hard. Grace held onto his shoulders as the wave of desire began to swell in her middle again. Harder. Faster. The pleasure grew and she pulled him closer, took him deeper. Still, she knew that it would never be enough.

She rode the wave of ecstasy higher and higher. It broke, and she cried out with her orgasm.

Camden thrust twice more and growled as he came.

Grace placed her lips on his, her pulse racing and

echoing in her ears. Yet it wasn't so loud that she couldn't hear the small voice inside her head.

What have you done, Grace? No matter what happens now, you'll never be exonerated. By having sex with Camden Kingsley, your innocence—along with your professionalism—will always be in doubt.

The truth gripped her by the throat until she couldn't swallow or even breathe. She slipped from his grip and fixed her underwear. It didn't matter that her heartbeat still raced. Or that her lips still tingled. Or even that her body still thrummed.

"I didn't mean for that to happen," she began. Her voice echoed inside her head, the words seeming to be spoken by someone else. All of the stress from the last day seemed to drop on her shoulders. How had she given in to the temptation to have sex with Camden? Never mind the fact that she'd been burning with desire. Now, all she wanted to do was get away. "I'm sorry." She stepped farther away, creating distance between them.

"Don't be sorry." Camden took a napkin from his pocket and dealt with the condom. Looking away, she gave him a moment of privacy.

She picked up her beer from the stone wall and took a long swallow. The alcohol exploded in her stomach like a bomb yet did nothing to stop her racing heart. "I should get back." She backed up, hooking her thumb toward the patio doors. "You know. The party."

Camden nodded. "I better go. If I find out anything about Grimaldi owning a gun, I'll ask Bryce to give you a call."

As if shocked by a faulty switch, she jolted and recoiled at the mention of her cousin's name. Bryce would call, not Camden himself. It was easy to figure out why. Camden Kingsley was about to walk out of Grace's life forever.

His gaze lingered on her face for a beat and then another.

Giving her one last smile, he turned and walked away.

Grace stood on the patio, breathless. Her eyes burned. She watched as he followed a path that led from the patio to the parking lot. The darkness swallowed him, and then he was gone.

As the first rays of the gray morning seeped through his curtains, Camden rubbed his gritty eyes. Saturday morning already? He'd spent the night tossing and turning, filled with regrets.

Making love to Grace Colton had been a mistake.

Walking away from her had been a tragedy.

His hands still recalled the feel of her body. He hardened with desire. There was more than merely the physical attraction. For years, Camden had observed the life of others, never really caring about much more than uncovering the facts. All that changed when he met Grace.

Was there any way to make a possible relationship between them work?

He shouldn't even bother with the question, though, because he already knew the answer.

Despite how he felt about Grace—or how she felt about him—being together was not in their future.

Setting his feet on the floor, Camden stood and ran his hand over his face. His lips still held the memory of Grace's kiss. His hands still remembered the feel of her body—muscular yet soft. His phone pinged with an incoming text. It was from Bryce.

Heading to office. Can you still meet?

Thank goodness the other man was an early riser. Camden would have gone crazy if he'd had to spend the entire day waiting for Bryce.

Camden typed out a message and hit Send.

See you then.

Bryce's simple reply:

Text me when you arrive.

Camden showered and dressed quickly, deciding on jeans and a T-shirt. Stepping from his condo, he felt his pulse race as he drove to Bryce's office.

Before he had a chance to send his text, the front door opened. Bryce Colton, dressed in a golf shirt and jeans, stood on the threshold. A holster, along with a gun, was strapped under his arm.

"Thanks for stopping by so early," said Bryce.

Sliding out of the car, Camden used the fob to lock the door. "Thanks for running Grimaldi's name through the database."

"I'd offer my services to any investigation. The FBI is here to help," Bryce said. "But I'm not going to lie, I'm glad you're here. Grace is my baby cousin, and I'll do everything in my power to find out what happened."

Grace. His pulse sped at the sound of her name. The

fact that they'd had sex should change everything. Still, he was here.

Stepping into the vestibule, Camden took in his surroundings. The floors and walls were covered in marble the color of ash. A patriotic mural filled the ceiling. Camden couldn't help himself; he was impressed.

A set of dual walk-through metal detectors led to a long hallway. At the end of the corridor stood a bank of elevators.

"You don't have to worry about those," said Bryce, tilting his head to the detectors. "They aren't on when the building's closed."

"You're at work."

"There's always something to keep me busy," said Bryce. "You know how it goes."

Camden walked between the two detectors. For the first time, he wondered if the agent was like him: working constantly because it was a calling. "I do know how it goes."

They took an elevator to the second floor, then walked down a long hallway. Motion-sensor lights clicked on as they approached. The hallway ended at a single door. It would have been unremarkable if not for the FBI seal— scales, a shield, olive branches and a banner with the words *Fidelity*, *Bravery* and *Integrity*—affixed to the wall.

The door was locked. Bryce keyed in a code on an electronic lock that was attached to the handle. He then scanned his thumbprint, and the latch clicked. Bryce turned the handle, and they entered a waiting room. Pictures of both the president of the United States and the US attorney general hung on the wall. Flags for both the USA and the state of Michigan flanked the framed photographs.

Camden couldn't ignore the thrill that danced along his skin. The whole setup was, well, cool and impressive. It was where important work was done to serve and protect not just the state but the entire nation.

"Right this way," said Bryce. Another door. Another security code and thumbprint scan.

Finally, they were in the inner sanctum of the FBI. It was much like any other office. Workspaces, with desks separated only by partitions, filled a large room. Yet the walls told a different story. A large picture of Len Davison, a man wanted in connection to several serial killings in the Grave Gulch area, was tacked on one wall. It was surrounded by photos of his victims. A timeline of the killings had been scrawled on a whiteboard. Another wall had a picture of Randall Bowe, the CSI investigator who had falsified evidence.

Bryce's cell phone began to ring. He glanced at the screen before opening the call. "Hey, Troy. You're up early."

He was silent for a moment, while the GGPD detective spoke.

"You're kidding, right?" His eyes went wide. Looking at Camden, he mouthed the words *Baldwin Bowe.*

Randall Bowe's brother? Camden's pulse spiked. Baldwin had gone off the radar and been near impossible to find.

"I'm here with Camden Kingsley," said Bryce. "I'm putting you on speakerphone."

Bryce engaged the app and set the phone on the desk.

"Troy," said Camden, "what happened? Baldwin Bowe's been a hard man to track down."

"It looks like he didn't want to be found until now," said Troy. The excitement in his voice was unmistakable. "I'm meeting with him soon and need backup." He continued. "There's a coffee shop near the park. Grave Gulch Coffee and Treats. There are tables on the street."

It was the same place Camden and Grace had shown pictures of the witnesses only the day before. "I know the one."

"Meet me there in ten minutes," said Troy.

"Ten minutes," Bryce echoed, and then the line went dead.

Chastity knew she had a headache before she opened her eyes. Her mouth was dry, and her tongue felt as if it'd been wrapped in cotton. Crap. How many bottles of cheap wine had she and Thad gone through the night before?

He lay beside her. Blankets were draped over his hips. His back was naked, and she traced the outline of his shoulder blade. Groaning, he batted her hand away in his sleep.

Chastity knew two things for certain. First, she'd never get back to sleep, and second, she needed a cup of coffee. A real latte—made with soy milk, by an actual barista—and not the crap they made from instant coffee.

Lying on her back, she stared at the ceiling. Her gaze outlined the water stain that looked like a rabbit. It was early for a Saturday, not much after nine o'clock. If she left now, would Thad even know she'd been gone?

Rolling off the mattress, she rummaged through the clothes that covered the floor. It took a minute to find a shirt without a stain and a pair of pants. After dressing silently, she slipped from the bedroom and pulled the door closed.

In the living room, she counted the empty bottles of wine. One on the coffee table. One on the kitchen counter. One on the floor, tipped on its side. She and Thad had finished three bottles of wine? No wonder her head hurt.

She grabbed her phone. Did she dare to look at what the news was reporting?

The temptation was strong, and she opened the TV station's app.

The app had created a separate tab. *GGPD: A Department Embroiled in Scandal.* She touched the link with her thumb.

Yesterday's article was pinned at the top.

Below were comments about the police.

She scrolled through them all in seconds.

Then she stopped. Someone had posted a video from the press conference. Chastity turned down the volume on her phone and pressed Play.

She watched the chief of police give her statement. As the woman spoke, Chastity's pulse raced. What did the cops know? Did they suspect that someone had taken the gun? Correction: not just someone. Thad and Chastity.

The video began to scan the crowd. The grim-faced protesters who held signs. The police inside, the interior of the building so dark that they were only shadows. Except one man, who stood near a window. He was tall. Dark-haired. Chastity would've found him attractive if she didn't love Thad so much.

The video ended, and she closed the app. Slipping her phone back into her pocket, she decided on a simple fact. The police were no closer to finding Thad and Chastity, the gun or even the truth.

A black hoodie lay over the arm of the sofa. She worked into the jacket and left the apartment without a backward glance.

On the street, the air was cool and bracing. She inhaled deeply, and the throbbing in her head lessened. After slipping on a pair of sunglasses, she pulled up the hood. It wasn't a great disguise but, she wasn't going to be outside for long.

Grave Gulch Coffee and Treats, her favorite coffee shop in the neighborhood, sat on the corner. Half a dozen tables filled the sidewalk. They were all empty, save for one guy sitting alone and twirling an old-school flip phone through his fingers. Pushing the door open with her shoulder, she entered the shop. The dark and nutty aroma of coffee brewing greeted her. Immediately, Chastity's headache disappeared. She'd been right to come out this morning.

"That's him," said Camden. A man sat at an outside table at Grave Gulch Coffee and Treats. He had short dark hair. Despite the fact that Baldwin was in a chair, Camden could tell that he was tall. He wore a T-shirt and jeans and had the look of a guy who knew how to throw a punch and take one. Troy was sitting opposite.

"That's Baldwin Bowe with your cousin," said Camden.

"I recognize him from the photos," said Bryce. They'd driven to the rendezvous. Turning off the car's ignition, he continued, "Let's go."

Baldwin looked up as Camden and Bryce exited the car. His expression gave away nothing. Without a word, the two men crossed the street and slid into seats on either side of Baldwin.

Camden nodded a greeting to Troy.

Bryce spoke first. "You're a hard man to find."

"Correction," said Baldwin. "I'm impossible to find. Unless I want to be found, that is."

The hairs on Camden's arm stood on end. "I'm sure you heard that your brother wants to talk to you."

"What if I don't want to talk to him?"

Camden said, "You know that your brother let some serious criminals go free."

"I'm not my brother," Baldwin growled.

"Who are you?" Troy asked.

"I'm just a guy who's trying to do the right thing."

"So where have you been?" Camden asked.

Baldwin held a small burner cell phone—the kind that made and received calls and did little else. He tapped the plastic casing on the table. "Around," he said, in answer to Camden's question.

"What about your brother? Has he been around with you, too?" Bryce asked.

"Randall?" Baldwin snorted. "I have no love for my brother. I definitely wouldn't hide him from the police."

Camden was an only child, yet he imagined that siblings should act like the Colton family: loving, supportive, encouraging. For a split second, his memories were flooded with a dozen images of Grace. Her smile. Her laugh. The way her brows came together when she was thinking. Shifting in the small seat, he turned away from the recollections. "Why no love for your brother?"

"Randall's a sneaky piece of garbage. He always has been. In fact, I don't blame his wife for cheating."

Troy redirected him. "He's got some kind of score to settle with you. You know that, right?" He removed a slip of paper from his pocket and slid it across the table.

"This is the number Randall gave to Chief Colton. He wants you to call."

"I assume you tried to trace it." Without looking at the number, Baldwin tucked it into his shirt pocket.

"Of course," Bryce replied. "It's registered to a burner phone, purchased with cash, at a convenience store outside of Grave Gulch. The phone hasn't been turned on, so there's no way to track it."

"That may change when you make a call," said Camden. The back of his neck itched, as if someone was watching him from behind. He glanced over his shoulder.

No one was there.

He looked back as Baldwin spoke. "If I call my brother, I need your word that you'll find him. Arrest him. He needs to be put away before more people get hurt."

"You have our word," said Bryce.

"Where can we find you?" Camden asked.

"If there's anything to report, I'll find you."

Obviously, Baldwin Bowe was being purposely evasive. He might've had his reasons. It's just that Camden wasn't willing to leave it alone. "Why don't you cut the crap?" he asked, being uncustomarily abrasive.

Baldwin sat back. "Excuse me?"

"You heard what I said. If you really want your brother caught and put away, you're going to have to cooperate with us." He flicked his thumb toward Bryce and Troy. "That means we need to find *you*."

"My job isn't one where I show up to an office or work regular hours," Baldwin began. He sighed. Maybe he really was ready to help find his brother. Or maybe he was just tired of hiding. He continued. "I've been working as a bounty hunter for years. But my typical client isn't a guy who's quit paying child support. Or someone who skipped their court date. The people who I find are really well hidden."

Camden nodded slowly. He was starting to get a picture of what Baldwin Bowe did for a living. More than that, he was coming to understand what kind of man he was.

"Ghost bounty hunter?" said Troy, putting a name to Baldwin's job.

"Of sorts." Leaning back in the seat, he folded his arms. "I work hard to operate under the radar, and that's where I plan to stay."

"Understood," said Bryce with a nod.

Again, Camden's neck itched. He glanced over his shoulder once more. This time, the door to the coffee shop swung shut as a young woman walked down the street, coffee cup in hand.

Camden only caught a glimpse of her reflection in the glass door. She looked familiar. But from where? Then it hit him. Gripping the edge of the table, he leaned forward. "That's her," he hissed.

"Her who?" Bryce asked, brows drawn together.

"The witness." Camden rose to his feet and stopped. In the split second that he'd turned away, the woman was gone. "Where in the hell did she go?"

"Witness? Go?" Bryce was on his feet, as well. "What're you talking about?"

"I swear that woman who just walked out of the shop looked exactly like the female witness to the shooting." Energy pent up in Camden's core made him feel like a compressed spring. He just didn't know which way to explode.

Troy scanned the street. "Where'd she go?"

"You looking for the girl in the hoodie?" Baldwin asked. "She went around the corner." Baldwin pointed to the right. "That way."

"I'll go after her," said Camden. And then to Bryce, "You come around the block. Troy, you stay here in case she comes back."

He didn't wait to see if the agent or the detective had anything else to say. Sprinting down the sidewalk. Camden skidded to a stop. Rows of brownstones, renovated into apartment buildings, lined both sides of the street. Cars were parked at the curb.

Yet the woman was gone.

Bryce sprinted up the street and skidded to a stop. Sweat dampened his brow, and his breaths came in sharp gasps. "Where'd she go?"

Turning in a slow circle, Camden shook his head. Hundreds of windows looked down on the street. The woman could be in any one of the dwellings. Or none at all. She might've gotten in a car and driven away before Camden even realized what he'd seen. Bryce's question still hung in the air. *Where'd she go?*

"I don't know where she is, man."

"Let's get back to Baldwin and from there call Shea. He can increase patrols in this neighborhood and put them on the lookout for the witness."

Camden nodded while he felt his cheeks sting with the failure. "Sure thing."

Camden and Bryce returned to the coffee shop. Troy and Baldwin Bowe were on their feet.

"No luck in finding her," said Bowe.

Camden shook his head. "None."

Lifting the slip of paper with Randall's number, Baldwin said, "Unless you need anything else, I'm outta here."

"You know," said Troy, "there's a lot of questions I have."

"I've got no answers for you," Baldwin said, walking backward. "We'll be in touch."

He rounded the corner. On his seat lay the burner phone.

Bryce cursed. "I guess our man has slipped back into the shadows. Who knows when we'll find him next?"

Picking up the phone, Camden said, "I don't think we'll find him. But as soon as he talks to his brother, he'll find us."

Chapter 12

Chastity crouched by the door. A paper cup was clutched to her chest. Her heartbeat hammered, and her stomach threatened to revolt. Why had she gone out?

Of course, the police were still looking for her and Thad.

When she walked into Grave Gulch Coffee and Treats, there had been one guy at the table. Then, when she came out, there were three more. Even worse, she'd recognized the dark-haired man. He was the same one in the video at the police press conference.

It had taken every bit of willpower to walk slowly by the men. But the second she rounded the corner, Chastity sprinted to her apartment. It was only luck that she was less than half a block away.

Two panes of a grimy window filled the top third of the door. Rising to her knees, Chastity peeked outside.

Nobody stood on the sidewalk. No cop car drove slowly down the street. Had she imagined it all?

There had been a table with four guys. That was a fact.

She tried to recall each detail. They all looked tough and, at the same time, professional. Had they been cops? Or had it been her imagination—a combo of runaway nerves, isolation and her hangover?

She stood. Her legs were wobbly. Her hands shook. Coffee sloshed out of the lid and onto her hoodie. "Damn," Chastity cursed.

"There you are." Thad's voice boomed from the top of the stairwell. He stood on the landing, looking down. Bare-chested, with abs and pecs that were well defined and covered in a fine sprinkling of hair. His sweats hung low at his hips, accentuating that sexy V-thing at his waist. God, he looked good—better than someone like Chastity deserved. One day soon she'd lose the extra weight that Thad kept mentioning. "Where the hell did you go?"

"The coffee shop." At least she got her coffee. Climbing the stairs, she continued. "I picked up a latte."

The door to the apartment stood open. "My head's killing me. Coffee sounds good." As Chastity brushed past him, he snagged the cup from her hand. "Thanks."

She opened her mouth to protest. Whatever she was about to say was forgotten as Thad placed his lips on hers. He tasted of stale wine and vape juice. "You do take care of me." Brushing his thumb over her breast, he added, "I like that."

Like a thousand butterflies had been let loose in her stomach, a fluttering filled her middle.

"Maybe we should go back to bed." With a smile, he

lifted the cup to his lips. Immediately, he gagged. Choking with each step, he moved to the adjacent kitchen.

Chastity followed. "Oh my god, Thad. What's the matter?"

He spit into the sink. "What the hell, Chas? That tastes like garbage. I hate soy milk." Flipping the lid off the cup, he dumped the drink down the drain. "You know that. I'm going back to bed."

Her throat was tight. Still, he would make love to her, and everything would be better, right?

"Okay, we can go to bed."

"We? I don't think so. I said that I'm going back." Without a backward glance, he wandered into the bedroom, leaving Chastity standing in the living room—alone and lonely. It was the same as it had been when she was a kid and her parents fought. Both of them so wrapped up in the argument they forgot she even existed.

Her eyes burned, and she moved to the kitchen. Opening a cabinet, she pulled out the instant coffee and a mug. After wiping at her eyes with her sleeve, she set the kettle on the stove to boil. As she measured a scoop of coffee powder into her cup, Chastity swore that her future would be different from her past.

All she needed was a new direction—and the courage to take the first step.

As a freshman in college, Grace had taken a psychology class. She remembered very little from that course, except that singing increased endorphins, a chemical in the brain that makes people happy.

At the time, it had been nothing more than a fact to be memorized and then repeated for a test. Yet, as Grace sat in the passenger seat of Madison's red sedan with a song blasting through the speakers, she knew that singing really had lifted her mood. For two hours, the entire trip to Kendall, the cousins had listened to Grace's playlist. They sang every word, even if they were never quite on key.

Don Henley's "The Boys of Summer" filled the car. Leaning together, they belted out the lyrics.

Even as she sang, her thoughts returned to last night. Had she really had sex with Camden on the patio, hidden only by the shadows? That was a stupid question to ask, even if in her own mind.

Obviously, they'd done the deed.

What now?

Or maybe she should be asking another question. What would happen if the truth came out? Grace shuddered at the possible headlines.

She couldn't change what happened. What's more, a small part of her didn't want to. Having sex with Camden had been the most natural thing in the world.

Maybe her mood was lighter because of him than the singing.

Did she have the right to be happy? Was it okay, just for now? But what about her future? Would she ever be the one to look for a wedding dress? "Thanks for inviting me to come with you."

"I wouldn't want to pick out my wedding dress with anyone else." They rolled past a sign that read *Welcome to Kendall*. "How're you doing, by the way?"

"Glad to be out of Grave Gulch."

Looking out the window, Grace studied the shopping district of Kendall as they drove past. The street was lined on both sides with boutiques and cafés. A used bookstore sat next to a jewelry store. Across from the bookshop was a store that specialized in crystals and herbs. A sandwich board sat on the sidewalk: *Madame Q's Tarot Card Readings. Today 12–5 p.m.*

"How's the investigation?" Madison asked.

Grace stared out the window. "There's not much to tell. There's still no evidence that proves my side of the story." She lifted one shoulder and let it drop. "I want my job back. I don't know if I'll get what I want, though."

After pulling into a parking spot across the street from the bridal salon, Madison turned to Grace. "You can't be out of options."

"There were two witnesses—a guy and girl. They saw everything. In fact, they approached the man who'd been shot. But now?" Grace shook her head. "They've disappeared."

"Disappeared? How can two people disappear?" Madison echoed. "Are they magicians?" she said jokingly.

Grace gave a quiet chuckle. "Maybe they are. But I've been asking myself the same question. How can two people just fade into the mist?"

"Have you come up with an answer?" Madison turned off the ignition. The car went still and silent.

"Maybe they were from out of town. Maybe they've left Grave Gulch and don't even know that we're looking for them."

"Or?"

"They know what they saw." Grace pushed the sunglasses to the top of her head and looked at her cousin. "In fact, I keep thinking that they might've even taken the gun. Because of that, they don't want to be found."

"What else can you do?"

It was a good question and one that Grace had asked

herself more than once. "I'm going to start by forgetting about the witnesses. Today is about you. Let's go look at that dress. You ready?"

Pressing her lips together, Madison stared out the windshield.

Yet again, Grace was filled with disquiet. Why the hesitancy? Did Madison love her fiancé? Did she even want to get married?

Honestly, Grace liked Alec. Still, she couldn't help but wonder if Madison simply had a plan for her life. College. Job. Marriage. Kids. And since marriage was next on her list, Alec was her best option for a husband.

She should say something. But what if Grace ruined her cousin's happiness?

Finally, the corners of Madison's mouth turned upward. A small smile played on her lips. "Actually, I am ready."

Grace opened the door and stepped from the car. It was late morning. The sun was shining, and the air was warm. In short, it was a perfect day. "All right, then. Let's go."

Madison exited her car. After using the fob to lock the doors, she held out her hand to Grace. "Let's go," she echoed.

As they crossed the street, Grace's mood was lighter than it had been in days.

Grace scanned the dresses displayed in the window. The gowns ranged from snowy white to cream to ivory to champagne and blush. Despite the various colors, the dresses had one thing in common. They all represented a dream come true. Someone had found their forever partner, and they were willing to devote their life to that person.

Madison had.

Melissa, Annalise and Desirée, too. Even Palmer had found someone he wanted to marry.

What about Grace? Would she ever find *the one*?

Her mind filled with images of Camden Kingsley. His hand on her elbow as they ran through the rain. His chest pressed into hers as they huddled in the doorway. And finally, her thoughts returned to the kiss. His touch. The moment he slid inside her. She sucked in a breath at the memory.

"You okay?" Madison asked. "You look a little…" Her words trailed off and she gazed just over Grace's shoulder.

Was now the time for Grace to confess all? "Something happened last night," she began. But Madison wasn't listening. Instead, she dug through her bag and pulled out her phone. Without a word, she snapped a picture of the street. Her hands shook.

It was Grace's turn to ask, "You okay?"

"Did you see him?" Madison asked, her voice shaking. Her skin was pale and sweat dotted her upper lip.

Grace turned. A guy, walking down the street, turned the corner. "Who's he?"

"I dunno, but he looked exactly like my brother Bryce, except with blond hair. Maybe dyed." She drew in a deep breath. "He looked exactly like my dad would look." Sighing, she shook her head. "I don't know where he went."

Whoever, or whatever, Madison saw was obviously gone. "C'mon." Hand on elbow, she steered Madison toward the boutique's door. "Let's go inside."

Madison dug her heels into the sidewalk, refusing to

budge. "I got a picture." She held up the phone. "It's a little blurry, but do you see what I mean?"

Grace leaned in close. "Wow," she whispered. For a moment, she was weightless with disbelief. "He definitely looks like Bryce. I'll give you that. What d'you think?"

Madison's dad had died in combat when all of the kids were young. Aunt Verity had never got over losing the love of her life.

Madison shook her head. "Honestly, I don't know." She paused.

"You want a cup of coffee?" Grace asked, pointing to a café half a block away. They still had time before the appointment at the bridal salon.

"Do I ever."

In silence, they walked to the restaurant. Several tables were scattered on the sidewalk. "You sit," said Madison. "I'll get the coffee and be right back."

"I can come in with you. Help with the cups."

"I'm not fragile," said Madison. "Seeing that guy, well, it freaked me out a bit. But I'm perfectly fine now."

"You sure?"

"Positive." Madison pushed the door open with her shoulder and disappeared inside.

Madison returned moments later, two white mugs in hand. "Here you go," she said, setting one of the cups in front of Grace. "Sugar, no milk."

"Aww. You remembered." She took a sip.

"That's because I love you. You're more than a cousin. You're my friend."

Grace shared those feelings. That fact cemented what she needed to do—and say. "Are you sure you want to get married? I'm worried that your moment of hesitation was more about Alec than your father."

"I saw something," she insisted. "Some*one*."

Grace recalled the picture Madison captured on her phone. "The guy who you saw definitely resembles your brother." Another thought occurred to Grace. "What're you going to say to Aunt Verity?" she asked.

Madison shook her head. "I don't know. Nothing. I mean, it's not my dad, right? It's just some man. There's no reason to make my mom sad about some random guy."

Grace took a sip of coffee for courage. She was a cop and went into lots of difficult situations every day. But this was different. If she said the wrong thing, her words could wound Madison. "Besides, you didn't answer my question. Do you really want to marry Alec?"

While stirring her coffee, Madison sighed. "I'm not sure what I want." She added quickly, "He's a great guy."

Grace nodded. "He is."

"Our life would be perfect. Both of us are teachers. We share a passion for instructing our students."

"That's true," Grace agreed. "But do you share a passion for each other?"

"The sex is good, if that's what you're asking."

"I've found that even bad sex can still be pretty good." After pausing a beat, she added, "I'm joking."

"Mostly," said Madison, smiling. With a sigh, she went on. "I care for Alec. I respect him. Maybe I'm not head over heels in love, but maybe I don't need to be. I just want a nice life with a nice man."

"If what you want is a nice life with a nice man, then I won't ever talk you out of your happiness. It's just that I've been wondering." She sipped her coffee again, not sure if she really wanted to continue the conversation. Actually, she didn't.

Madison coaxed her. "You've been wondering what?"

Grace had decided not to say anything, yet she couldn't help herself. "What's going on?"

"I always thought that once I found the dress, everything would feel different. I'd be ready to plan the wedding."

"And you aren't?"

Madison said nothing. The silence was an answer in itself.

Grace tried again. "Why aren't you sure about the wedding?"

"I don't know," said Madison, dropping her gaze to the table.

"Is it Alec?"

With a shake of her head, Madison said, "No. He's great."

"There's a difference between great and wanting to spend the rest of your life with someone." Again, Camden's face came to mind.

"I want to marry Alec. It's just… I know either one of my uncles will fill in, but my dad won't be there to walk me down the aisle."

"Oh, honey." She reached for Madison's hand. Grace was lucky to have both of her parents, and she could only imagine the hole that must take up a big part of Madison's heart. "Wherever your dad is, he's looking down on you right now and smiling."

"You think?" A single tear snaked down Madison's cheek.

"I know." She riffled through her bag for a pack of tissues. Holding them out to Madison, she said, "I just wonder if all the reluctance about picking a dress has more to do with wanting more than safety than it does with finding the perfect dress."

Madison shrugged. "I'll think about what you said."

"I just want you to be happy, so that's all."

Madison smiled. "I want the same for me—and you, too."

The conversation hit a snag. For a long moment, the two women just sat, sipping their coffees. She wanted to tell Madison about what happened with Camden last night. Did she dare?

"So, what's the verdict on the dress?" Grace finally asked.

"Since I don't have a verdict on the wedding yet, I guess I shouldn't be worried about the dress."

Grace drank the last swallow of her coffee. There had been a definite tone to her cousin's voice. What had it been? Disappointment? Resignation? Then she knew: it had been relief.

"You ready?" Madison asked, getting to her feet.

"If you are." Grace stood, as well. They walked past the bridal boutique. The large window was filled with dresses. Pausing, Grace looked inside and saw her reflection superimposed on a wedding gown. As she stood there, she had but two thoughts. What would it feel like to be getting married? And what was Camden Kingsley doing at that exact moment?

Sitting on his sofa after meeting Baldwin Bowe and losing the female witness, Camden knew his job to be objective about all investigations. However, this time was different. This time, he'd become personally involved with the subject, Grace Colton.

Actually, he was more than personally involved. He'd taken her as his lover. He needed to get off the case now before things got more complicated.

Picking up the phone from the coffee table, he placed the call without another thought.

Arielle answered on the third ring. "Camden?" The DA's voice was overly loud. In the background he could hear a cheering crowd. "Are you there?"

"I'm here," he yelled back.

"Give me a second."

"Sorry to interrupt," Camden began. It was noon on a Saturday. He should've guessed that she'd be busy. Maybe he shouldn't have called at all. "I have news."

"Good or bad?"

"A little of both. We made contact with Baldwin Bowe." Camden spent a few minutes telling the story of the meeting at the coffee shop. He included the details of Baldwin's job as a ghost bounty hunter and his acrimonious relationship with his brother. Camden continued, "He took the number for Randall and left his own burner behind."

"That's better than good news. That's actually great news," said Arielle. Her voice was so bright that Camden's phone practically glowed. "Anything else?"

"I saw someone who resembled the female witness from the shooting."

"Really? What did she say?"

"I never got a chance to speak to her. She seemed to…" Camden paused and rubbed the back of his neck. "She seemed to disappear."

"That is bad news," said Arielle.

"There's more." Camden inhaled. "I'm taking a leave of absence."

"You're doing what? The phone must have lousy reception at the park. It sounded like you said you're taking leave."

"I am, Arielle. I need…" What should he say next? *I need a break. Time off. Time to evaluate my career.* No, he owed her honesty at the very least. "Grace Colton's case has become more than a job for me."

The other line was filled with silence. Had the call dropped?

"You there?" he asked.

"I'm still here," she said, her words clipped. "Now I know what you've been trying to tell me and why." She didn't wait for him to reply. "You have feelings for Grace Colton, don't you?"

There was no denying the truth. Yet how had she guessed? "It's not something I planned."

"I'll give you today to think things through. Because if you take a leave now, I'll do everything in my power to make sure there's no job for you later." With that, Arielle ended the call.

The DA's words were like a knife to his chest, with the last little bit of a twist—just to be certain that it hurt like hell. She'd get him fired from a job? *Him?* Seriously?

Did it matter if he had to turn his back on the truth? Did he really want to keep his job if it meant staying away from Grace?

Maybe he should be asking another question. What did Grace want from him?

Well, as far as he was concerned, there was only one way to find out.

Chapter 13

The drive back to Grave Gulch from Kendall was bleak and overcast. A bank of dark clouds hung low in the sky, and rain fell. The wipers moved back and forth. Grace stared at the trail on the windshield. The continual *swish*, *swish*, *swish* lulled her into a trance.

She kept asking herself a single question. What was she supposed to do about Camden Kingsley?

What would Melissa do?

Well, that question was easy to answer. Melissa would never allow herself to get into a such a mess.

Grace had to put Camden out of her mind, her life and her heart. It's just that sometimes doing the right thing was so damned hard.

"I have to say," Madison said, glancing at Grace, "you look miserable."

"Then, I look better than I feel." Grace gave a feeble laugh.

"You want to start your playlist?"

She looked out the side window. The dark and dreary weather matched her mood perfectly. "Not really."

"What's going on? Are you worried about the Internal Affairs investigation?"

"Among other things?"

"What *other things*?"

Grace silently cursed. She hadn't meant to drag Madison into what had happened with Camden last night. If she didn't want to talk to her cousin, she never should've given such an evasive answer. "I screwed up."

"What happened?"

"You know the IA investigator? Camden?"

"The sexy guy you brought to Palmer's party last night?"

"He's the one," she confirmed.

"And?"

"And last night we kissed." There, she'd said it. In truth, it had been so much more than just a kiss.

"Really?" Madison gaped at Grace.

"Hey, eyes back on the road," Grace said, using her best cop voice.

"Yes, Officer Colton. But what happened? I mean, aside from you kissing that dreamy guy." Madison took the exit that led to downtown Grave Gulch. Pulling up to a stoplight, she turned. "You have to tell me. What happened?"

"Well," Grace began, "we went out to the patio and... I don't know. His lips were on mine. Mine were on his. Hands were touching lots of interesting places." There was no way that she was going to admit to having had sex with Camden. Okay, she'd thought about sharing with Madison a little bit earlier, but there was no way she was going to drag her cousin into her mess. "But that's not the point of the story."

"It seems like a pretty solid story to me. Do you like him?"

"What's there to not like?" Her insides felt as if they'd been filled with mud. It was disappointment. "He's handsome."

"I noticed," said Madison, with a smile. "Trust me."

"He's smart. He's dedicated. Honest. He has integrity. My middle fills with butterflies every time he's around. And if he smiles?" She shook her head. "Forget about it. I can't even." Grace sighed and leaned her head on the window. They were in Grace's neighborhood. Soon, she'd be home. Then, she'd hide in her apartment, shutting away her worries along with the rest of the world. "Basically, he's perfect."

"Okay, so why are you miserable?"

"He's with IA." She paused before adding the most damning part of all. "And he's investigating me."

"Oh," Madison slumped in her seat, a birthday balloon losing air. "I didn't think about it that way. I can see how the kissing and the touching could be a problem, then."

"Beyond being unprofessional, what if he thinks that I'm trying to influence the investigation? What if he thinks that I let this happen to distract him? What if he thinks Robert Grimaldi didn't have a gun and my whole story is BS?" Once she started to worry, it was impossible to turn it off. "What if he hates me?"

"I might not be the best person to give you advice on your love life. Still, I don't blame you for being upset. There could definitely be consequences."

It was a nice way of saying that if the situation ever

became public, the GGPD would have to fire Grace—and Camden would lose his job, too. "I know."

"But you like him?" Madison asked, her voice soothing.

"I do like him a lot."

"That's a problem, then." Madison exhaled, as the car stopped once again at a traffic signal. "What are you going to do?"

"There's only one way out of this mess. I can't see Camden anymore." Grace shook her head.

"That's probably wise," said Madison. She turned onto Grace's street.

"What do I say to him?"

"I'm not sure what you should say." Madison pulled into a parking place in front of Grace's building. "Whatever it is, you have to figure it out now."

Before she got the chance to ask what Madison meant, Grace's eyes were drawn to the steps leading to her building. Leaning on the rail, there stood Camden Kingsley.

Camden watched as a car pulled up next to the curb. It was Grace. If someone had asked him how he knew, he wasn't sure that he could put it into words. It was just something he sensed—not with his mind but his heart and his soul.

The passenger door opened, and she stepped from the car. His pulse raced.

"Hey. I didn't expect to see you here."

"I hope you don't mind," he began. Camden felt a pull—like iron to a magnet—drawing him to her. "I think we should talk."

"About the case?"

"About us," he said.

"First, I need to say goodbye." She glanced over her shoulder. With a wave, the woman behind the wheel drove off. "That was my cousin," Grace added. "I guess she had to go."

"I guess so." Was it his imagination or was Grace distant?

He asked, "Is there someplace we can talk?"

"What about here?"

No. It wasn't his imagination. There was something different about Grace. Well, he didn't need to waste time skirting the facts. "I quit my job."

"Your job? You quit?" she echoed. Grace would never give up being a police officer for anything—even an affair. "How can you walk away from your job? I thought you were devoted to your career."

"I am."

"Then, why?"

"You."

"Me?" She held up her palms. He'd quit? That was something Grace would never do. "You have to think this through."

"I have," he began.

"I know what happened last night was completely unprofessional. It was a mistake. If we just avoid each other, then nobody has to quit anything."

Camden's cheeks stung, as if he'd been slapped. To be honest, he didn't know what kind of reaction he had expected. Still, this wasn't it. *A mistake? He was a mistake?*

Or maybe *mistake* was the perfect word. He'd been mistaken about Grace and their connection. True, he didn't get serious about most of the women he dated.

But he'd always been a good judge of character. How had he been so wrong this time?

Then the idea hit him, and he went cold. "Was last night an act? Was everything between us a ruse?"

"No, Camden. That's not it."

She reached for him. Her fingertips brushed the back of his hand. He shook off the touch.

"What is it, then?" he asked, filled with fury.

"I wish the circumstances were different. I wish I could be with you—that we could be together. I can't. We can't. It'd ruin both of our careers."

"Correction. It'll only ruin *your* job." Even he heard the venom in his tone. He didn't care. "I already quit."

"I didn't ask you to leave the DA's office. If you'd come to me first, maybe we could've figured this out."

Then he knew why it hurt so bad. Camden was willing to sacrifice everything for Grace. And she wasn't able to do the same for him. His anger vanished, leaving the landscape of his soul as nothing but a charred wasteland. He swallowed. What else was there to say?

His phone began to trill. The ringing was loud on the quiet street. Camden checked the caller ID. Bryce Colton. What'd Bryce have to say? Had Baldwin Bowe called back? If he wasn't working with the DA, then Randall Bowe wasn't his concern anymore, either.

"Go ahead," said Grace with a flick of her wrist. "I can tell that you want to answer it."

He swiped the call open. "What d'you have for me, man?"

"I was able to run Robert Grimaldi's name through the firearm registry for several states. Not all of them have a database, but he didn't turn up in the ones that do."

"So, he's never registered a gun?" Camden asked,

his heart slammed into his chest. Was this another dead end to his attempts to prove that Grace's story was true?

"Like I said, several states don't monitor gun ownership. He could've crossed into Pennsylvania and bought a gun. It'd be a legal purchase, and he'd never show up because they don't keep records." Bryce paused. "Or the gun might be stolen. Bought illegally. There's lots of other ways that Grimaldi might've gotten his hands on a firearm. But if you're hoping to pressure him because he made a false statement to you, owning a gun won't work."

"Thanks for checking. I owe you a favor."

"I'll call it in someday. Gotta go."

The call ended. The line was dead. Still, Camden held the phone to his ear. The echo of his pulse resonated in the base of his skull. Only a moment ago, he'd been wounded. What else was he supposed to call it? He wanted Grace, but she clearly didn't want him in return.

Now, though, Camden had a different set of questions. Had he been duped? Was everything he'd been told—or heard from the police—meant to protect Grace Colton?

He placed his phone in his pocket.

"I'll ask you this for the last time." He drew in a deep breath and looked at Grace. "Are you positive that Robert Grimaldi had a gun?"

"Positive."

"Is there any way, at all, that you might've been mistaken?"

"None."

"Are you sure?"

Instead of answering the question, she turned to him. "Who was on the phone?"

Had Camden been a fool from the beginning? Certainly, he'd been a fool last night when he'd had sex with her on the patio. Finally, he saw how recklessly he'd acted. But had he been so enamored with Grace that he never thought the unthinkable? *Could* she have shot an unarmed civilian? "Why won't you answer the question?"

"Why won't you tell me who was on the phone? The call obviously changed your mood."

Fair enough. He shrugged. "It was your cousin, Bryce. He ran Robert Grimaldi's name through every firearm registry in the country."

"And?"

"And Grimaldi's name didn't come up."

"Oh."

Oh? Was that all she had to say? "You don't seem surprised."

"There are lots of states without databases. You said so yourself."

So he had. Still, Camden wasn't in the mood to be patronized. As if quitting his job over Grace Colton wasn't bad enough, Camden had compromised his character for nothing. Hell, he'd thrown away his dad's legacy. The fact that he'd been blind left him ill and filled with self-loathing. "Is there any way you could be mistaken about what you saw?"

Grace lifted her chin. "I know that Grimaldi had a gun. What's more, I don't think I like what you're implying."

"And what's that?"

She drew in a deep breath. "I've been lying to you all along."

Implying, hell. Camden was starting to think that might be the truth. He said nothing.

"In fact," she continued, "why don't you just go?"

* * *

Had Grace just told to Camden to leave? She had. Well, he didn't need to be told twice.

Stewing in the juices of his own anger, he'd gone directly from Grace's apartment to the DA's office. Having found some empty boxes in recycling, he stood in his office. One box was only halfway filled—yet it contained all of his personal belongings. There were two commendations. A picture of Camden with his state-police-academy class at graduation. A photograph of his father in uniform. He had a picture with his mom—also from the day he graduated from the state-police academy. A couple of coffee cups. A house plant, which needed water.

In a second box, he had all of the equipment belonging to the IA. His ID. His gun. His laptop. All the gear used for surveillance: a camera, a microphone, a wireless transmitter and receiver.

How many hours had he spent in this very room? Yet it took him only minutes to clear away any evidence that he'd ever been here at all. Wasn't that how he lived, too?

Never making connections.

Never having relationships.

Never really caring about anyone—and only searching for the truth.

That was, until he met Grace.

Regret sat heavy on his shoulders. Maybe it was better to be alone. He'd forgotten how much caring about another person could hurt.

"I didn't expect to see you here." Arielle stood at his door.

"I figured I'd take some time to get packed up. Save myself from coming in on Monday morning."

Arielle leaned on the doorjamb. "We have to talk, but I definitely don't want you to quit."

"I thought that you swore to get me fired."

She sighed. "I take that back."

Camden's pencil holder was an old tea tin that his grandmother had given him when he was in high school. Dumping the pens and pencils into a desk drawer, he placed the tin in the box. "I was wrong about everything with Grace Colton."

"Are you saying that Grimaldi didn't have a gun?"

"Not exactly."

"Are you saying that Grace lied to you? Or that she gave a false statement?"

"I'm not saying that, either."

"What are you saying, then?"

Now, that was a good question. "There's no way to prove Grace's version of events. Furthermore, I've been focused on proving that she was innocent, not on finding the facts."

"I won't argue with you there."

"I've lost your confidence. I should go."

"Obviously I can't force you to stay with Internal Affairs. Just know that everyone screws up," she said, "especially where the heart is concerned."

"Not me," said Camden. He picked up the box of his belongings.

"Why, because you don't have a heart? I know you're with Internal Affairs, but I always thought the heartless thing was a joke."

"I have a heart," said Camden, ignoring the fact that Arielle's joke was a little funny. In fact, he knew that he had a heart, because right now his was breaking.

"I understand that love and attraction and passion make us all do crazy things."

"You do?"

"You don't have to sound surprised. I might be fifty-two years old, but I'm not dead. Besides, I have kids. You know where they come from."

Camden held the box in one hand and lifted the other palm in surrender. "I don't need the biology lesson, but thanks. I do have to ask, what're you getting at?"

"You tried to tell me about Grace from the beginning. I respect that, and I'm sorry that I didn't listen. Stay or go—the choice is yours."

Grace stayed on the sidewalk long after Camden had driven away. Her low back was tight from time in shoes that were much more cute than comfortable. Pulling her phone from her bag, she placed a call.

Madison answered. "How'd it go?"

"Horrible," she said, her throat raw. Since she'd joined the force, being a good police officer had been her only priority. Even after having sex with Camden, she'd never intended for her focus to change.

Maybe that had been her first mistake.

"How are you?" Madison asked.

"Horrible," Grace said again. "Overwhelmed."

"Are you still at home?"

Technically, she was standing in front of her building. "I am."

"Hold on one second. I'll be right over."

Grace's legs felt like they'd been dipped in concrete. Slowly, she walked up the short flight of steps to the front door. Just as she slid the key into the lock, Madison parked at the curb.

"That was fast," said Grace, as her cousin stepped from her car.

"I didn't go far."

"I'm glad." She opened the door.

"Let's get to your apartment, and you can tell me everything."

Within minutes, they were sitting on Grace's sofa. Madison made both of them cups of tea. Grace held the steaming mug in her hands.

Tucking her feet beneath her, Madison asked, "What went so horribly?"

"He quit his job for me."

"He what?" Madison asked, her jaw slack.

"Yeah, he wanted to help me prove my innocence, and he quit."

"I can see why you'd be horrified. A great guy wants to make sure that you're treated fairly." She shivered with the willies. "Awful stuff."

"Can you be serious? Please?"

"I'm sorry for teasing, but I don't understand why you're upset. You met a lovely guy. He cares about you. You care about him. On top of it all, he's willing to sacrifice everything for you."

Grace wasn't sure that she understood, either. It was sort of like all the advice and warnings she'd been given after the shooting. True, her family meant well, but did they really think she couldn't make the right choices? "Maybe I don't want to be taken care of. I might be the Colton baby, but I'm not actually a child."

"In a perfect world, what would you have wanted from Camden?"

It was a good question and one which Grace didn't

have a ready answer for. She sipped her tea. "I wish he had talked to me first. Told me what he planned to do."

"Then what would you have done?"

"I don't know. I mean, we only met a few days ago. It seems a little hasty to change our lives for one another." She knew what her cousin was trying to do: make Grace see that her situation wasn't as awful as she originally thought. She wasn't ready to calm down or to forgive Camden, though. "He accused me of lying about the gun. He asked me if I was mistaken."

"Are you? Lying or mistaken?"

"Of course not."

"But you're offended that he asked?"

"Damn straight."

"Can I tell you what I see?" Madison stretched out her final word, and Grace knew she wouldn't like the picture her cousin wanted to present. "You're in a tough situation. But it's not impossible. If you care for Camden, you might have to make some sacrifices, but you two can be together. Look at Troy and Evangeline. But they talked to each other and worked it out." Madison's words hung in the air. "If you want to be with Camden, you can. If you don't, you never have to see him again. The choice is up to you, Grace. The question is, what do you want?"

Camden stood in his office. On the desk sat the two boxes. He needed to take one with him. But which should he choose?

True, he'd overreacted to Grace's rejection.

He could've handled the whole situation a little bit— okay, make that a whole lot—better.

Even without the romance in question, he still had a choice to make.

If he'd been wrong about Grace, then his personal and professional judgment was fried. There was no need for him to stay at Internal Affairs. Camden would never again trust himself.

It was just that he was so damn sure that Grimaldi had a gun—forget that there wasn't a single fact to prove that theory.

Was it him? Was he wrong?

No gun had been found at the scene.

Nobody had called the police with the witnesses' identities.

In fact, nobody had seen them at all since the night of the shooting.

Correction: Camden had seen the female witness. He was certain that she'd run from him.

It brought up an interesting question. How had she known he was working with the cops? He wasn't exactly in the public eye.

Then again…

He took his phone from his pocket and opened the app for the TV station out of Kendall.

A story about the press conference at GGPD appeared first. It was accompanied by dozens of comments and a video. He pressed the play arrow. The camera focused on Melissa as the briefing began. Then with Melissa's voice still in the background, the aspect moved and panned the crowd.

"Well, I have a second announcement to make. I can see that the citizens of Grave Gulch have lost confidence in the GGPD and in our ability to keep peace in the city. But it's my responsibility to maintain a trust between the town and the police department. I haven't. Therefore, I'll be stepping down as chief of police."

Behind the podium, a group of police officers were gathered inside. Most of the people were little more than shadowy figures, yet a single face was recognizable.

It was Camden's.

Picking up a box from his desk, he walked out the door.

Chapter 14

Grace's career was in tatters. Her love life was a wreck. Sitting on the sofa, she didn't know which was worse—or how she could make either one right. The indecision ate at her.

Her phone rang. It was Camden. She sucked in a breath. What was she supposed to say? Did she want to apologize? Ignore the call? Tell him to leave her alone?

"I didn't know if you'd call me again," she said, answering the phone.

"I think there's a lot for us to talk about, but there's something I need to show you. Can you let me in?"

"In?"

"Look outside."

Grace moved to her window. Pulling aside the curtain, she looked onto the street. Camden stood on the sidewalk, cardboard box in hand. He saw her and waved.

That same old fluttering erupted in her belly, traveling down her arms and legs until her toes tingled.

"Give me a second," she said into the phone.

On the street, he gave her a *thumbs-up*.

Within seconds, she was standing at the front door. Camden was at her side.

"I'm not sure where to begin," she said.

He held up the box. "There's something I want to show you, first."

"Come up to my place," she said.

They said nothing as they walked up to her apartment. Inside, Camden put the box on her kitchen table. It settled with a thunk.

"What's in there?"

He opened the lid and lifted out a picture of a man who looked an awful lot like Camden. "This is my dad," he said, handing her the photo.

"He looks nice. Detroit beat cop, right?"

"My dad was charged with unauthorized use of force, too. IA was called." He paused. "The investigation didn't go well for him. It was easier to blame my dad than have the public indict the entire department."

Grace stepped closer to him. She wanted to touch him again. Did she dare? "I'm sorry."

"It's why…" he began.

"It's why you do what you do. Why you're always fair. And why you're always looking for the truth."

"There's more, though."

"Oh?"

"It's what happened with him afterward." Camden paused. "He, well, he took his own life because of it. I was fifteen years old."

"Oh, Camden, I am so, so sorry." Her chest ached as

it opened to a bottomless well of grief. She needed to console him. But how? She touched his arm. "Sincerely."

"I never talk about, but it's always with me."

"What happened to your mom?"

"She still lives in Detroit. I don't see her a lot, even though I should."

"Family is a good thing to have."

"After being around the Coltons for the past two days, I'm starting to think that they are. A good family, I mean."

Grace traced the side of his face with her finger. He leaned in to her touch. "You're a good man, Camden Kingsley."

"Am I?" He reached for her hand. She wound her fingers through his, and he pulled her close. He caressed the inside of her wrist with his thumb.

"You are."

He shook his head. "If I was a good guy, I never would have made love to you last night. I never would've taken advantage."

"You act like I didn't have a say-so in what happened. You aren't to blame. For anything."

"There's more, though." He unloaded the box. There was a wireless microphone. A camera with a long-range lens. A remote receiver for the mic.

"What's all of this for?" she asked.

"This is what we're going to use to prove that Robert Grimaldi had a gun."

Camden's plan was simple, direct and all the more difficult in its simplicity.

He started by telling Grace, "I saw the female witness this morning."

"You what?" Grace's tone was incredulous. "How'd you see her? What happened?"

"I was with your cousin Bryce this morning."

"What were you doing with him?"

Grace had about a million questions. He told the story about meeting Bryce at the FBI office. The call from her brother, Troy. Camden going with Bryce to meet with Randall's brother because of his involvement in the case. The woman who came out of the coffee shop and then vanished. He ended with, "I didn't get a great look at the woman, but I swear it was her."

"What d'you think? Where'd she go?"

"At first, I assumed it was all just a string of coincidences. Maybe the lady I saw looked like the witness, but was it her?" He shrugged. "Then, as far as the disappearance, Bryce and I figured it was a car parked nearby. I mean, even if it was the witness, she'd have no reason to run from me. Then I saw this." He played the press-conference video on his phone.

Grace chewed on her bottom lip. "I saw it yesterday. There's footage of you in the film."

"Exactly." He stopped the video at the moment his face was visible.

"So what're you thinking?"

"I think that this woman lives near Grave Gulch Coffee and Treats. I think she knows that the police want to talk to her, and that's why she ran."

"It also means she has something to hide."

"She has something to hide," he repeated. "But we know more about her."

"Which is?"

This was the part that he loved—when all the pieces fell into place, and the puzzle became a picture. "She keeps track of what's posted about the story. Although, no surprise there. Most criminals do. But I think she's a fan of this reporter—Harper Sullivan."

"I don't disagree with anything you're saying, but how does that help us at all?"

Camden's eyes were bright with hope and anticipation. "If we could get a specific kind of story on the news—one that reaches out to the witness—I think she might react. But this was the place where my plan falls apart. To make that happen, we have to get the reporter to work with us."

Grace lifted a brow. Her cousin Stanton had connections to the media, through his love, reporter Dominique. "I think I know someone who might help…"

It took only a few texts to get a number for Harper Sullivan. After a short call, she agreed to meet at Grace's apartment. On the phone Grace had given few details, but as she settled on a chair, Camden knew that to get the reporter's cooperation, they had to be more than honest: they had to be compelling.

Grace sat on one end of the sofa; Camden was on the other side. Harper sat in a chair and faced them both. Camden glanced at his watch—two thirty—as Grace started the conversation.

"We have reason to believe that the witnesses to Thursday night's shooting live near Grave Gulch Coffee and Treats. We also think she follows your reporting online. I'd like to use the TV station's platform to reach out."

Harper stared at Grace. Several seconds passed. "You what?"

"My gut tells me that this witness might feel guilty for hiding. I think reaching out personally could help her find the courage to contact the authorities."

"I'd like to help you, Grace. Trust me, nobody wants to find the truth more than I do. But I'll be honest. This isn't how our station typically works."

"Think of it this way. The TV station will get an exclusive interview with Grace," said Camden. Harper lifted a brow. From the look, he could tell she wasn't convinced. After pausing, he added, "We can give you a heads-up if the interview leads to an arrest."

Harper's eyes widened as she drew in a short breath. Both gestures were subtle, gone as quickly as they came. Yet he was trained to look for the almost imperceptible and, moreover, discern what it meant. Right now, Sullivan was hooked. But was she interested enough for Camden to reel her in?

"Arrest for what?"

"Tampering with evidence," said Grace.

"The missing gun?" Harper asked.

Camden had been right. The reporter was smart.

With a quick nod, Grace echoed, "The missing gun."

Harper wrote in her notebook. "What else can you tell me? Something I haven't already heard."

"They're in Grave Gulch." Camden leaned forward. "Hiding from the police. They might have a firearm, along with a willingness to break the law. We need to reach them—the woman, in particular. You say you want to keep the community safe, but are you really ready to help?"

Tapping her pen on the paper, Harper sighed. "I'll do . Tell me what you need."

4:11 p.m.

Chastity had done little all day...beyond refreshing the TV station's app, that is. Nothing had been posted to the site or app since the release of this morning's stories.

Maybe she'd gotten it all wrong. Maybe the guy she saw was, well, just a guy and not the same one from the press-conference video. Maybe him being at the coffee shop had nothing to do with Chastity, and the problem really was in her imagination.

Rolling her shoulders, she smirked.

Yeah, it was all just imagination.

What would it hurt to refresh the app one last time?

A new article appeared at the top of the list. The head-line read: *Witness Sought in Police Shooting. Cop Asks for Community Help.*

There, next to an embedded video, was the sketch of Chastity. She studied the image. The nose on the draw-ing was too big. Still, it was a decent likeness. If she and Thad had bothered to make any friends in Grave Gulch, certainly someone would've recognized her already.

An entire month in one place and not a single friend— except Thad.

She glanced at the open bedroom door. The curtains were still drawn, leaving the room gloomy. Yet his form, draped over the bed, was unmistakable—as were the snores and the stench of stale booze and BO.

Chastity glanced back to the phone in her hand. A triangle-shaped Play button was superimposed on the video. Drawing in a deep breath, she pressed it.

The fuzzy image cleared, and the face of a blonde woman filled the screen. Chastity swallowed. It was the cop she'd seen on the street. Funny, at the time sh hadn't realized that the officer was young—for a cop, anyway. In fact, she wasn't much older than Chastity.

A caption read: *Officer Grace Colton, accused of shooting an unarmed civilian, has been put on administrative leave pending the results of an investigation.*

"Officer Colton" came an off-camera voice. Was that a reporter? Chastity assumed so. "What do you want our viewers to know about the witnesses you saw at the scene of the shooting?"

Grace looked directly into the camera. Chastity shivered, though she certainly wasn't cold. Was it excitement? Trepidation?

The video continued to play. "First, I know that they're still in the area. The female witness was seen this morning. She knows that the police want to speak to her, but she's hiding."

"What if she doesn't want to be found? What will you do then?" the reporter's voice asked.

"I'd like to make a direct plea." Sitting taller, Grace continued. "We both know what you saw, and I can only guess why you haven't come forward. Maybe you don't like the police much. Or maybe you're worried about getting into trouble because you ran. If you're hiding, then you know what really happened. If you care about the community—you need to tell the truth. I want you to know you can come to me." Grace paused. The seconds passed like an eternity, and a breath was trapped in Chastity's chest. "I can help. If you let me, I can be your friend."

Friend. The word echoed through the silent room, ~~l~~ouder than cannon fire.

~~C~~ould Chastity and Grace really be friends? Grace ~~had~~ been right. Chastity did need help. Could she trust the cop, though? Hadn't she tried that before? That time, her trust had been completely misplaced.

Yet her gaze was drawn to Thad's computer system. Multiple monitors, keyboards and a server all sat on a folding table.

She'd met Thad in the first week of college, both of them majoring in IT. The professor paired them to work together on a project. Chastity still recalled the feeling of her stomach being tied in knots as the teams were announced.

Thad was in his last year of school and the best-looking guy in a room filled with men. He had an easy smile that Chastity, barely out of high school, had felt in her toes. The first time he smiled *at her*—well, she felt it in an entirely different part of her body.

Did it matter that once they'd become a couple, she dropped out of school and worked at a fast-food restaurant to help pay for Thad's degree? Honestly, it made sense that one of them work while the other went to school. Right? Besides, Thad was closer to graduating than she had been.

She might not have a degree yet. Still, she knew her way around the internet better than most. Taking a deep breath, Chastity rose from the sofa and walked quietly across the room. She closed the bedroom door. After taking a seat at the workstation, she booted up Thad's computer. It wouldn't take her long to find a number for Grace Colton—no matter how well she protected her account.

Once she got the number, then what? Well, Chast would have to make some tough choices.

4:26 p.m.

The interview had gone live only moments earlier. Sitting on her sofa, Grace couldn't slow the racing drumbeat of her pulse. Nor could she stop from asking a single question. What if the plan didn't work?

Leaning back into the cushion, she sighed.

Camden sat beside her. She glanced his way. His dark hair was tousled. Stubble covered his cheeks and chin. He was exquisite, and her stomach tightened.

Her phone pinged with an incoming text. Grace glanced at the screen. The message came from a blocked number. Her pulse picked up speed.

I saw your interview on the TV station's site.

She held up the phone for Camden to see.

"That was fast," he said. "You think it's the witness?"

That's exactly what she thought—or hoped, at least. She tapped out her reply.

You did? Who's this?

Three dots danced in the reply field as the other person responded. The seconds stretched out.

"Come on," Camden urged. "Come on."

Ping.

Grace read the message out loud. "*A friend.*" She paused. "A friend?"

"It's the witness." Camden gave her wrist a squeeze. "They're repeating the last lines in your interview, you remember?"

"*I can help,*" she repeated her earlier words. "*If you let me, I can be your friend.*"

"She wants your help," said Camden. "My guess, she feels trapped and needs a way out."

Grace exhaled. Did she dare to hope this nightmare was finally ending? "What do I do? What do I say?"

"You want to try and meet with her," said Camden. "That's the end game." He paused. "Ask her if she saw something."

"*I need all the friends I can get.*" Grace spoke while typing the message. "*Did you see something?*" She sent the text.

The dots flashed in the text field again.

"She's thinking about what to say," said Camden.

Grace tried to swallow. Her mouth was too dry.

The phone pinged with another message.

I know what happened...

Grace texted back.

How?

The reply:

I heard something at a party.

Camden said, "It's the witness, for sure."

"How do you know?"

"The text is a lie. The witnesses haven't been out. They haven't spoken to anyone. Nobody around here has heard anything."

Grace:

Do you know who saw the shooting?

Unknown number:

I've heard some names mentioned.

Grace replied.

Who???

Grace watched the text field. She waited a minute. Then a minute more. Five minutes passed It was then she asked another question aloud. "What if this is a random prankster?"

Camden shifted where he sat. His shoulder grazed hers. Grace wanted to lean in to him and ask him to hold her once more. She sat up taller.

"That's a fair question. You need to get her to interact with you more."

"So, what do I do? You're the expert in getting people to tell the truth."

"Be honest with her. Tell her you're worried that she's a scam. Then suggest a meeting."

"What good will a meeting do? What if I talk to her and she still doesn't want to come forward?" She lifted her phone, letting the dropped thread prove her point. "I don't see this person being overly eager to chat with the police."

"That's why you're lucky I'm here. I brought all my surveillance equipment. Camera. Microphone and receiver. You wear the wire. I'll park at the end of the block. If you get this person to talk to you, I can record every word spoken."

"Is this legal? Will this be admissible at a trial?" She knew the answer to the first question. Michigan was a "one-party" state. Simply put, one party in a conversation could legally record what was being said without notifying the other. Truly, she didn't know if the recording would stand up in a trial, or not.

Camden said, "Right now, let's see what we get. If we can prove your story, then this case may never go to court."

On a certain level, the whole setup felt sneaky to Grace. True, she wasn't pretending to be someone—or something—she wasn't. If the witness was willing to meet. If the witness had anything important to share. *If. If. If.*

Grace typed a message before holding up the phone for Camden to read.

"Looks good," he said.

She pressed the Send button. "It's done," she said. "Now all we can do is hope that she replies…"

Chastity's chest was tight; her breastbone hurt. Contacting Grace Colton had been a mistake. The police weren't to be trusted. They'd failed her before. All those years ago, they'd failed her mother, as well.

Yet, she reread the text.

If you saw something, we need to talk. There's a coffee shop near the park. Grave Gulch Coffee and Treats. Meet me there in 20 mins?

It was almost five o'clock in the evening. Thad was still in bed. She knew the weekend routine. Drink too much and stay up late on Friday. Sleep all day Saturday. Up again at 9:00 p.m., ready for another round of bingeing on booze.

Okay, she was only nineteen years old. But was this the life she wanted?

Now was the time that Chastity needed to decide about her loyalty. Was it to Thad? Or the truth?

She felt the gun's presence, tucked into the drawer and hidden under a stack of papers. In her mind's eye she saw it, dangerous and deadly. Having it in her house wasn't actually making the world a better place. In fact, it was the opposite.

It was true that nobody actually liked the cops. Unless they needed help.

On top of that, Grace Colton had already seen Chastity—and Thad, too. If Chastity showed up at the meeting, the police officer would know that Chastity hadn't heard rumors or stories at a party. She'd been the one who'd caused all the trouble by grabbing the weapon and refusing to come forward. Was she really willing to take that kind of heat? What if leaving the scene was a crime? Certainly, taking the gun would be illegal.

After tapping in her message, she hit Send. Leaning back into the sofa, she sighed and looked at the screen one last time.

I'll be there, the message read.

She'd told Grace Colton that she'd meet with her. But there was something else she had to decide. Was Chastity really willing to tell the cop everything she knew?

Chapter 15

Grace sat near the window of Grave Gulch Coffee and Treats. For what actually might be the hundredth time, she checked her phone.

The time was five thirty.

She hadn't missed a single message.

The witness was almost twenty minutes late.

Moreover, she hadn't bothered to text with an excuse. Nor had she suggested a new meeting time.

A lot of police work was waiting around for something to happen. Grace knew better. It was time to face facts. The woman wasn't going to show.

A lump stuck in her throat. She set the phone down and reached for a cup of coffee, now lukewarm, and gagged down a sip.

Her phone vibrated. She scooped it up and opened the call. Heart racing, Grace was breathless. "Hello?"

"Hey." It was Camden. At this very moment, he sat in his car that was parked at the end of the street. He also had his camera, equipped with a lens powerful enough to get clear photos of anyone entering the coffee shop, even from a block away. Beyond the camera, Grace wore a small microphone, the size of a pen cap. It was taped between her breasts and hidden by her bra. The microphone recorded every noise within twenty feet and transmitted it to a broadcaster in Camden's car.

"You see anything?" she asked.

"Nothing on the street."

The invisible kernel in Grace's throat hardened as it filled with disappointment. Without the witness, she had no other way to clear her name or save her career.

"Anything in the coffee shop?"

"Nope," she said, her voice cracking.

"Tell me what you see."

Grace scanned the shop. Ten small tables filled the room; less than half were occupied. Nearest to Grace was a mother staring at her cell phone, while her two children fought with swizzle sticks. At the table next to the door sat a guy with a beard and a laptop who muttered at the screen as he typed. An elderly couple was huddled in the corner, bent over two cups of coffee and a single blueberry scone. Their happiness was almost palpable, and Grace wondered if she'd ever find the kind of love that could last a lifetime.

"There's nothing to see."

"Hold on," he interrupted. "I have another call."

"Go ahead," she said, dark humor starting to take over. "I've got nowhere else to be and nothing else to do."

Camden was gone for less than a minute before he was back on the line. "That was your cousin Bryce."

Bryce? When had the two men become so chummy? "What's he want?"

"Someone called. They think they saw Len Davison at a local campground. Right now, Bryce needs backup."

"From you?"

"From me, but I don't need to leave if you need me."

"There's no way I'm going to stop you from searching for Davison." She dropped her voice to keep the conversation from being overheard by her fellow patrons. "Go," she said. "I'll be fine."

"Really, I can't leave you alone. You aren't even an active cop."

His words stung, like a slap to the face. "Excuse me?" Even Grace heard the steely tone of her voice.

"I didn't mean it that way…"

She didn't have the energy to argue with him. "I'm hanging up now. You go." She ended the call. A moment later a sleek silver car passed the window, and she knew that Camden had driven away. Her eyes were dry and gritty. She screwed them shut.

Inhale. Exhale. Just breathe.

Well, there was nothing more for Grace to do—other than finish her coffee and maybe order one of the blueberry scones.

Opening her eyes, she lifted the cup to her lips and took a small sip. The door opened. A person stepped into the coffee shop wearing a hoodie and a large pair of sunglasses. Even with the features hidden, Grace recognized her at once.

It was the female witness.

Camden dropped his foot onto the accelerator, and his car shot down the road. The rendezvous point, located at a secluded state park outside of town, was still several miles away. At this speed, he'd be there soon.

As he drove, he cataloged his lengthy list of problems. First was the most obvious. Without being able to prove her innocence, Grace would be considered guilty. Even if Camden could show that Robert Grimaldi owned a gun, even if Arielle Parks didn't file criminal charges, Grace would lose her job.

Certainly, there was more that could be done. But what? Right now, he was fresh out of ideas.

Another looming problem was much more immediate. Technically, he'd taken leave from his work. It enabled him to help Grace without the implication of favoritism—and yeah, he did favor Grace Colton a lot.

Nevertheless, facts were facts. Only a few hours before, he'd stepped away from his job. It meant that he shouldn't even be racing down the tree-lined road to help Bryce Colton. In reality, his presence could muck up any subsequent prosecutions.

Camden gripped the steering wheel as his imagination took over for a single moment. Sitting on the witness stand, Camden would be faced with a sly defense attorney.

Mr. Kingsley, can you explain why you assisted Special Agent Colton in the apprehension of Len Davison? Make sure you include the details about why you were there, especially since you weren't technically working for Internal Affairs.

Camden turned off the main road. With less than a mile to the rendezvous, he didn't have a plausible reason for helping the Fed.

It meant only one thing.

Camden had to tell Bryce everything.

The shores of Lake Michigan were filled with recreational areas. There were several near Grave Gulch. A sign pointed to the park's entrance. A narrow drive was lined on both sides with a thick forest. In the distance, sun glinted off the gunmetal-gray water of the lake.

During the summer, this was a popular destination. At any time from Memorial Day to Labor Day, the park would be busy with picnickers, swimmers and boaters. But the season had ended weeks before. Now, a single car was parked near the entrance. Bryce Colton sat on the trunk. He stood as Camden pulled to a stop.

"Thanks for coming on such short notice," said Bryce as Camden opened the door. "Looks like I'm calling in that favor you owe pretty quickly."

"Before we get started, I need to come clean."

"Come clean?" Bryce echoed. "About what?"

"Technically, I'm on leave."

Bryce gaped. "This is news to me, man. Why?"

Camden knew he was wasting time by not being forthright. "It's Grace."

"My cousin?" Bryce drew his brows together. "What happened to her?"

"I've become…" Camden searched for the right word. "Attached."

"Like, how attached?"

"Attached enough." He exhaled. "Listen, I'm willing to step away from my job for her. I have to help Grace prove that she's innocent." Camden searched for the right words. He continued, "You gotta know that I could mess up your investigation. Or bring any arrests into question at trial."

"As far as I'm concerned, following this lead is more important. If it makes you feel better, I'll deputize you a a task force officer. Because what I need now is someone I can count on. And you just told me everything I need to know."

"Which is what?"

"If you're the kind of guy who's willing to give up everything for the truth, then you're the kind of guy who I can count on."

It might not have been the perfect answer. Still, it was enough for Camden. "You have a lead?"

"Sure do. This afternoon, there was a woman walking her dog. She saw someone and swears it was Len Davison."

A road, barely big enough for two cars to pass side by side, led to the water's edge. Was this how the Len Davison investigation ended? Him spotted by a woman who was walking her dog?

"Swears?" Camden echoed Bryce's earlier choice of word. "That's sounds pretty certain."

Bryce grunted. "It is, and yet..."

Camden picked up the thread of conversation that Bryce had let unravel. "What else did the woman say?"

"She went on a bit about keeping close tabs on the press coverage about Davison. She also mentioned her name several times, in case I need to pass it on to any reporters."

"Sounds a little dubious," said Camden.

"I was thinking the same thing. She said that the guy was camping. But all the campgrounds are closed for the season."

"Living rough follows Davison's MO."

Bryce nodded. "Right again. Besides, we have to follow up on every lead. Just because someone wants a little publicity doesn't mean they're lying."

"What's the plan?" Camden asked. "Where's everyone else? Air support? State police? Canine units?"

A search for the serial killer should involve more than two people.

"For the moment, it's just us. We'll search the area where the man was seen. If there's reason to suspect it was Len, we call in the rest of the troops."

So the mission was just reconnaissance.

"Give me a second." He reached into the car's glove box.

On a day-to-day basis, Camden had little use for his weapon. He kept the Glock 9 mm in his glove box, which was kept locked. The pistol was stored in a holster, and Camden removed them both. Sliding back the sight, he chambered a round. After he secured the gun back in the holster, he threaded both onto his belt. Taking a moment to adjust the entire rig on his hip, he untucked his shirt and let the tail hide the firearm.

"You ready?" asked Bryce, sliding a gun into the shoulder holster he wore. He donned a jacket, and the sidearm was no longer visible.

Bryce's question hung in the air. Was Camden ready?

He nodded once. "Let's roll."

They didn't stay on the road, which ran directly to the lake's shore. Instead, the duo took a path that led through the woods. The sun now hung on the western horizon. Still, there would be hours of twilight before it became fully dark. The half-light leached the forest of its colors, turning everything murky and muted.

Then Camden caught a glimpse of bright red through the trees. Was it a person? Pulse spiking, he dropped his hand to his Glock.

A moment later Bryce tapped him on the shoulder, a

silent command to stop. "I think this is it. We've found what the woman saw."

Camden nodded.

Less than fifty yards away, a campsite was hidden at the base of a large tree. The tent was little more than two plastic tarps held up by a frame. A firepit, just a divot in the earth, was surrounded with stones. A banked fire smoldered. Several cans of food were stacked next to a pot that was propped up on a nearby rock. A cord, stretched between two branches, held several articles of tattered and frayed clothing.

A red jacket hung limply and swayed slightly with the breeze. It was that coat which Camden had seen first. Keeping his hand close to his gun, he whispered back. "We've definitely found a campsite. The question is, who's been staying here?"

As if on cue, a person emerged from the tent. Narrowing his eyes, Camden peered through the woods. It was a man—that much was obvious from the build and the thick brown mustache and beard. His dark hair was lanky, dirty and tangled.

He'd seen pictures of the serial killer and imagined that he'd recognize him on sight. But with the distance, the trees and the waning light, Camden couldn't be certain.

He wore a sweatshirt with frayed cuffs and a pair of ripped and stained jeans. Camden didn't see a weapon—a gun or even a knife. From this distance, what he saw meant next to nothing.

The man went down on one knee next to the pile of cans. After lifting one from the stack, he scanned the label.

Without question, the guy had been living out of

doors for a while. Moreover, he had the hungry look that came with desperation.

But there was one question that was yet to be answered.

Was this man Len Davison, the serial killer wanted by the GGPD?

Bryce took a step. Underfoot, a twig snapped. In the quiet woods, the sound ricocheted off the trees.

"Damn it," Bryce mouthed.

Camden's gut clenched as the guy slowly glanced over his shoulder. At fifty yards, Camden could clearly see the man, even through the trees.

It meant that the guy could see them, but only if he knew where to look. For the span of a heartbeat, he scanned the woods. His eyes were narrowed, and his brows drawn together. If Camden had to guess, he'd say that the guy hadn't seen them—yet.

Then his gaze stopped. He looked directly at Camden. The two men made eye contact. There was no use in trying to hide now. Resting one hand near the gun at his hip, Camden raised his other. "Hey," he said. "I'm with Internal Affairs. This is Special Agent Colton with the FBI. Do you have a minute to chat with us?"

The man slowly rose to his feet. For an instant, Camden was certain that he would cooperate. Without a word, the man turned and sprinted farther into the woods.

The woman took off her sunglasses and slid into the seat across from Grace. She was young—under twenty years old, by Grace's estimation. She stared at her hands, and Grace shifted in her place.

The small microphone that was taped to her chest shuddered with each beat of her heart. Even though she'd seen Camden drive away, she glanced at the window, hoping beyond hope that he'd come back. His car wasn't on the street. Of course: he was gone. All the same, without him to capture the images, there would be no evidence that the woman had been here at all.

Would the meeting even matter?

"You alone?" the woman asked, her eyes trained on the table.

Nodding, Grace said, "I am."

"Anybody on the street?" The woman looked toward the large window.

"Nobody."

The witness sat in silence. Grace knew it was up to her to start a dialogue. She was new on the police force, but she'd been taught that the best way to connect with a suspect was to build a rapport.

"I'm glad you're here," she said. "I'd started to think that you wouldn't come at all."

"To be honest, I'm still not sure that I should've."

"But you did come," said Grace quickly, before the woman could talk herself out of confessing what she knew. Or, worse, leave. "It means you're ready to do the right thing."

She gave a snort-laugh. "If you say so."

"You are here," Grace said again, putting more force in her words. "And you were there on Thursday night, too. I saw you."

"If you say so." She paused before adding, "*Cop.*"

There was enough venom in the single word that it sounded like a curse.

Grace's temperature rose, along with her temper. After everything she'd been through, this woman—and her attitude—was the last thing she wanted to deal with.

Sitting back in her seat, Grace folded her arms across her chest. "Okay, then, why did you show up? It's certainly not to help. Or to do the right thing." She flicked her wrist toward the door. "Go back to hiding. Go back to not showing your face in public."

The woman looked up. Her eyes were wide. "That's not…" Her voice trailed off, thick with emotion.

Grace tried to muster some sympathy. Despite all the trouble this person and her friend had caused by running off—and possibly taking the gun—she could imagine how meeting with Grace would be personally difficult. She decided to try another tactic. "The guy you were with…"

"What about him?"

"He doesn't know that you're here, does he?"

"Thad?" She shook her head and gave a chuckle. "He's clueless that I've even left the apartment."

It just seemed like chitchat. In reality, the woman had shared a good bit of important information. Grace cataloged what she now knew: the witness lived in a nearby apartment with a guy named Thad, who also happened to be the other witness.

"Clueless?" Grace echoed, matching the woman's laugh with one of her own. "How?"

"He's still asleep."

"Really?" Grace glanced outside. The sun had set, turning the sky orange and pink. "He's been asleep all day? Does he work nights?"

"Hungover is more like it. But yeah, he's been out most of the day."

"That must be hard on you."

The woman shrugged. "Sometimes."

"I'm Grace, by the way."

"Yeah, I know. I saw your video."

Grace nodded and then waited a beat. "You are?"

"Chastity."

Yes! I have names for both witnesses. "Chastity what?"

"Just Chastity."

"Okay." She paused a beat. "You want a coffee or something?"

Chastity shook her head. "I'm okay for now."

Just like in the textbook, Grace had followed all the rules for building a bond with a subject. Yet, she had one more question. Now what?

She was still mad at Camden for his "not an active cop" comment. All the same, he was a hell of an investigator and had given her decent advice. What had he said? Oh, yeah. *Be honest.*

And honestly, Grace was anxious to find out what Chastity knew—and what else she might say. "Do you mind telling me what you saw on Thursday night?"

Scratching the side of her face, Chastity sighed. "It was really dark."

Was this another dead end? "You seemed upset that night. You had to have seen something."

"I know that you fired a gun. I could see the flash of flames coming out of the end part."

"The muzzle?"

"I guess that's what you call it."

"Thad approached the man who was shot. Do you know what was said?"

Dropping her gaze to the table, Chastity traced a whorl in the wood with her fingernail. "I'm starting to think that coming was a bad idea. Maybe I should go."

Damn. Grace had been too direct. She'd pushed Chastity too hard. Now she'd scared off the one person who could help clear her name. It also confirmed Grace's suspicion: Chastity definitely had something to hide.

"Don't go," she said quickly. "I mean, you just got here. You want a coffee?"

"You've already asked me about that, and I've already told you I'm not interested." Pushing back from the table, she stood. "Besides, you lied in your video. You don't want to help me. You just need me. That's it." With a roll of her eyes, she added, "I hope that they hang you for what you've done, cop."

Grace had been taught how to deal with members of the public who were difficult or hostile. But she'd never been told how to deal with someone who was as mercurial as Chastity. It left her with one thing to do—rely on her instincts. The question was, would it be enough?

Camden had said that Chastity was looking for a friend. Could Grace be that friend and find out the truth at the same time?

"You're right," Grace said with an exhale. "I want to clear my name. But you're wrong when you say that I don't want to help. I do. Right now, you're caught in a trap that you set. You can't go anywhere in Grave Gulch without being turned in to the police. But if you talk to me, I can help clear your name, as well."

"Or I can stay in my apartment. Face it, all of this will eventually blow over..." Her words trailed off as her decisive tone weakened.

"Is that what Thad told you?"

Chastity dropped back into her seat. "Maybe that's what I told him."

Thad was the one who made all the decisions. Why

break the law, though? Did Chastity's love for Thad leave her blind? Or was there something else?

Grace asked, "You don't like the police much, do you?"

"Let's just say that the police haven't always been on the job when it comes to protecting and serving."

Grace would bet good money there was a lot more to Chastity's story. "So what happened?"

"Nothing," said Chastity. It was clearly a lie.

"Most everyone in my family works for the Grave Gulch Police Department—except for a few people. Like my cousin Bryce."

"What's he do?"

"He's a special agent with the FBI." The mention of her cousin brought back Camden's abrupt exit. She couldn't help but wonder if they'd actually found the serial killer—and if everyone was safe.

"Sounds like he's a cop, too."

"I guess," said Grace. "Just with a fancier badge."

Her small joke earned a smirk from Chastity. "Must be nice to have such a close family."

"Most of the time, it is. We all gravitated to law enforcement for a specific reason." Grace continued, launching into the story she hadn't planned to share. "My dad was married years ago to another woman. Amanda's the mom of Troy and Desiree, my half siblings. Anyway, when Troy and Desiree were little, Amanda was murdered. To this day, the killer's never been found."

"Why go into law enforcement? The police failed you like they fail everyone else. It's not a reason to be a cop."

"That's just the thing. The pain my family felt is something we want to keep others from feeling, too. We want to do our job."

Leaning back in her chair, Chastity folded her arms tight across her chest. Grace didn't need any police training to understand the body language.

Chastity was trying to protect herself. But why?

Was the younger woman trying to keep Grace out?

Or was she trying to put up an emotional wall before Grace had a chance to get in?

"Hey," Grace said, her voice low and soft. "We all have past hurts. I think you have one that involves the police. I'm sorry for whatever happened."

A fat tear snaked down the side of Chastity's cheek. She wiped it away with her sleeve. "It wasn't me. It was my mom. My dad." Exhaling, she shook her head. "He liked to drink and fight. Sometimes, well, he hit my mom."

"That must've been a hard way to grow up."

"The thing is, at first you don't know better. Then you realize that your family isn't like everyone else's. When that day comes, well, it sucks. From then on, all you want is to look normal. But one day..." She wiped away another tear and turned to look out the window.

It was then that Grace realized she'd been holding her breath. "But one day..." she coaxed.

"One day I couldn't stand it anymore. I called 9-1-1. A police officer showed up. My dad spoke to him outside. I watched from my bedroom window. I couldn't hear what they were saying, but it didn't matter. I could tell. They started off all serious, heads bowed together. Then my dad must've said something funny because the cop laughed. A minute or two later, they were slapping each other on the back. It was just like they'd been friends since forever. The cop left, and my dad came back into the house."

Grace was afraid of the answer, yet she had to ask. "What happened then?"

"My dad *told* me." She hooked air quotes around the word. Grace assumed that the telling was closer to yelling. "He explained to the cop that I was just a bratty teenager, bent on getting my dad in trouble. He lied. But what's worse, the cop never checked it out. He never talked to my mom, who had a black eye. He never asked to see me. The cop just talked to my dad, who gave him some BS answer, and left."

Chastity's voice had risen. The elderly couple glanced over. Chastity slouched in her seat.

"I can't speak for that police officer, but you have every right to be mad at him." Grace knew what she had to do now—much as she hated the sacrifice. Shoving back from the table, she stood. "We both know that Robert Grimaldi had a gun. I saw it, and you did, too. I'm not going to ask you to come forward. I'll handle whatever happens to me. Well, thanks for showing up."

"Wait." Chastity was on her feet. "What will happen?"

Grace was already across the room. Without a word, she opened the door and stepped into the cool evening air.

Chastity followed. They both stood on the empty sidewalk. "What will happen?" she asked again.

"To be honest, I don't know."

"I mean, there's some other way to prove that guy had a gun, right?"

Grace shook her head. "That's the thing. There isn't."

"What'll happen to you? Let me guess. You'll get a few weeks off with pay. It'll be like a vacation."

"I know for a fact that I'll lose my job. With an unauthorized use of force on my résumé, I'll never work in law enforcement again. Hell, it'll be hard to get hired anywhere. Who wants to hire an unstable cop? Then, there's the worst-case scenario."

"What's worse than losing your job? Or not getting another one?"

"I'll end up in jail."

"They can't do that." Chastity's voice had risen again. "You didn't do anything wrong."

"Without video or a witness or even the gun, I have no proof. It's my word against Grimaldi's." After the last few days, Grace was exhausted. She only wanted to go home and sleep. When she woke, what then? Well, then she'd have to figure out the rest of her life.

"You're wrong," said Chastity. "You do have a witness. You have me."

"Are you willing to speak to the authorities now?"

Chastity gave a quick nod. "I figure there have to be at least some good cops out there. It seems like you're one of them. You should keep your job. Right?"

Grace's shoulders relaxed, letting go of tension she didn't realize that she'd been holding. "Right," she echoed.

"And that's not all. I know something about the gun."

"What about the gun?" Grace asked, her voice a whisper.

"I know where it is."

"You do? Where?"

Chastity looked up and down the street. "I have it. It's in my apartment. We've wiped off all the prints, so you won't be able to tie me or Thad to the gun."

Did Chastity really have the gun? There was no reason for her lie. She knew it really didn't matter. It'd be foolish for Grace to go into an apartment where a desperate and dangerous man had a weapon—especially since she didn't have a sidearm of her own—or backup. Just thinking the single word hit her like a slap to the face. Her cheeks burned and her eyes stung.

Camden had said many things and all of them had turned out to be true.

Right now, she wasn't officially on duty. That meant she couldn't call in the help she needed.

Which meant her next move should be what? They definitely never covered this scenario at the police academy. In an instant, she knew that sending Camden away had been wrong, because without him she was truly on her own.

Chapter 16

Camden sprinted through the woods. He jumped over a felled tree at the same moment a branch lashed his arm. Ignoring the sting of broken flesh, he focused on his quarry. The man from the campsite ran ahead. The sun had slipped below the horizon, and the fugitive was little more than a shadow. What was worse, if he wasn't captured quickly, then night would fall. In the darkness, he'd be impossible to find.

Next to Camden, matching him stride for stride, was Bryce. Then the special agent pulled ahead, although the extra speed wasn't enough.

Catching the suspect was going to take not just stamina but a strategy, as well.

The man turned, veering to the right. It was then that Camden understood his plan. The suspect need not outrun the police. He only needed to get to the lake first and a rowboat that sat on the sand. There, he could get away in the water.

Peeling away from the direct pursuit, Camden cut a path toward the shore. If his guess was right, he'd be able to intercept the man as he ran for the water. If he was wrong? Well, then he'd just left Bryce on his own.

Skidding to a stop at the tree line, Camden wiped sweat from his brow. There was a rustling in the trees an instant before the man burst onto the shoreline. He was less than a dozen yards from where Camden waited.

Launching forward, Camden sprinted across the sandy beach. Just as the man waded into the water, Camden dove. He grabbed the man by the middle, pushing them both down with a splash.

Bryce was right behind. Grabbing the man by the back of his shirt, the special agent hauled the suspect to his feet.

"Let me go," the man growled. He threw a punch. The man's fist missed Camden's chin by inches.

"You know I'm not going to do that," said Bryce, his breath labored. "We can do this the easy way, where you calm down. Or my friend and I can wrestle you into cuffs. Your choice, but you aren't going anywhere."

"This is total crap. Police harassment." Yet, the man placed his hands behind his back, intertwining his fingers. To Camden, it looked like the guy might have been arrested more than once. Bryce produced a set of cuffs from his jacket pocket and slipped them onto the man's wrists.

The pause gave Camden time to think. Would Len Davison instinctively know how to respond to an arrest? That brought up another question worth asking. Would the serial killer give up without much of a fight?

"What d'you want?" the man asked, his voice hoarse.

"We need to talk." Bryce led the man to the shore.

"Is it about the campsite? I know it's past the season, that's why I came here. My old lady kicked me out last week. I got out of jail in July and haven't been able to get back on my feet. I just need a few days more to straighten some things out. To begin with, her loser brother owes me money."

In his time with IA, Camden had investigated more than one high-functioning sociopath: charming, calculating, with an inclination toward violence if things didn't go their way. In his estimation, this guy didn't come across as suffering from an antisocial personality disorder.

Most sociopaths had a high IQ. The guy they'd just apprehended seemed a little dimmer than most—likely not a sociopath, then.

"What's your name?" Camden asked, while patting down the guy for anything that might be used as a weapon. In his back pocket was a wallet.

"Hank Ford." Camden opened the wallet.

There was still enough light to read the license. Hank Ford was a resident of Grave Gulch. Beyond that, the picture on the license matched that of the man in their custody—who only had a passing resemblance in age, race and build to Len Davison.

Still, Camden quizzed Hank on his date of birth, address and social security number.

He knew all the right information.

What Camden didn't know was what to do with the guy now.

He moved several feet away from Hank Ford. Lowering his voice, he asked Bryce, "What d'you think? Is this Davison?"

"My gut tells me it's not."

"Mine, too. But after everything he's done, it's not a big deal to steal a wallet and pose as someone else."

"We need to compare fingerprints or DNA."

Camden agreed. "Both will be on file if Mr. Ford was incarcerated." He paused. "I hate to turn him back to the system."

"Maybe there's a little more that we can do," said Bryce. Stepping closer to Hank, the special agent said, "You can't be camping out here."

"Where am I supposed to go?" Hank asked. "What can I do?"

Bryce said, "There's a shelter in town run by a church. They can give you a bed, a shower and a hot meal. More than that, they've helped plenty of people find a job and a permanent residence. How's that sound to you?"

Hank nodded eagerly. "Sounds good. I haven't really had any decent food in a week."

Since Camden was technically on leave, a patrol officer was called to process Mr. Ford. Assuming that his story checked out, Ford, along with his scant belongings, would be taken to the shelter. It took only minutes for the man to be secured in the back seat of the police cruiser for the ride back to Grave Gulch.

As the taillights faded to nothing, Camden admitted that he'd done some good with his day. Then, just as quickly, his thoughts went to Grace. Where was she now, and what was she doing?

Chastity's apartment building was around the corner from Grave Gulch Coffee and Treats. Grace stood on the sidewalk and waited.

While working the key into the door, Chastity spoke. "I have one favor to ask. You can't implicate me or Thad in any of this. I mean, I'll talk to the police and tell them what I saw. But you can't tell them who gave you the gun."

Honestly, Grace wasn't sure that was a promise she could make. "I swear that I'll do what I can."

She unlatched the lock. "I guess that's enough."

The door opened to a dingy square of vinyl tile that hadn't seen a broom in months. A side wall was filled with a bank of mailboxes. It looked like there were four apartments on each floor, two in the front of the building and two in the back. A set of stairs led upward.

"We're on the third floor." Chastity began to climb the steps.

Without comment, Grace followed.

They stopped on the landing. Chastity moved to the unit at the front right corner. "Wait here," she said, producing a second key from the ring. After working it into the door's lock, she continued. "I'll get the gun and then be right back." Opening the door, she slid inside.

Grace leaned against the wall and closed her eyes. She wanted to pray that this was all about to end. She knew enough not to hope—not yet, at least.

The scent of old wine and stale body odor filled the apartment. Closing the door, Chastity pressed her back to the wall. The curtains were open, letting in the last light of day. She glanced into the bedroom. A pile of blankets was draped over the mattress edge, but she couldn't see Thad in the gloom.

Still, the metallic taste of panic coated her tongue. Her heartbeat raced. Thad would be pissed at Chastity for turning over the gun. But when they were able to leave the apartment, he'd thank her. Right?

Walking quietly to the end of the sofa, she knelt in front of the small table and pulled on the handle. The drawer didn't move. She tugged again, harder this time. The wood creaked as the drawer opened an inch.

Damn.

Chastity froze and held her breath. The room was silent. Holding the corners, she walked the drawer forward. A stack of bills sat atop a loose-leaf textbook. She moved it all aside and sucked in a quick breath. The drawer was empty. Chastity rifled through the drawer once more, despite the fact that the gun was undoubtedly missing.

Straining, she listened for Thad's quiet snores as he slept. There was nothing.

Moving on tiptoe, she crossed the living room and peeked through the open door. The bed was empty. Thad wasn't here.

Leaning against the wall, Grace exhaled. A spark of excitement warmed her chest. Was the nightmare really about to end?

If it did, what did that mean for her and Camden?

A relationship between them would raise more than a few eyebrows. An IA investigator involved with a cop?

He was worth a couple of sideways glances.

The apartment door opened slowly, and Grace pushed off the wall. She stopped, her heart thundering. Chastity stood in the apartment. Her eyes were moist and rimmed in red. "He's gone," she said.

Grace could guess the answer. Still, she asked, "Who's gone?"

"Thad," said Chastity as the first fat tear rolled down her cheek. "And what's more, he's taken the gun with him."

Grace went cold. Thad had taken the single piece of evidence that could prove her innocence. Yet there was more. Thad was armed, on the loose, and there was no telling what he might do. Or who he might hurt.

Driving back to Grave Gulch, Camden broke more than one speed limit.

Did he and Grace have a future together?

There was only one way to find out. Using the controls on his steering wheel, he placed a call. The phone rang four times before being answered by voice mail.

"This is Grace." Her tone was so cheerful that he smiled. "You know what to do at the beep."

The phone started recording. "Hey, it's me. Camden. I'd really like to see you soon." He paused. What else was there to say? "Call me back." He ended the call.

Without a plan, he drove to her place. The apartment was dark—not even the flicker of light from the TV or computer screen.

Obviously, she wasn't home.

But where would she have gone?

With all her Colton kin, Grace could be almost anywhere.

Settling back into the seat, he shook his head. Right now, he had no choice but to wait for her to call him. Too bad that waiting was the last thing he wanted to do.

He pictured her, sitting at the table, glancing his way as he drove by. Her shoulders were rounded. Her slouched posture made it look as if she were exhausted.

But he knew better. She was more than tired, she was defeated. The witness was the key to proving her version of the shooting.

And they'd been a no-show.

Or had they?

Camden called Grace a second time. Once again, the phone went straight to voice mail. He hung up without leaving a message.

Could it be that Grace was still at the coffee shop? Had the witness shown up after all?

Camden drove to Grave Gulch Coffee and Treats. His car idled as he counted over a dozen patrons. None of them were Grace.

But he'd seen something out of the corner of his eye. A glint of light and color. What had it been?

He glanced to the console between the seats. There, wedged between two cup holders, sat the black plastic audio receiver. It was the same one that was attached to the microphone Grace wore. A set of red lights flashed. It meant one thing: voices were being picked up.

He reached for the volume control. His fingertips brushed the dial, and he stopped. Should he be listening to Grace?

If she were having a private conversation, she'd know enough to remove the wire. Right?

Without another thought, he turned up the volume.

"Who's gone?" she asked. Her voice was a breathless whisper.

"Thad," said a female. "And what's more, he's taken the gun with him."

And what's more, he's taken the gun with him.

The woman's words echoed in Camden's mind—leaving no room for thought.

Camden was a creature of the rational and logical. He pushed all emotion aside. If he was picking up the broadcast, it meant that Grace was close. He drove, turning right at the next corner. It was the same path he'd taken that morning when following the witness.

The street was narrow, quiet and dark. Late-model cars were parked at both curbs. Brick buildings rose up on either side, three and four stories tall. They were all filled with apartments.

Just as he had stood on the street this morning, looking for where the witness had gone, Camden now stared at each and every window. Grace was close. He knew that for a fact.

But where?

Grace assessed her situation. In a word, it was bad. She smothered a curse with her hand and wondered, what next?

"I think," said Chastity, wiping her face with her sleeve. "I can find him."

Grace lifted her brow. "How?"

A folding table with several monitors and a hard drive sat in the corner. Chastity moved to one of the keyboards and began to type. "I should be able to find his phone," she began. "Damn it."

"Damn it?" Grace echoed. "*Damn it* doesn't sound good. What's wrong?"

"Nothing's good. And a lot is wrong." A loud *ping* came from the bedroom. "Thad left his phone.

must've known what I was doing and wanted to get rid of the gun before I could give it to you."

Grace pushed open the bedroom door. The stink of body odor, stale wine and tropical-scented vape smoke filled the small room. The cell sat in the middle of the mattress. She picked it up and silenced the alarm.

Yet, she couldn't help but ask herself a single question. "How'd he know you were meeting with me?" Grace handed Chastity the phone. "Was it a guess?"

Chastity gave a slow shake of her head. "I don't know," she began. "Or maybe I do…"

She typed onto the keyboard. The screen filled with a text exchange. Grace read the first few messages.

It began with:

I saw your interview on the TV station's site.

Followed by:

You did? Who's this?

And then:

I know what happened…

"These are our texts," said Grace. "Was he able to hack into your phone?"

"He was able to access my account," said Chastity. "Not exactly a hack and not exactly hard, either. If you know what you're doing."

"That brings up an important question, Chastity. Do you know what you're doing on a computer?"

She sat up taller. "Of course. I'm better than Thad."

"Good." Grace's pulse began to race as she formed a plan. "Because if he can search through your account, can you search through his?"

Chapter 17

Chastity had a decision to make. Sure, she'd contacted the police about the gun. Was she willing to lead them to Thad? Especially since it was obvious that he was trying to destroy or hide evidence?

She already knew. She was going to do the right thing. It was people like her dad, or the cop from all those years ago or even Thad, who thought that rules weren't meant for them. Those were the people who had to be stopped.

Exhaling, she picked up his cell. "We have to assume that he left his phone so he couldn't be tracked," she said.

"That's smart of him," said Grace. "Where do you think he went? Do you have a car?"

Chastity shook her head. "No car."

"Could he have gotten a ride from someone? A friend?"

Chastity wasn't about to admit they had no friends. Still, she opened his text messages.

Nothing.

"Do we assume he's close?" Grace asked. "What would he do with the gun?"

It was a good question. Thad designed games. He always inserted a way to escape in every situation. Real life would be no different. Yet Grace's question still hung in the air.

"What would he do with the gun?" Chastity repeated. Then she recalled. He did have a plan. They were supposed to lay low for weeks, then… "He's going to throw the gun into Lake Michigan."

"How would he get there without a car? Ride share?" Grace answered her own query. "That wouldn't make sense. Whoever drove Thad would be one more witness."

"Let's see what he looked up on his phone." She scrolled through his internet history. "There's nothing."

"But if he left his phone so you couldn't track him, then I doubt he left any clues on it, either."

Grace was right and Chastity's jaw tightened with frustration. As she leaned back in the chair, her eye was drawn to Thad's computer system. She entered some keystrokes.

An internet history appeared. "It looks like he deleted some of his searches, but I can work around that." It took only a few seconds and Chastity had recovered everything.

Grace read from over her shoulder. "Grave Gulch Car Sharing. He rented a car?"

Chastity continued to type. A map, along with a flashing red dot, appeared on the screen. Chastity pointed to the dot. "There he is." Her mouth was dry. "That's the car Thad rented."

* * *

Grace bounded down the stairs from the apartment to the street level. Chastity had transferred all of the data from Thad's car share to her phone and was at her side.

They knew where Thad was at this moment, but where was he going? How would they catch him?

Grace opened the door to the sidewalk as a set of headlights cut through the gathering darkness and she glanced down the street. It was a sleek, silver sedan. Her heart skipped a beat.

"Camden?" She whispered his name.

Chastity followed her gaze. Eyes narrowed, she asked, "Who's that?"

The car pulled to the curb and the passenger-side window rolled down without a sound. Camden leaned across the seat. He lifted his chin. "Hey."

Grace exhaled. "Hey."

"Who's he?" Chastity asked, her voice brittle.

"He's the guy who'll help us get that gun."

"The gun?" Camden echoed. "You mean to tell me that you've found Robert Grimaldi's gun?"

Chastity bit the cuticle of her thumb. The nailbed filled with blood. "I know you. I saw you on the video. You were at the press conference yesterday."

He gave a quick nod. "That's me."

Grace would never know why Camden appearing in the online video made him someone that Chastity could trust. Or maybe the younger woman was just tired of hiding, and running, and lying. In the end, it really didn't matter.

"I know where he is," she said, holding up her phone. The GPS hadn't updated in several minutes, leaving the pinpoint for his car on the outskirts of Grave Gulch. "I'm not sure where he's going."

Camden put the gearshift into Park and the doors automatically unlocked. "I know where he's headed. Get in."

Grace slipped into the passenger seat as Chastity got into the back.

"You know where he's going?" Grace pulled the door shut and put on her seat belt. "How?"

"That road leads to a state park on the shores of Lake Michigan. I was just there."

Was that where Camden and her cousin had been searching for the serial killer? Grace glanced over her shoulder. Certainly, they shouldn't talk about an open investigation in front of Chastity.

Camden must have guessed at her hesitation to continue the conversation. He added, "It wasn't him."

"Lake Michigan?" Chastity echoed from the back seat. "It's what he planned to do with the gun from the beginning."

"So, this guy is who? Your boyfriend?" He glanced at Chastity through the rearview mirror.

For half a second, Grace wondered how Camden knew about the relationship between Chastity and Thad. Or for that matter, how he had found her in the first place. Then she saw the receiver that was tucked between the seats. For the first time in nearly an hour, she felt the tiny microphone taped to her chest.

Had Camden been listening to her? She had to assume so. In the end, there was only one thing that mattered. He was here. Could Grace finally let go of the dread and despair of the last two days? Was everything going to finally turn out okay?

"I think I should tell you," said Chastity, her voice barely rising above the revving engine and the road noise, "Thad won't let you arrest him. He's hell-bent on winning."

Grace turned in her seat, so she could see the other woman. "This isn't a game."

"It is to him," she said. "Winning or losing, that's all there is."

"If the police find him, he'll go to jail. There is no other choice," Camden said.

"There is one more choice." The car suddenly felt cold. Goose flesh covered Grace's arms and she quelled a shiver. Before she could ask what Thad planned, Chastity spoke. "He'll die before he loses. That, or he'll kill someone else."

Camden tightened his grip on the steering wheel and dropped his foot onto the accelerator. There was no way he was letting another criminal go free. "I'm calling backup." Using the controls on the steering wheel, he contacted Bryce Colton. Since he was heading back to the park they'd just left, Camden might get lucky. The Fed might still be nearby.

"This is Agent Colton."

"Bryce, I'm heading back to the park in pursuit of the male who witnessed the shooting. He has the gun and is driving a…"

From the back seat, Chastity said, "Blue, hybrid hatchback."

"Blue, hybrid hatchback," he repeated. "Any chance you're around?"

"Sorry, man. I'm no help at all. I'm headed in the opposite direction. Someone called in another sighting of Len Davison."

Is that all the Fed did with his day? "I'll call Troy."

"And Brett," Bryce suggested. He paused. "You do good work. Not many guys like us left who only focus on the job."

Camden placed the two calls, gave the information and got the response he hoped to hear from both. "On the way."

Yet, as he spoke and planned, his mind worked through a completely different set of problems. Camden wondered if what Bryce said was true. Was Camden only focused on the job?

That used to be the case.

Was it still true, or had Grace changed everything?

The park entrance was dark. In the distance, the water of Lake Michigan reflected the night sky.

"Where is he?" Grace whispered, even though the area seemed to be empty.

Chastity looked at the phone. The screen illuminated her from beneath. Grace recalled all those sleepovers as a kid when her siblings and cousins took turns telling scary stories and used a flashlight to cast ghoulish shadows on their faces. But this was no childhood party.

"The app still won't update," said Chastity. She sucked in a breath. "Unless…"

"Unless what?" Camden turned off the engine and the lights.

"Unless," Chastity said, "he disabled it from his end."

Camden cursed.

Grace's stomach dropped to her shoes. "Think about

it," she said. "He's still on the way here, even if he thought to disable the app."

In the dark, Camden's profile was a shadow. Grace's fingers itched with the need to touch him. But now wasn't the time. "You might be right, Grace," he said, his words seeming to come out from nowhere and everywhere all at once. "We should pull off the main road and wait to see if he shows up."

Without turning on the lights, he drove toward the lake. A narrow dirt path ran into the woods. Camden maneuvered the car into the space so that the nose faced out and the road was visible, yet their auto was hidden by the shadows.

"We should tell Brett and Troy where we are right now," she said. "They should be here soon."

Grace placed two brief calls. Both men less than five minutes away. Then there was nothing to do besides wait—and hope that Thad was really coming to the park. There was so much she wanted to say to Camden. To ask him. Did they have a future together? Is that what she wanted?

Yet, she sat without speaking. She couldn't have the conversation with Chastity in the back seat.

A blue car sped past.

"It's him," said Chastity.

"Coming up on foot is the best plan," said Camden. He retrieved a gun from the glove box of his car. He slipped the firearm into the waistband of his jeans at his back.

Grace unclipped her seat belt. "Let's go."

"Go?" Camden echoed. "You can't go anywhere."

"Don't bring up the bull about me not being a cop.

I might be on administrative leave, but I'm as dedicated to upholding justice as anyone on the force."

Camden let out a long exhale. "Is there anything I can say to convince you to stay?"

"You heard what Troy and Brett said. They're still five minutes out. This is going to be over before they get here." She saw the flash in his eyes and knew that she'd hit on a nerve. Since his father's death, he'd been trying to save the world all on his own. Reaching for his arm, she continued, "Camden, you cannot do this alone. We're better together."

"You win." He exhaled. "But you have to do as I say."

Grace smiled. "Yes, sir."

"Chastity," he continued, "you have to stay in the car."

"I won't go anywhere," the young woman said.

Grace and Camden exited the car. Keeping to the tree line, they walked quietly and quickly to the water's edge and the blue car.

"Where is he?" Camden asked at the same moment Grace noticed that the car was empty.

She swallowed down a wave of despair that rose from her middle. Were they too late? Had Thad already thrown the gun into the water? Would Grace ever truly clear her name?

Then she heard a metallic click. Soft, but unmistakable, it was the sound of a safety being released from a gun.

Camden heard the noise. The hair at the nape of his neck stood straight. Someone was standing behind them and that was bad enough. What was worse—the person had a gun, and they were ready to use it.

His own firearm was tucked into the small of his

back, hidden by his jacket. Could he draw, turn and fire before the assailant got off a shot? He thought not.

Holding up his hands in mock surrender, Camden asked, "What d'you want?"

"I'm not going to jail."

Camden glanced over his shoulder. A guy, brown hair covered by a beanie, held the gun in both hands. With his feet planted on the ground, he looked like he'd learned to shoot by playing laser tag.

"You Thad?" Camden asked, turning slowly. He had one objective—to disarm the suspect.

"How'd you know my name? You a cop?"

"I'm with Internal Affairs, so I'm worse. I'm a cop's cop."

"Listen," said Grace as she turned to face Thad, as well. "I think we can work our way out of this mess. All of us. You hand over the gun and let us go. We don't have to say anything about how it was found…"

"Chastity might be a moron." Thad aimed the gun at Grace. "But I'm not. I don't believe you for a minute. I'm not going to jail, now or ever. But you do bring up an interesting point. I don't know how this all ends, especially since all of you cops are corrupt." He cursed quietly and narrowed his eyes. "Besides, she's definitely guilty. Which is good for me, because I can't have any witnesses."

Camden's blood went cold. No witnesses?

Before Camden could speak, Thad rolled back his shoulders. "Say your prayers now, both of you. It's time for you to die."

In her short time on the force, Grace had faced more than one dangerous individual. Yet, Thad had two things that made him different. He had a gun and enough desperation to use it.

"Walk towards the water," he snarled.

Before that moment, Grace had wondered how the simple threat of violence had the ability to make people compliant—even to the point of putting themselves in greater danger. At that instant, she understood.

It was all about survival. If you cooperated, you might live.

Hands up and palms out, she walked toward the lake.

Thad had a gun. He was all emotion and no lucid thought.

Could she get him to think?

"You can't do it, you know."

A sheen of sweat covered Thad's brow. "What d'you mean?"

Grace needed something—anything—to use as a weapon. There was a boat several yards away. Was there an oar inside? She had no way of knowing.

"What d'you mean?" he asked again. "I can't do what?"

Camden said, "Kill us and get away with it."

"Oh, yeah?" Thad laughed at the statement. "You don't think I can pull this trigger and end your life?"

"You can shoot us, if you want." Grace veered toward the boat. "But murder is messy business. There'll be blood everywhere. I don't care what you do with the gun. Our DNA will be all over this beach. There are other cops on the way right now and that brings up another important question. Do you really think you can get rid of two corpses before they show? I don't."

"Stop walking. Shut up and let me think," Thad growled. Was there a slight tremor in his voice?

"Thad, just let us go." Camden glanced at Grace. Was he willing her to move forward? Or warning her to stay put?

She took another step to the side, another step closer to the boat. He continued, "You're already in deep trouble. Don't make it worse."

Grace's chest was tight. Her focus was razor-sharp but also divided.

There was Thad, anxious and ill, along with his gun.

Could she make him see how killing her—a police officer—would make his situation go from bad to beyond terrible?

There was also the boat. It was her only means of attack, escape and survival.

She knew one thing: unless she did something, she would die on this beach. Shifting her weight to the left, she scooted her foot a fraction of an inch. Thad seemed not to notice. She moved again—and then, once more.

"What're you doing, cop?" he snarled.

Grace froze.

"Stop fidgeting. It's giving me a headache. Hell, I already have a headache."

Camden said, "You don't want to break the law."

"Couldn't you have just left me alone?" Thad drew in a ragged breath. "Because of you, now I'm a criminal? And it's the cops who are corrupt. It doesn't matter that the guy on the street pulled his gun first. She—" he hitched his chin toward Grace "—deserves to die."

Grace understood the truth, and it chilled her soul. Thad was more than frantic. He was unhinged. She'd never be able to reason with him. Which meant she had to act.

Without another thought, she sprinted toward the boat.

At that moment, all hell broke loose.

* * *

Camden watched as Thad turned toward Grace and hooked his thumb onto the hammer. He pulled it back with a *click* that Camden felt in his teeth. A round was in the chamber.

Yet Thad's attention was on Grace and that was all Camden needed to draw and aim his own weapon. "Move another inch, and I'll paint the beach with your brains," Camden said.

Thad didn't bother to turn around.

"You think I care what happens now? I'd rather die than go to jail."

Only moments before, time had been slow, yet now it raced. Thad lifted the gun, aiming at his own head.

"No!" Camden launched himself at the other man, while slipping his gun back into the waistband of his jeans. As he approached, Thad whirled around and slammed the weapon into the side of Camden's head. For a moment, his vision went black.

He grabbed Thad's arm. They both fell to the sand. Holding Thad's wrist, he pulled back. Thad screamed in pain. Thad's gun fired. Where had the shot gone? Where was Grace?

"You…" Thad held tight to the gun. Snarling, he slammed his skull into the bridge of Camden's nose.

Camden's skull ached, yet he refused to let go. Shifting his body weight, he flipped over, pinning Thad's arm behind his back. Camden pried one finger loose and then another. As he heard the crunch of tires on gravel, three sets of headlights swept over the beach. Finally, the backup.

Guns drawn, Brett Shea, Daniel Coleman, Troy Colton and two others ran toward the water's edge. The fight seemed to leave Thad. Brett dragged Thad to his feet. "You're coming with us," he growled, cuffing the witness's hands behind his back.

Camden rose to his feet. A round had been fired, but where had the bullet gone? Where was Grace? Was she okay? The sand shifted and he listed to the side. "My car." He pointed to where he'd parked. "The female witness is in my car."

One of the uniformed officers said, "I'll get her."

"What happened?" Grace ran over to Camden and wrapped her arms around his middle. God, it felt so good to hold her that his head buzzed. "The gun went off."

"I don't know where the bullet went." A halo surrounded the headlights. A pain drove through his brow and his thoughts seemed lost in a mist.

"Camden? Camden!" Grace's voice echoed, as if she were yelling at him from beneath the waves. "Are you okay?"

He tried to nod, but his head wouldn't move.

Grace called out, "Brett. Daniel. Someone! I need an ambulance."

Brett slipped his arm under Camden's shoulder and lowered him back to the beach. "Looks like you got hit in the head. An ambulance is on the way. You need to sit until it shows up."

"I've got this." Grace knelt at his side. "Brett, you secure the scene."

The wail of a far-off siren grew louder, the noise drove into his brain.

"Sounds like the ambulance," said Grace.

Camden's eyes were heavy. Blackness surrounded him on all sides, like he was in a tunnel. He was tired, so tired. It would be so easy to rest, just for a minute.

"Stay awake, Camden. You'll be okay." She choked on her words. "For me, you have to be okay."

"I'll do anything for you," he said, his hand on hers.

Then he stopped fighting and stepped into the darkness.

A pair of EMTs rushed toward the shore at the same moment that Camden lost consciousness.

"We have this," one of them told Grace.

She still held Camden and didn't want to let go of him.

"Grace," said Troy. His hand was on her arm. "Let the EMTs do their work."

Her brother was right. She stood. Her hands shook. Her legs trembled. Her eyes burned, and her throat was raw. Despite everything she'd been taught about being a police officer, nothing had prepared her for this moment. "Will he be okay?" she asked Troy.

"I hope so."

"Officer Coleman, call the hospital," one EMT said. Camden was strapped to a gurney. An oxygen mask covered his nose and mouth. An IV was attached to his arm. "This guy has a head injury. We need a scan to determine if there's a brain bleed."

"I'm on it," said Daniel. He used his mic to connect with Dispatch.

"Camden's getting the best treatment." Troy still had hold of her arm. "Let's get out of their way so they can get their job done."

Grace didn't want to leave Camden's side, but she let him lead her to the waiting police cruisers. Hands secured behind her back with flex-cuffs, Chastity sat in the back of a black-and-white police car. A patrol offi cer read her the Miranda rights. "You have the right to remain silent." *Blah, blah, blah.*

Grace glanced at the other woman. Rage boiled up from her gut, leaving her hot and sweating. She clenched her fists and looked away.

"Grace, wait," Chastity called out. "I want to talk to you."

That was the last thing Grace wanted. In fact, what she wanted more than anything was to be furious. "If you hadn't interfered the other night, then none of this would've happened."

"I'm sorry for everything."

Grace wasn't in the mood to be forgiving. But she said, "If you're actually sorry, you have to tell the truth."

"I know. I will. I just wanted to apologize."

Would Chastity really take responsibility? Would she be honest about what she'd done? Would she really be able to start over?

After all, she had helped find Thad, so maybe she would change.

She gave a small nod.

"Let me take you home," said Troy. "Or, better yet, I'll drop you off at Dad and Leanne's house."

"I'm not going to lie. I want my mom right now."

"No shame in that." He opened the passenger door to his police car, a blue SUV. "Let's go."

Grace shook her head. "There's someplace else I need to be."

"Where's that?"

A pair of EMTs walked toward the waiting ambulance. One held the top of a stretcher, the other carried the foot. Camden was under a sheet and secured with straps.

"Take me to the hospital. I need to be with Camden."

* * *

Grace sat in the waiting room at Grave Gulch Hospital. On a Saturday evening, the room was deserted—except for her. Grace held an unopened pack of graham crackers and stared at a muted TV that hung on the wall.

"Troy said I'd find you here."

Grace looked up as Melissa stepped into the room. "Hey."

"You know I never wanted any of this to happen, right? I might've said some harsh things about Camden, but it was because I was worried about you." She paused. "Turns out I was wasting my time being concerned. He's a great guy."

"I'm not mad at you, I promise. I'm just worried."

"What'd they say about Camden's condition?"

"He's getting a scan. I was told that the concussion was severe, but there might be other problems." Grace glanced at the clock on the wall. It was half-past ten. "He's already been gone for more than an hour. Not sure how much longer it'll take." She paused. "What's going on with the case?"

"Brett talked to Chastity Shoals, the female witness. She's confessed to hiding the gun and confirms that it was taken from Robert Grimaldi. She also told Brett that Grimaldi pulled his gun on you. The serial number matches a gun that was reported stolen from Grimaldi's mother. In short, your name's been cleared. On Monday, you'll be reinstated to the force."

Obviously, that was good news. Still, she couldn't help but wonder. "Was all of this worth it?"

"Sometimes finding justice is messy business. Aside from you being exonerated, there's more good news. Some of the protesters are meeting with the mayor, Arielle and Brett on Monday. It seems that this episode has opened up a dialogue."

Okay, that was more good news. "Why's Brett going to the meeting and not you?"

"Because he's the police chief."

"If my name gets cleared, then your name will be cleared, too. Aren't you going back to work?"

"It's like I said at Palmer's party. Antonio and I are thinking about the future. I won't be coming back to the GGPD."

"You what? Why?"

"Well, I got some pretty surprising news this morning." Melissa rested her hand on her abdomen.

The gesture was a not-too-subtle hint. "A baby? Are you kidding? Congrats!" Grace opened her arms for an embrace.

Melissa laughed. "The Colton family just keeps growing and growing."

"Family is nice," she said. Yet, her mind was drawn to the picture of Camden's father—a man whose death had shaped his son's life. Certainly, Camden deserved all the happiness a family could bring.

A dark-haired woman in scrubs, lab coat and surgical cap entered the waiting room.

"Are you Grace Colton?" the doctor asked. A badge hung on a lanyard around her neck. It read: *Dr. Shah*.

"I am." Grace was on her feet, though she didn't remember standing. "How's Camden?"

"I can't say much since you aren't a family member, but we're done with all the tests."

"Can I see him?"

"We sedated him in case there was any swelling in

the brain. Now that I've seen the scan, we'll take him off the meds. He should be up for a visit in a few hours."

"Thanks for the update," said Grace.

The doctor said, "You're welcome" and then left.

"Why don't I give you a ride home?" Melissa offered.

"You know," said Grace, "I think I'm going to stay here and wait for Camden to wake up."

"Are you kidding? You heard what the doctor said. It could be hours."

How long would it take to get from Detroit to Grave Gulch? A few hours seemed about right. "Don't worry about me. Besides, I have to make a call."

Camden stood at the end of a long tunnel. It looked familiar. Yet how did he know? There were no features, it was simply dark. A light shone in the distance, but to him it looked like it was miles away.

He wanted to stay in the darkness, where it was quiet and warm.

Then he heard a woman's voice. "Camden? Can you hear me?"

He knew the woman's face. She had blue eyes and hair that shone like gold in the sunshine.

"Camden?"

The light was brighter now. He was almost at the end of the tunnel. Would the woman be waiting for him?

"Camden. It's me, Grace."

Grace. Grace. Grace. His heartbeat resonated with her name.

He burst from the tunnel and opened his eyes. He squinted against the glare and the throbbing pain in his head.

"Where am I?" he croaked. It felt like he'd swallowed glass. What the hell?

"You're in the hospital with a concussion."

Just his head? The localized pain had spread, and now his whole body hurt. His eyes were dry, yet he peeled them open. Grace looked down on him. He touched her face. She was warm and soft and real. "You're here."

"Of course I'm here. Where else would I be?"

Camden couldn't focus on much, but he did remember her rather large and tight-knit clan. "At another family party," he said.

She laughed, although he hadn't meant it as a joke. Well, maybe it was a little funny. "No parties on a Sunday morning."

Sunday morning? The last thing Camden remembered was that it had been Saturday evening. The fog surrounding his thoughts cleared, and he recalled the park. The witnesses. The gun.

He tried to sit up. His head swam, and his stomach churned. "What now?"

"There's someone who wants to see you."

Grace stepped aside, and for the first time, Camden realized that someone else was in the room. He screwed his eyes shut. Maybe he was seeing things. Opening his eyes again, he said, "Mom?"

His mother stood near the door, clasping her hands. "I got a call from your girlfriend about what happened. I came. I hope you don't mind."

Camden's eyes watered. "It's good to see you." He paused, yet there was so much he wanted to say.

"I'll let the doctor know that you're awake," said Grace. He saw through her ploy. She just wanted to give Camden and his mom a moment alone.

His mother waited until Grace had left the room before moving closer to his bed. "I know we don't talk much. But I like that girl. She's a keeper."

At one time, the Kingsleys had been a happy family. Then his dad had fallen victim to his shame and disgrace, taking not only his own life but the joy from those he left behind. Could Camden and his mother, well, maybe not rebuild that old relationship, but could they create something new? And if they did, he'd have Grace to thank.

"You know, Mom, I think that you're right."

Epilogue

Grace stood at the foot of the hospital bed a few days later. Camden sat on the edge of the mattress. Dr. Murielle Shah held a stack of papers. "These are all the discharge orders. I expect you to follow all protocols." She tapped him on the knee with the pages. "Got it?"

"Got it."

She turned her gaze to Grace.

"Got it," Grace echoed. She'd read through the pages already and knew what needed to be done.

Grace had been Camden's constant companion since the he took a blow to the head two and a half days prior. She'd gone home for short periods, to change and shower. But otherwise, they'd been together. At the beginning of the following week, he'd be returning to his job with Internal Affairs. Until then, he needed to rest but he wasn't going home. To allow him more time to heal, it was decided that he'd stay with Grace. After Camden went back to work, she'd be returning to the GGPD. She'd seen the counselor, the shooting had been ruled as justified, and in a few more days she'd be back at work, like she'd wanted from the beginning.

Having Camden at her place wasn't a sacrifice. She liked his company. For the past few days, they'd talked. Laughed. Watched reruns on TV and laughed some more.

An orderly with a wheelchair came into the room as the doctor left. "Ready to go home?" he asked Camden.

Camden looked at Grace and smiled.

Wow, he did know how to release those butterflies in her belly.

He said, "Sure am."

The orderly wheeled Camden through the hospital and out the front door. He stopped the wheelchair in front of Grace's car.

"What's that?" Camden asked.

Her car was old. And okay, maybe there was some rust and a few dents, but it had been hers since high school. "Hey, it still runs." Grace got behind the steering wheel as the orderly helped Camden into the passenger seat. She started the engine, and the car whined.

"Still runs?" Camden echoed.

Grace ignored the comment and put the gearshift into Drive. It lurched forward.

"Maybe I should get you a new car."

"Are we that serious?"

"I'm not sure, but this one…" He shook his head. "I just can't put it into words."

"First, I walk everywhere. Second, it still runs. Third,

everyone in my family learned to drive in this car. It's like an heirloom or something. Finally, I've had this car since I was sixteen."

"Sixteen, huh? Why am I not surprised?" he teased. And then, "If you like the car, I like it for you. You could get a nicer car… Something that an adult would drive."

She'd gone through a lot in the past week. Melissa was no longer at the GGPD, leaving Grace without her mentor and champion. For the first time, she was on her own. She'd been Camden's advocate at the hospital, and now he was her responsibility.

Maybe she was a bona fide grown-up, after all.

"I'll think about a new car," she said, parking in front of her building.

It took only a few minutes to get Camden up to her apartment. She led him to her room. "You should get some rest," she said, helping him onto the bed.

"I haven't done much besides rest the last few days." He kicked off his shoes and lay back. "You could stay with me."

His voice was dark and seductive. Was he suggesting what she thought he was? A thrill danced along her skin until her toes tingled. "You just got out of the hospital."

Twining his fingers through hers, Camden pulled her to him. Grace didn't resist. "Don't you think I should celebrate being alive?"

"You have a point." The thing was, she wanted him, too. "I don't want to hurt you."

"The only way you'll hurt me is if you don't kiss me now."

Leaning in to him, Grace brushed her lips on his. She sighed, and Camden slipped his tongue into her mouth. His hand slid under her shirt. Under her bra. He teased her nipple, rolling it between finger and thumb, until it was hard.

"Oh, Camden."

"Take off your shirt," he ordered. "Your bra."

She did as she was told, slipping the fabric over her head.

"Take off your pants. Your panties."

She did as he bid. He stared at her, his eyes filled with desire, and Grace felt beautiful. "Come here," he whispered, his voice intoxicating. "And kiss me."

Camden reached for her, his hand tracing her body. His touch like a moving prayer. She kissed him, hungrily, as she unbuttoned his shirt. The muscles of his pecs were firm. She moved her kiss lower, running her tongue over his well-defined abs—just to taste the salt of his skin.

He was hard and pressed against the fly of his jeans. Grace traced him with her fingertip. Camden hissed. "You're driving me crazy."

"I am?" she teased, flicking her tongue over his flat nipple.

"I want to touch you." He reached between her thighs and slid a finger inside her. "You're so hot. So tight. So wet."

She unbuttoned the fly of his jeans. Grace spit on her palm before reaching inside his shorts. She ran her hand up and down Camden's length. His fingers were inside her. She matched her strokes to his thrusts. His breath came harder and faster. She felt herself swirling upward, to the place where she would break into pieces of ecstasy, desire and longing.

"You need to stop." Camden reached for her wrist. "Or I'm going to come undone."

"Maybe that's what I want. To drive you wild."

"You do drive me wild." He placed his mouth on hers, separated the seam between her lips with his tongue and deepened the kiss. "But I want to be inside you."

Grace wanted to explore every inch of Camden, yet the desire to have him inside her was stronger.

There was a box of condoms in the drawer of her nightstand. Sadly, they'd been there for a while. Still, they hadn't expired. She reached for the handle and opened the drawer.

She held up the foil packet. "Can I help you with this?"

"I was hoping you'd offer."

He stripped out of his jeans and shorts. God, Camden was perfection. And he was about to be hers. Grace rolled the condom down his length and straddled him. She lowered herself onto him in one slow stroke. Camden gripped her ass as Grace rode his sex. Having him inside her was a beautiful torture. He touched the top of her sex. Every nerve ending tingled. She was caught in the pleasure; it pulled her from her body, drawing her higher and higher. At the moment Grace thought she could go no further, she cried out.

Settling back in her body, Grace leaned forward and placed her lips on Camden's.

He stroked the side of her breast. She licked the side of his neck, tasting the salt of his skin. He growled with desire.

So, this is what he likes? She nipped his flesh and ran her tongue over the lobe of his ear.

Breathing hard, he held her hips. She ground down on his pelvis as he cried out.

"That was magnificent." Panting, he placed a kiss on her lips. "You are magnificent."

Grace felt pretty damn magnificent. For the first time in, well, forever she felt a complete connection with another person. Was she in love? Honestly, she couldn't wait to find out.

"I have to admit it." She rolled off Camden. "I feel pretty damn magnificent right now."

Camden stood. "Bathroom?"

"Down the hall. You'll see it. The apartment's small."

"Be right back. Have to take care of the condom."

Grace slid under the blankets and Camden was back in less than a minute.

"Hey." Grace saw one of those smiles that landed with a tingle in her belly.

"Hey yourself," she said.

"Can I join you?" he asked, kneeling on the edge of the bed.

"Sure."

She lifted the comforter. He slipped between the covers and lay on his back. Grace rested her head on his shoulder. Camden's heartbeat was strong and steady. Grace could feel the pull of sleep dragging her under. She knew she should wonder what the future would hold for her and Camden. Soon, he'd go back to Internal Affairs. She'd still be a cop.

However, this moment was perfect. Did she really want to ruin it with worry? Rolling to her belly, she met his gaze. "I was just thinking."

"Oh, yeah?" he asked. "About what?"

"I'm not sure how our story will end, Camden. But for now, you're the only one I want."

"Grace." He kissed her softly. "I couldn't have said it better myself."

* * * * *

Check out the previous books in
The Coltons of Grave Gulch *series:*

Colton's Dangerous Liaison *by Regan Black*
Colton's Killer Pursuit *by Tara Taylor Quinn*
Colton's Nursery Hideout *by Dana Nussio*
Colton Bullseye *by Geri Krotow*
Guarding Colton's Child *by Lara Lacombe*
Colton's Covert Witness *by Addison Fox*
Rescued by the Colton Cowboy
by Deborah Fletcher Mello
Colton K-9 Target *by Justine Davis*

And don't miss the next book

Uncovering Colton's Family Secret
by Linda O. Johnston

Available in November 2021 from
Harlequin Romantic Suspense!

**WE HOPE YOU ENJOYED
THIS BOOK FROM**

◆HARLEQUIN

**ROMANTIC
SUSPENSE**

Danger. Passion. Drama.

These heart-racing page-turners will keep you guessing
to the very end. Experience the thrill of unexpected
plot twists and irresistible chemistry.

4 NEW BOOKS AVAILABLE EVERY MONTH!

#2155 COLTON 911: DESPERATE RANSOM
Colton 911: Chicago • by Cindy Dees
When lawyer Myles Colton is drawn into a high-profile case involving a notorious gang, his marriage begins to crack. And when someone threatens Faith and their four-year-old, Jack, forcing them into hiding, the marriage is further strained. But then Jack is kidnapped, and that's the final straw. Can this family survive against all odds?

#2156 UNCOVERING COLTON'S FAMILY SECRET
The Coltons of Grave Gulch • by Linda O. Johnston
While Madison Colton is on the tail of a man who looks suspiciously like her dead father, she ends up crossing paths with US marshal Oren Margulies. He tries to send her away from this potential connection to her father. A gunrunner threatens her life, and Oren is the one to protect her, which leads to a surprising attraction.

#2157 OPERATION WHISTLEBLOWER
Cutter's Code • by Justine Davis
Parker Ward lost everything after testifying against his boss. So when his friend ends up in a similar situation, he'll do anything to help. Including team up with the Foxworth Foundation, a group he's not certain he trusts—even if the pretty police detective, Carly Devon, has him wondering if he might have something to give after all...

#2158 UNDER THE RANCHER'S PROTECTION
Midnight Pass, Texas • by Addison Fox
Fifth-generation Texas rancher Ace Reynolds has never forgotten Veronica Torres. She's returned to Midnight Pass, but what haunted her in Houston hasn't abated. Ace is determined to protect her, but the threat may go deeper than either of them imagined...

"You doing okay?"

"Yeah. I'm fine."

Ace's gaze searched Veronica's face. "I wasn't trying to scare you earlier."

"I didn't think that. At all. It doesn't seem real, but I know that it is."

"I know my family has seen more than its fair share of bad happenings around here and I'm not asking for trouble, but there was something off about that guy. I'm not going to ignore it or pretend my gut isn't blaring like a siren."

Ignore it? Had she been so wrapped up in her frustration that she'd given him that impression?

"Once again, my inability to speak to you with any measure of my normal civility left the absolute wrong impression. I'm grateful to you."

Those sexy green eyes widened, but he said nothing, so he continued on.

"You were watching out for me and I couldn't even manage the most basic level of appreciation." She stood, suddenly unable to sit still. "I am grateful. More than you know. I just—"

Before she could say anything—before the awful, terrible words could spill out—Ace was there, those big strong arms wrapped around her.

Just like she'd wanted all along.

"What happened?"

Her face was pressed to his chest, but it gave an added layer of protection to say what she needed to say. To let the terrible words spill out. Words she'd sworn to herself she'd never say again after she got through the horror of police statements and endless questions by drug company lawyers and even more endless questions by insurance lawyers.

She'd said them all over and over, even when it seemed as if no one was listening.

Or worse, that they even believed her.

But she'd said them each time she'd been asked. And then she'd sworn to bury them all.

His arms tightened, his strength pouring into her. "You can tell me."

"I know."

Don't miss
Under the Rancher's Protection *by Addison Fox,*
available November 2021 wherever
Harlequin Romantic Suspense
books and ebooks are sold.

Harlequin.com

Get 4 FREE REWARDS!

We'll send you 2 FREE Books plus <u>2 FREE Mystery Gifts.</u>

Harlequin Romantic Suspense books are heart-racing page-turners with unexpected plot twists and irresistible chemistry that will keep you guessing to the very end.

FREE Value Over $20

YES! Please send me 2 FREE Harlequin Romantic Suspense novels books and my 2 FREE gifts (gifts are worth about $10 retail). After receiving them, if I don't wish to receive any more books, I can return the shipping statement marked "cancel." If I don't cancel, I will receive 4 brand-new novels every month and be billed just $4.99 per book in the U.S. or $5.74 per book in Canada. That's a savings of at least 13% off the cover price! It's quite a bargain! Shipping and handling is just 50¢ per book in the U.S. and $1.25 per book in Canada.* I understand that accepting the 2 free books and gifts places me under no obligation to buy anything. I can always return a shipment and cancel at any time. The free books and gifts are mine to keep no matter what I decide.

240/340 HDN GNMZ

Name (please print)

Address   Apt. #

City   State/Province   Zip/Postal Code

Email: Please check this box ☐ if you would like to receive newsletters and promotional emails from Harlequin Enterprises ULC and its affiliates. You can unsubscribe anytime.

Mail to the **Harlequin Reader Service:**
IN U.S.A.: P.O. Box 1341, Buffalo, NY 14240-8531
IN CANADA: P.O. Box 603, Fort Erie, Ontario L2A 5X3

Want to try 2 free books from another series! Call 1-800-873-8635 or visit www.ReaderService.com.

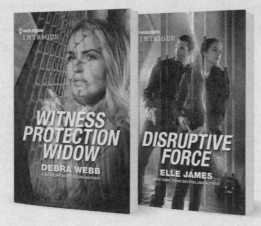